Never Throw a Seven

By
Jerry Schuessler

PublishAmerica
Baltimore

ISBN: 1-4241-7088-5
PUBLISHED BY PUBLISHAMERICA, LLLP
www.publishamerica.com
Baltimore

Printed in the United States of America

This book is dedicated to my wife, Jeanette,
Who is a treasure beyond belief!

ACKNOWLEDGEMENTS

My special thanks have to go out to Bob Scheck, Pat Varville, Paula Ulreich, Mary Ciszek and Bob Hall, for their many thoughtful suggestions regarding the manuscript. *No one man does it alone*!

I would also like to thank the people at PublishAmerica. They took a chance on a rookie and I'm grateful!

To Ken Bennett, Len Harvey, Jim Heavey, Jim Knight, Steve Schneider and Eddie Trelevan, whose names appear in the book. I hope you enjoy your alter egos. And to Julius Rimdzious (1925-2003), the man who taught me this crazy game.

I would also be somewhat remiss were I not to acknowledge the help I received from Saint Jude, patron saint of the impossible, and the Miraculous Infant Jesus of Prague, in putting this book together. I have a daily devotion to each.

– Jerry Schuessler.

Preface

Whoa! Hold it! Back up a second!

STOP RIGHT THERE!

If you were expecting a Bible on gin rummy, you've made a mistake. Turn right around, go back to the counter and get a refund. That's right, go and get your money back. *You're in the wrong place*!

This is more of a story about big money card games, and a card player.

Never Throw a Seven tells the story of how one man, Kenny Allen, while in the Army learns about becoming a soldier, card games and life. It also features Eddie Colquitt. Kenny knew him in high school. Eddie is his teacher and once again becomes his mentor and *savior* twenty-five years later, long after the two of them have left the service. Along the way you'll run into the Sitkowitz brothers. They are the likeable villains in our story. (Boo! Hiss)!

You'll also meet *Old Man Kards*. He is one of the gambling gods who will in many cases have the last word on whether you're a winner or a loser. He is distantly related to Lady Luck, but nowhere near as nice.

True, there are some pointers in here, pointers about the opponent. You'll be shown how to get into his head, how to *out think him, out drink him,* and if a few breaks come your way, how to lighten up his wallet a bit. Kenny for a while forgets all this, loses big time, and Eddie has to straighten him out. The outrageous ending has Kenny eating crow and plotting his revenge.

I'm one of the few men in this country who can tell you why people win and why they lose at cards. In the pages of this book, I'm going to share this while telling you a story. The text borders on the hilarious at times, is fast paced, informative and includes a trip to Las Vegas where the "big dogs" (*real* card players) live!

Jerry Schuessler
Arlington Heights, Illinois.
November 2006

PART ONE

Chapter 1
NEVER THROW A SEVEN!

"Thank god for the Cubs!" I heard as I walked into the room.

Eddie Colquitt turned around and looked at me. He was seated at a card table in Itasca Country Club, and was watching the Chicago Cubs on television.

This to me is an exercise in futility. The Cubs haven't been in the World Series since 1945, and haven't won the damned thing since Teddy Roosevelt was in office. Hell, anyone can have a bad century! I hear it again. *"Thank God for the Cubs!"*

I stood there and looked around the place. The card room itself is something to behold. It's about 1500 square feet of plush. Your feet kind of sink into the carpeting as you make your way around. Glancing at the cushioned chairs surrounding the card tables you can't but help smile at the thought that creeps into your head. Some things are built for comfort, some things are built for speed!

These chairs were definitely built for comfort. The four walls are lined with plasma television sets that have pictures so clear they are mirror like in appearance. There must be six or seven of them.

Adjacent to the card playing area, there are leather sofas, ash stands and cocktail tables containing popcorn, peanuts, and cheese with crackers. Is everything low-cal? *Of course!*

There are action photographs hanging on the walls, photographs of notable golf stars, Tiger Woods, Phil Mickelson, Jack Nicklaus and Arnold Palmer to name a few.

It was the Fourth of July and things were quiet. Everyone, it seemed, was out on the golf course. I looked at Eddie sitting there. He was dressed in his usual attire, white slacks, a red and white flowered shirt along with red socks and white shoes. When he is out of earshot we refer to it as his uniform. His blond wavy hair along with the ready smile he always seemed to wear made him resemble quite a few movie stars, past and present. Me? I don't dress nearly as flashy, nor am I quite as good looking. My name is Kenny Allen and my appearance, tall, brown hair, and slightly overweight, could best be described as inconspicuous. I kind of favor the white slacks with a navy blue golf shirt type of outfit when I go to the club. In my opinion the white bottoms with the navy top look terrific on anyone, male or female, no matter what the rest of the issue looks like!

"Why 'Thank *God for the Cubs*'?" I asked.

Eddie looked at me, took a sip from the drink he was holding and said; "Every time someone tells me some piece of shit rock star or rapper is super talented because he sells a lot of records, I remind him the Cubs fill up Wrigley Field every time they play!"

I sat down, looked at him and smiled. I had to agree.

"Why are you just sitting there?" I asked, "Nothing to do?"

"Well," he said, "the two used car lots I own are closed because of the holiday, and I thought I'd just hang around here and see if I could find me a gin game. Maybe you'd be interested?"

I thought for a moment. "Yeah," I said, realizing I was in the same boat. My construction company was shut down for the same reason. Eddie got up and went over to a table next to the bar and came back with two decks of Bicycles a pencil and two gin pads.

"Hey Pooch," he said. He always used these words when he was thinking of doing a number on somebody. I should have taken warning. "Hey Pooch," he repeated, "the last time we played together you took a grand off me. I'll tell you what, I'll play you one game of gin. One game to a hundred fifty points for the thousand!" I gave him a long look while I considered this.

I am a firm believer in an opponent who loses a lot of money should get it back the same way he lost it. I usually shied away from raising the stakes. Thinking for a moment I considered his proposition. My luck had been running hot for the last month or so, the good cards were coming in, and *Old Man Kards*, that grand old god of card players, was being nice to me.

"Let me get this straight," I said. "If I win, I'm up two grand, if I lose, we're back to square one!"

"That's about it," he said, giving me that quick grin of his.

I grinned myself, and said those words I said many years ago when I agreed to sell cars for him. *"I'm your man!"*

So we sat down and began to play. It was an interesting game that seesawed back and forth. First he would be ahead, then me. Finally it got down to where he had a hundred and thirty-six points and I had a hundred–forty. Both of us were at the stage of the game where, with a little bit of luck, it could quickly be ended. Eddie, I was sure, had three spreads in his hand, as did I. My hand was the three spreads and a lone ace. It was my turn to play.

I drew the seven of diamonds. This merited some thought. Sevens normally are not the greatest of discards, there are just too many ways the other guy can use them. They sit right there in the middle of the deck and are extremely volatile. I thought for a moment. I could knock the hand—— Nah! Forget about that! If Eddie was lying in the weeds with a couple of cards he could play off he could easily undercut me and back out of the game.

How about the ace? I could discard the ace. The problem was no aces had been played. None were in the discard pile. Eddie probably had two or three of them in his hand. The seven seemed reasonably safe. It couldn't be used for three sevens as two sevens had already been played. The only way Eddie could use this card would be to complete a diamond run, a seven-eight-nine or, to add onto an existing eight-nine-ten diamond combination. This seemed unlikely because the jack of diamonds had been played long ago, as had the six. How do I play it? Throw the seven? Throw the ace? *Son of a bitch, son of a bitch!*

Holding the corner of the card, the seven of diamonds, between my thumb and forefinger, I flicked my wrist and sent it spinning toward the discard pile, glancing at Eddie as I did.

A quick look at his eyes told me I was dead. *Call the priest and send for the undertaker.* One glance at those eyes told me the hand was lost, the game was over and the thousand bucks were gone!

Eddie didn't say a word; he just looked at me and laid his hand down on the discard pile next to my seven of diamonds. He had been holding three kings, three queens and, oh yes, the 8-9-10-of diamonds. *GIN!*

He got up from the table, looked at me again, and headed for the bar. A kibitzer, who had walked in a minute or so ago, a man by the name of Ken Bennett, smiled and said, "*Never throw a seven!*"

Chapter 2
DO YOU KNOW EDDIE COLQUITT?

"Do you know Eddie Colquitt?" I'm asked. I hear the question and I smile. Do I know Eddie Colquitt? Hell, throughout the years there has been more money transferred from my pockets to his at the card tables that anyone with a lick of sense can shake a stick at. *Do I know Eddie Colquitt?*

It is a sunny day in January at Itasca Country Club in Illinois. It is much too cold and snowy for golf, but just perfect to be seated by a window, admiring the snow and trees on the golf course, and playing gin rummy. There is a glass of Absolut on the rocks near my right hand, and I allow my mind to wander. I am mentally a pleasant thousand miles away when I realize my daydreaming is being interrupted.

I detach myself from my reverie and say to my companions,

"Do I know Eddie Colquitt?" I pause for a moment and then go on. "Let me put it this way. Many years ago, near the turn of the century, say, 1919, two Mexican gentlemen, caballeros as it were, are seated at a bar in a cantina, just south of Tijuana.

"The bar is made of mahogany and has a glossy top. It's just right for sliding beer mugs or whiskey bottles along. You can see this type of bar in all the John Wayne movies. If I try, I can almost visualize the 'Duke' catching a bottle sliding along the bar top with one hand and pouring himself a shot with the other. It was that kind of a bar.

"Behind the bar, above the whiskey and tequila bottles are two five feet wide by four-foot high plate glass mirrors, with an equal five foot by four-foot space in between. In the middle of this space is a very large portrait of Pancho Villa, the notorious bandit and revolutionist. He is seen mounted on a big black horse."

"'Ah, Pancho Villa!' says the gentleman on the left side of the portrait, 'He mucho mallo hombre (Big bad man)!'

"'You mean you know Pancho Villa?' says the other gentleman, gesturing at the picture.

"'Do I know Pancho Villa? —*Do I know Pancho Villa?* — I was walking in the desert not far from here. It was noon, about this time of day, when I came upon a man all dressed in black. He wore black shiny high-topped boots, a black chimarra (jacket), and a black sombrero. Around his shoulders were *bandoleros* holding bright shiny brass bullets. He is astride a big black horse, and, in each hand he holds a *pistola*.

"'Pancho Villa!' I say, 'Estoy correcto (Am I correct)?'"

"'Senor Pancho Villa to you, campasino (Peasant).'

"'Hola (Hello) Senor Pancho Villa!' I say.

"'Pancho Villa looks down his nose and sneers. 'Hombre,' he says, pointing the pistolas at me. 'Kita te la sombrero (take off your hat).'

"'I take off my hat.

"'*Hombre,*' he says again waving the pistolas, 'Cagata in la sombrero (shit in your hat).'

"'What do you do?' asked the gentleman on the right.

"'*What do I do?* He is Pancho Villa, I am campasino, I drop my pants, squat down and I shit in my hat.'

"'*NO!*'

"'*YES!*'

"'Then Pancho Villa looks at me and says, '*Hombre*, comida la cagata (eat the shit)!'

"'What do you do?'

"'Hey, he is Pancho Villa and he has the two pistolas pointed at me. I get on my knees. It is very hot and I am miserable. The best I can do is a weak sniff. Pancho Villa is very amused. He smiles, then he chuckles, then he lets out a huge belly laugh. 'Ho, Ho, Ho!' He laughs so loud he excites the horse. He really scares the animal. The startled horse rears up on his hind legs pitching Pancho Villa from the saddle. He tumbles to the ground the two pistolas come flying toward me and I catch them. Now the situation is reversed, the shoe is on the other foot.

"'I point the two pistolas at Pancho Villa.

"'Hombre!' I say, 'Kita te la sombrero! (Take off your hat)!'

"'And you ask me, 'Do I know Pancho Villa? —— I have *lunch* with Pancho Villa!'"

I look at my gin rummy buddies, "And you ask me if I know Eddie Colquitt!" I say, "I have *lunch* with Eddie Colquitt!"

Not only do I have lunch with him, I *buy* his lunch, and sometimes his wife's lunch, and his family's dinner, and then some. People like me have helped put Eddie's kids through college. *Eddie Colquitt indeed*!

Eddie is a close friend, and a gin rummy player *par-excellence*, an expert who has written two books on the subject. You can call him up at any time of night or day and he'll come right over and play you for any amount of money you desire. In for a nickel, in for a dollar, that's Eddie, but just like our caballero friend turned the tables on Pancho Villa, the tables can be turned on Eddie, and he can be had!

My name is Kenny Allen, and I'm seventy. I'm a retired paratrooper, car salesman, bricklayer, contractor, and homebuilder. If you try real hard you might be able to say all that without tripping over it. Like I said, I'm seventy, but don't you worry your little head. You're not going to have to sit there and listen to the ranting of some old fart, because a lot of the story you're about to read happened a long time ago.

What do I look like? Well that depends. Many years ago people said I resembled John Wayne. This is hard to understand because I'm not Irish. I'm probably as big as he was, right now anyway. Maybe it's the nose, it's been broken once. This happened when it got into an argument with a concrete building block that was flying through the air. It's got a little bend in it, just like the 'Duke's,' but am I Irish? Nope. Not a chance. My dad was German–French and my mother was mostly Polish, so I guess I'm a Kraut Pollack who is fairly good looking, although my mother always referred to my brother as her "*best looking son.*"

I'm six-foot-one and I weigh two–twenty. I have blue eyes, brown hair and tough guy looks. When I'm slim-trim and in condition I look like my mother's side of the family. When I'm out of shape and overweight (which is most of the time), I resemble my dad's. If you can make any sense out of all that you're a better man than I am!

Possibly I do have good looks, but nothing like when a lot of this story took place. Then I was really slim and trim. Do you remember Charlton Heston when he was young and agile, and in his prime? Well there I was, young and agile, slim, trim and full of piss and vinegar. And I did do *many* terrific things when I was younger. How? Stick around, my friend, stick around.

Chapter 3
THE SITKOWITZ BROTHERS

Ice fishing? Po perked up his ears. *Did I hear Ice Fishing? Please God, anything but that!* he thought.

Po was a Golden Retriever and he was seated on the rear seat of a Buick Rendezvous SUV being driven by his master's brother, Leon Sasecasewicz. The name Sasecasewicz is a very old long Polish name, very difficult to pronounce. Most their friends got by this by calling them Sitkowitz. Po looked around. He looked out of the two rear windows. There was snow on the sides of the highway and a sun in the clear blue skies that had a mind of its own, refusing to cooperate as far as generating even a tiny bit of heat. It was cold, and the wind was blowing.

Riding in the SUV with the windows closed was no fun. No fun at all! Not like in the summer time when Po could ride along with his head poked out of the window, his tongue hanging out, and feeling the wind flow over his face. Now that was fun, enjoyable and terrific! But ice fishing? Forget it!

Po's real name was "Polack," or at least that's what his master, Anton, named him when he was a pup. One of his friends remarked the dog had a Polish face, so Anton began calling him "Polack." This lasted until about the second or third time Anton went outside to call him. A number of his neighbors turned their heads around and Anton decided right then and there it was time to shorten the dog's name to "Po."

Looking at the floor of the SUV Po decided he must have misunderstood. There was no fishing pole, no tackle box, and no axe. These are items of necessity for ice fishing.

Po hated ice fishing. Who in their right mind would go out in the middle of nowhere, into the snow and cold, chop a hole in the ice on some God-forsaken frozen body of water, sit there with a pole in his hands and freeze his ass off for hours on end.

He looked at the floor of the SUV again. All he saw was some kind of a net, a double barreled shotgun, and four short sticks taped together with a kind of a piece of string sticking out. He didn't know about the net or the gun, what they were for, but the four short sticks looked like some variation of Po's favorite game, "Chase the stick!"

Now that was great sport. Anton, his master, would bend over, pick up a stick and throw it as far as he could. Po would be off like a shot, run as fast as he could, chase down the stick, pick it up in his mouth, and run like the wind back to Anton and drop it at his feet. Anton would smile, pat Po on his head, maybe give him a cookie, and say "Good dog!" This would then be repeated. Anton would bend over, pick up the stick and throw it again and off Po would scamper, retrieve it, and bring it back to Anton. What could be more exciting? This was life at its best! Po could do this all day, all night, all week.

Sometimes Po would look at some of the other things Anton would do to keep himself amused. Things like, play cards, chase women, drink beer, eat kielbasa and dance the polka. Who the hell would want to do stupid things like that when he could go out and play "Chase the stick?"

"It's like this!" Leon was telling his brother, "I ran into Eddie Colquitt last week at a golf outing at Itasca Country Club. He's a member there and we just sort of bumped into one another."

"You mean the same Eddie Colquitt we knew at Shabonna Park when we were kids many years ago?"

"One and the same," continued Leon, nodding his head.

"How's he doing?"

"Pretty well," replied Leon, "He's got a few used car lots going for him that turn out a good buck, and he plays a lot of golf and gin."

Anton thought a bit.

"Yeah!" he said, "I did hear he was a pretty fair gin rummy player."

"Better that that," Leon said, "Much better, he's considered some kind of expert on the game. He pals around with another name out of the past, Kenny Allen. The two of them partner up a lot in golf and much more at gin, and they get along just fine. I do think the two of us should take them on in a gin game as soon as I can arrange it

"We're going to fleece them?" Anton inquired.

"No," said Leon, "we can't do that. Eddie's much too smart for most of our tricks, but Kenny likes a few cocktails while he's playing, so we'll make the most out of that."

This would seem to give the impression Leon and Anton were expert or professional gin rummy players. They were not. They were only better than average. Truth of the matter was they were bumblers. They were always looking for the short cut. They were always looking for an edge over the other guy.

Leon always believed in having this edge. Some of the time it worked out, most of the time, no. He and his brother were seldom illegal, just close to it. In gin rummy and pinochle they had little tricks, tricks like speaking Polish to one another when they were partners. They always claimed they were not disclosing information about the hand they were playing, or the opponents' hand.

They would say they were just talking baseball, or the weather, but unless you spoke the language yourself, how could you be sure? In poker it was the same. One brother would signal the other in Polish when he had a dynamite hand. The other brother would raise the bet like crazy then drop out near the end of the hand, thus helping create a huge pot.

Anton looked at the evergreens on the shoreline all covered with snow.

"Tell me," he said, looking at Leon, "Exactly what do you have planned for us today?"

Leon pulled the SUV off the highway and onto the ice surface of Geneva Lake. The lake is a spring fed body of water some fifty miles or so west of Chicago. The lake itself is so popular in the summer months the bars and restaurants in the adjoining town, Lake Geneva, are very crowded. They are all jammed with wall-to-wall people. In the winter months the hydrogen bomb could go off and no one would be there to notice.

The lake completely freezes by the end of January, and the ice is thick enough to support quite a few cars, or SUV's. Leon paused to take in the surrounding landscape to make sure no other vehicles were near. There were none. It was a Monday morning, the weekend ice fishers had long since departed, and Leon didn't really expect to see anyone around. He pulled the vehicle to a stop, looked at Anton and explained his set-up.

"Here's my idea" Leon began. "I don't particularly care to freeze my butt waiting for some fish that may or not be hungry to come along, and I sure as hell don't feel like chopping a hole through this god-dam ice"

He looked at the frozen shoreline, and the snow that covered the surface of the ice and shivered. "Just the thought of it makes me cold" He clapped his hands together and went on.

"I figure we could shovel off an area of maybe fifteen feet square, throw four sticks of dynamite taped together into the middle, and wait for the explosion. When it happens, it will blow a hole in the ice and stun any fish that are nearby. He pointed toward the ice. "We'll be able to see them floating on the surface. The more active ones we'll shoot with the shotgun. Then all we have to do is scoop them up with the net, put them in these garbage bags I brought along, and be on our way. The whole thing should take less than an hour, and we'll have

19

fifty or sixty fish apiece. We should have enough to keep us in filets for a month or two, and then we come back out here and do it again."

Anton grabbed the shovel, got out of the SUV, and walked some sixty feet away. He cleared an area fifteen feet by fifteen feet, and came back to the SUV. Leon handed him the four sticks dynamite with the wick taped on. He then produced a Zippo lighter from his pocket, spun the wheel and lit the fuse. He then flung the four sticks dynamite into the clearing in the snow.

Po bolted from the SUV like he was shot out of a cannon.

GALUMP-GALUMP- GALUMP- GALUMP! Swiftly he closed the distance to the dynamite. Picking it up in his mouth he turned, and with the speed of summer lightning, he made his way back to Anton. He dropped the dynamite at Anton's feet and looked up with pleading eyes. His breath was coming hard and rapidly. "*Heh-eh-heh-eh-heh-eh-heh.*" His tongue was hanging out and saliva was forming on his jowls.

Anton, quite taken by surprise, picked up the four sticks of dynamite and heaved them right back into the square.

GALUMP-GALUMP-GALUMP-GALUMP. Po again became the hunter. This was Chase the stick at its best! —— Leon seeing where all this was heading reached back, grabbed the shotgun, handed it to Anton and said " If he comes back here again with that dynamite in his mouth, shoot the son of a bitch, he'll blow us both to kingdom come!"

GALUMP-GALUMP-GALUMP-GALUMP! Po was on his way back.

"Shoot that fricken dog!" yelled Leon.

POW——POW! Went the shotgun!

Unfortunately the sawed off was loaded with birdshot and did about as much damage to Po's epidermis as would a flock of mosquitoes. What did happen was the explosions and accompanying flashes frightened the dog to the extent, that his instincts told him to seek refuge. Refuge in this case was beneath the SUV and this is where he went!

GALUMP-GALUMP-GALUMP-GALUMP-SKIDDDDD! There he reclined on all fours with the dynamite and flickering fuse cradled between his front paws. He was the picture of contentment.

"Get him out from under that van!" screamed Leon, "He'll blow the god-dam thing up!"

Anton did the only thing he could think of. He used a Polish word, well not really Polish, just a something he made up word. Whenever he would want Po to come to him quickly, at all costs, he would shout the word, "*SAWTAYDYROBISCH!*" This in Polish dog talk means "Get your bony ass over here or I'll kick it a few times!" Anton had kicked Po's bony rear end so many times he obeyed instantly. In a flash he was by Anton's side. Unfortunately again, he had left the dynamite and flickering fuse back underneath the Buick Rendezvous.

"*BLAM!*"

Bouranelli's Principal, which deals with air currents, could probably explain why the force of the blast went downward, instead of up, but that's what happened. It blew a hole in the ice that covered most of the fifteen square feet. The ice crackled, then gave way. The SUV seemed to shudder, then slowly began to sink out of sight, first the front end, then the rear. It sort of resembled a movie of a ship sinking at sea. The demise of the Buick Rendezvous left our heroes with nothing to do, short of the uttering of many words too vile for these pages, but to make their way to the highway, and hitch hike back to Chicago.

To compound the matter, everything near and dear to them was in the SUV.

Their street shoes, the car and house keys, and oh yes, their wallets, were still in the Buick Rendezvous. To further compound the matter, a week later the insurance company refused to honor the claim, citing the vehicle was being used for illegal purposes.

'Bon Voyage New Titanic, you're the greatest ship on the blue!"

Chapter 4
A FEW IMPORTANT NAMES

If one were driving north from the state of Florida heading toward Chicago, and wanted to travel by way of the great interstate highway system, he would have no choice but to run smack dab into the city of Nashville, Tennessee. This city is one of the major hubs in the system that handles no fewer than six interstate highways that pass through its confines. To get to Chicago from Nashville via the system one has but two choices to make. Drive north on I-65 to I-80 in Illinois, which will put you pretty close, or drive northwest on I-24 to I-57 in Illinois which terminates at I-80, and this, needless to say, will also put you pretty close.

I-65, except for a cup of coffee in Kentucky, takes one through the state of Indiana, which is "Nada! *Nada in absoluto.*" Think of the word *wilderness* and you'll have Indiana in the palm of your hand. I-24, on the other hand, is a scenic adventure through northwest Tennessee and southern Kentucky. As you travel on this route you will encounter two very important names in our story, Clarksville, Tennessee, and Hopkinsville, Kentucky. Fort Campbell Kentucky, another important name, seems to have been thrown in right between the two of them.

Fort Campbell, Kentucky, located on US. Highway 41, a short distance from I-24, is actually a misnomer. It gives the impression the military reservation is in the state of Kentucky. While it has a Kentucky mailing address and the main gate is there, ninety-five percent of the post is in the state of Tennessee.

Clarksville, Tennessee, had its beginning in the late 1700s when George Rogers Clark was in the process of launching his expedition across the Midwest and eventually northwest to the mouth of the Columbia River, into what is now the State of Oregon.

His stepping-off point was a settlement in northern Tennessee along the banks of the Cumberland River. It was here he met Merriwether Lewis. Together they began exploring the great wilderness then known as the Northwest Territory. These were the famous Lewis and Clark Expeditions that in 1802 opened up the Northwest Passage.

During this time, due to bad weather, rough terrain or just plain human lethargy, a great deal of time was spent in tents or at campfires waiting for one thing or another to happen. During these waiting periods, the playing of a card game still in its infancy, gin rummy, helped pass the time.

In December 1803 one of the soldiers in the accompanying military detachment heard an exclamation from the tent housing Rogers and Clark

"You son of a bitch!" it was heard, "If it weren't for your *'friggin'* luck you'd never win a hand!"

"I wonder what that was all about?" asked Private Appleby.

"Who knows, with those two!" answered Sergeant Morris with a shrug of his shoulders. Together the made their way from the tent and resumed their patrol.

Clarksville, named after George Rogers Clark, today is a thriving community of over a hundred thousand people, many of which are ex-soldiers who decided to stay and make their living there. The weather is decent, the scenery beautiful, and the living easy, mostly because it is a soldier town with the main economy military related.

Hopkinsville, Kentucky, is named after the famed educator and financier Johns Hopkins. This town located some eighty miles north of Clarksville boasts a population of the same amount, and has a more established downtown area. Johns Hopkins, besides being a noted teacher and philanthropist, was, at one time, given credit for the now famous statement one hears when one's partner is caught with a fistful of unrelated high cards near the end of the deck, when the call is ten.

"Hey, asshole, get rid of the bombs!"

Fort Campbell is named in honor of Col. William Bowen Campbell of the First Tennessee Volunteers known as "The Bloody First" of Civil War fame. Fort Campbell, until the outbreak of WW 11 was known as Camp Campbell. The term camp, when used in regard to a military reservation designates a temporary situation. In the early 1940's, because of the war, the government poured so much money into the engineering, development and reconstruction of the place; they decided it would be better to declare it a permanent facility, a fort. At this time there was a desperate need for forts because of the vast amount of human beings being channeled through their gates for training.

This training plus the haircuts, changes in diets and physical and attitude changes that take place when one is awakened at five–thirty (0530 hrs.) in the morning, then pushed at a hectic pace until five–thirty (1730hrs.) in the evening goes on for sixteen weeks and is known as basic training.

In the early1940s, (1941-1945), these human beings, (bodies, as they were called), were groomed, mostly successfully, to become soldiers. They were to be sent to such distant reaches of the globe as Europe (ETO), or the Far East (FECOM). These operations were known as pipeline. These new soldiers quickly picked up a game unknown to most of them. It was called gin rummy.

It is not hard to understand, because of the vast amount of time-spent waiting, there was ample time for card playing. Playing cards, therefore, were in short supply. It is not surprising the makers of Bicycle playing cards had to put on a second shift.

"*Get rid of the bombs!*" almost became a battle cry.

On the northwest side of Chicago there is park by the name of Shabonna. Shabonna is the Indian word meaning portage. Portage is the act of putting one's canoe on one's shoulders and carrying it from one river to another when the first river ceased to be going in the direction the Indian desired. A famous Indian chief, Chief Shabonna, developed the system. The Indian, having a desire for the many goods the white man had to trade, would journey to the settlement known as Fort Dearborn, later to be called Chicago. He would paddle his canoe down what is now known as the DesPlaines River, then exit at the far reaches of the settlement, travel overland on territory, part of which is now called Shabonna Park, until he reached the banks of The Chicago River. From here He could paddle downstream to Lake Michigan and Chicago where he would carry on his trade.

Considering the vast amount of time and energy involved for the Indian to get his goods to market, and the way he was taken advantage of (robbed) by the white man during these bartering sessions, it's a wonder the effort was made at all. The end result was the Indian massacring the city, taking his goods, changing rivers again and heading south for St. Louis on the Mississippi saying "To Hell with Chicago!"

It's also a wonder the white man didn't teach the Indian to play cards. He would have gotten his goods much easier.

At the field house at Shabonna Park there is a room set up for card playing. During the late forties and early fifties we would be in there every night during the cold weather, and it was here I first met Eddie Colquitt. I remember the first time I played pinochle with him. He totaled up his points, totaled up mine, looked at me and said, "Count your few!" Then he reached over took my money and walked away.

Eddie was a few years older than me, but if you were between the ages of thirteen and eighteen, chances are you were at the park, and in the card room. Even in those early days Eddie knew his way around a deck of cards. Most of the time it was pinochle, poker, or black jack, but even then, Eddie was fooling around with a form of rummy quite strange to the rest of us. That was Eddie, always one step ahead.

When the Korean War broke out Eddie was one of the first to go. Drafted for two years and extended for another, Eddie saw action in Korea before being permanently stationed at Fort Campbell, Kentucky. Meanwhile, the Army wasn't neglecting me.

THE UNITED STATES OF AMERICA, WASHINGTON DC.
GREETING: Your friends and neighbors have empowered me to have your name placed in a draft for selection into the service of the Armed Forces of this country. You are to report to the Selective Service office May 24, 1953, 7:00 am, Chicago, Illinois, for induction into the Army of the United States of America.
Dwight D. Eisenhower,
President of the United States.

I remember kissing my mother goodbye and leaving home. My dad drove me to the Draft Board in downtown Chicago. We shook hands. He wished me luck and I was on my way to becoming a soldier.

The Selective Service facility was a real picnic. The day began with us filling out a fifty-page questionnaire regarding our life histories, our health, hobbies and education. This took two and a half hours and was done fully clothed. The physical exam that followed was not. Try to picture a hundred and fifty twenty-year-old recruits stark naked standing in this line, or that line and you'll get the idea.

Was it cold? You may ask. Hell yes it was cold, and the Army didn't bother to heat the place. I guess they figured since it was spring (late May), heating the building was a thing of the past. We basked in a balmy temperature of fifty-five degrees. This was the first of many arguments I had with the Army, but not the last.

About three in the afternoon we were taken by bus to the North Shore train station for a trip north of the city to Fort Sheridan. This trip took roughly an hour and a half.

Fort Sheridan, until the Army in its down-sizing program closed it, was the major replacement center for Army personnel in the Midwest part of the country. It was a beautiful and well-maintained facility. It's unfortunate the Army decided to shut it down.

We were there for about a week being processed into the service. This involved moving from one building to clothing, receiving shots and attending classes denoting what each inoculation was for. After this we went to the barbershops where the Army presented each man its own idea of what a haircut should look like. I remember the average time for a haircut was about thirty seconds. I looked at myself in a mirror and figured the haircut had cost me some seventeen pounds.

Our sixth day began at six am. (0600 hrs) We got on busses for Fort Campbell Kentucky. This trip took us down US. Highways "45" and "41" and was long before the interstate highways, President Eisenhower envisioned, were built. The trip, including stops for lunch (afternoon chow), and dinner (evening chow), took sixteen hours.

The reception at Fort Campbell was unforgettable. It compared unfavorably to my first day of practice for college football. We got off those busses and ran into a form of harassment and hazing the like of which none of us had ever seen. *"Go here! Go there! Do this! Do that! Run! Run! Run!"* This went on until midnight. Then we were allowed to draw mattresses, pillows and bed sheets. (We were becoming experts at drawing equipment). "Get a good night's sleep!" we were told. "You're getting up at 0530."

The main theme of basic training, as far as the Army is concerned, is to teach each man to be a killer. That's right, a killer. A soldier is involved in the defense of his country, and sometimes this means killing other people. To put this product on the market, so to speak, the Army has to take a normal (sometimes) civilian who is used to his own ways, good or bad, been mollycoddled, pampered, or otherwise allowed to degenerate, reduce him to a state of nothingness, then build him back up again. Hence the hazing and harassment, and it had already started.

The first two weeks were spent on survival in the field. After that came cold weather training, tropical training, firing the rifle, bayonet training, hand grenade training, running the infiltration course, and most of all physical training. The American soldier, when he leaves basic, has been whipped into the best physical condition of his life. It takes eight weeks to master most of these traits, and at that point the G.I. is almost the best-trained soldier in the world. He was almost the best, but not quite. This would take another eight weeks of advanced infantry training.

Finally, after four months of the Army, we were considered soldiers and ready for assignment. There were people going to Korea, Japan, Germany, and to other posts in the world, in addition to assignments in the United States. I was fortunate. I was re-assigned to the same company I took basic with. Our regiment was being brought up to full combat strength and would now be considered a regimental combat team (RCT).

I would be staying at Fort Campbell for a while. Basic training was now a thing of the past and all of us were granted a fifteen-day leave. I took a look at my leave papers, smiled, and decided to hitch hike to Chicago.

Chapter 5
JODY

Transportation has always been a problem in the service. Not just the Army, but the Navy and Marine Corps as well. This would be transportation both on and off post. An Army post, such as Fort Campbell, is not unlike a city, there are the main business areas where Division headquarters, the main administration buildings, the post office and the main Post Exchange are located. This would be considered the downtown area.

As one moves out from the center, the neighborhoods come into play. Located here are the branch PX's, theaters, NCO (noncommissioned officers) clubs, officer's clubs medical and dental facilities, schools, branch post offices and other official offices of the United States Army.

In a typical Army post there is usually one principal division of the Army that makes its home there. At Fort Campbell when I was there, it was the 11th Airborne Division fresh from the south Pacific and World War II. An Army division is comprised of three regiments, four battalions to a regiment, four companies to a battalion and four platoons to a company. It is at these company levels where the barracks are located and the troops reside. Just one quick glance would illustrate how a division needs a lot of real estate to spread out and settle down.

If a GI (Soldier) wished to get from square one, his barracks, to the PX the library or the theater to see a movie for instance, he would have to resort to shoe leather. This is an old but reliable means of transportation. One foot is placed in front of the other and a method of locomotion called walking is performed. That is, of course, unless he was one of the fortunate few who had private transportation. A car.

There are many taxicabs to be found on Army posts. Many career soldiers would take their mustering out pay when leaving the service, invest in a vehicle, buy a license and go into the taxicab business. There are always people with a few bucks who could afford a taxi, but not your average recruit just out of basic. The only time he could afford a taxi was on payday.

Payday at Fort Campbell was a bizarre affair. It began at 0700 hours with the reveille **formation on the Company street**. The troops were then sent back to the barracks to pack everything military they owned into the two packs, they had been issued, light and heavy. A horse shoe roll, comprised of his blanket, rolled up into his half tent (shelter half), was strapped around these two packs that were hooked together, light on top, heavy on the bottom. This assembly was known as the full field pack.

The GI would then fall out again to the company street for a formation. This formation would march to battalion headquarters, be formed into a. battalion formation which would proceed to regimental headquarters. The regiment, along with the other regiments, would then take part in the Eleventh Airborne Division Payday Parade.

The entire division would pass in review in front of the commanding general. The general would be up on a platform with the Division Band on the right and spectators on the left. The band would be playing a Sousa March, and *almost* everybody felt patriotic.

Upon passing in review each battalion would move to its own battalion inspection area, be broken back down to companies and the monthly payday inspection would take place. Each man accompanied by his buddy would build a small tent using one of the half tents they each carried (shelter halves). Each man would then place all his equipment on blankets laid out in front of the tent.

The company commander, accompanied by the Platoon Leader a second lieutenant, and the Company First Sergeant would come by and inspect each platoon. This entourage would be followed by the Platoon Sergeant who would be taking notes. The inspection was done mainly to ensure each man had all his proper equipment, which had been issued to him. Upon completion of this procedure each man would pack up his belongings and be marched back to the barracks for "Pay call."

Every man would line up alphabetically and would proceed to a table at which was seated the Company Executive officer who acted as paymaster. The GI upon receiving an envelope containing cash, and a statement, would enter another series of lines consisting of people he owed money to, such as funds he owed the Army for lost or damaged equipment discovered in the full field inspection, and upon clearing this segment he would encounter another line. In this line were various non commissioned officers unofficially in the brokerage business who the soldier may have borrowed money from during the month. If there was any cash left over after all this, it belonged to the GI.

On payday, or the three or four days following, most soldiers had a few bucks, unless they had bad luck in a crap game or card game. These were the fortunate who could afford to ride in taxicabs for a short time. There would be ample time for walking during the coming month. I think the Army planned it that way.

I was planning to travel to Chicago during the fifteen days of leave I had coming. I hadn't seen my parents for a while and a taxicab was a luxury I just couldn't afford. It would take the pittance I had just received to get there and back. I was planning to use a mode of transportation military men have used for years. I would go to the highway, raise my arm, stick out my thumb, and hope! I decided to hoof it the three miles it was to the main gate.

In my walk to the gate I had plenty of time to observe the many facets of the post still in operation. I was officially off duty, but the Army functions "24 / 7." Twenty-four hours a day, seven days a week. There was a platoon heading my way, marching from one destination to another. I heard it long before I saw it. I was hearing the same chant the Army has used since the early days of World War Two. "Sound off." Listening to this chant I could hear them extolling the virtues of "Jody."

Jody was, and still is the "Sweetheart" of the American GI. She is slim, trim, gorgeous, voluptuous, tall, not too tall, well built, slim, cute, perky, short, blond, brunette, maybe a redhead, beautiful eyes, (the kind men get lost in), a great hair-do, an up sweep, maybe worn full length, bangs possibly, great legs, an hour glass figure, looks that could make a man drive his car into a fireplug, super personality, easy to talk to, maybe a little stuck up, a tingling laugh, the girl next door, but, sophisticated, and *sexy*. In a nut shell, "*Jody!*"

I remember the first time I heard of her. It was in a movie called *Battleground*, a story of "The Battle of the Bulge" in Belgium during the closing days of World War II. An American platoon, having been cut off for a month by elements of the German Army was preparing to withdraw after being relieved. A squad leader, played by James Whitmore, had just given his squad "About Face," and was preparing to march them to a rear echelon area. It was cold, cold enough to turn a man's breath to steam, and there was plenty of snow on the ground.

"Hut-Two-*Tha-ree* Four. Hut-Two-*Tha-ree* Four!"

"Hey Sarge," cried a squad member played by Van Johnson. "What ever happened to Jody?"

The sergeant, played by James Whitmore let his face break out in a tobacco-stained toothy grin. He spit out some juice from the wad in his cheek and nodded. He let out a loud command.

"Okay, pick it up!—— Hut-Two- *Tha- ree*-Four! Hut- Two- *Tha-ree*-four!"

"You had a good home but you left!" (Sergeant).
"You're right!" (Response).
"You had a good home but you left!" (Sergeant).
"You're right!" (Response).
"Jody was there when you left! (Sergeant).
"You're right!" (Response).
"Jody was there when you left!" (Sergeant).
"You're right!" (Response).
"Sound Off!" (Sergeant)
"One two!" (Response).
"Sound Off!" (Sergeant).
"Three - Four!" (Response).
"Cadence count!" (Sergeant).
"One- Two- Three- Four,
" One two— *Three four*!" (Response.)

The camera moves back for a panoramic shot, and down the snow covered road marches the squad. Fade out, end of movie. That was during World War II. Jody was also there during the Korean War because I was hearing about her when I made my trek from the barracks to gate three out by highway "41."

"You left Jody- a- way out west!" (Sergeant).
"We left Jody- a- way out west!" (Response).
"You thought this Army life was best!" (Sergeant).
"We thought this Army life was best.!) (Response).
"Now she's someone else's wife!" (Sergeant).
"Now she's someone else's wife!" (Response).
"And you'll be-a- marchin' the rest of your life!" (Sergeant).
"Sound off?" (Sergeant).
"Airborne!" (Response).
"Sound off' (Sergeant).
"Airborne!" (Response).
"Break it on down! (Sergeant).
"A-I-R-B-0-R -N-E!" (Response).

Maybe she made an appearance during "Nam" or "Desert Dtorm," probably, I don't know, I wasn't there. I was too busy enjoying the "Life of Riley" as a civilian. I was drinking beer, making money, and playing golf and gin rummy. Every once in awhile I would take a trip to Florida with my family. When we did we would make a side trip and visit Fort Campbell. At that time it wasn't difficult at all to walk onto an Army post. There would be an MP. At the gate, he would stop you and ask you to state your business for being on the post. You would then be directed to a visitor's section where you would be issued a pass to where you wanted to go. The MPs at that time were wearing Class "A" uniforms and spit shined polished boots with white laces.

All of a sudden "9-11" happened. If there was ever a time when I felt proud of an American president, it was when President Bush struck back at the madmen who committed that atrocity against our country. That organization that had lunatics fly airplanes into our buildings then stood in the streets of this nation, this *very* nation, and cheered. I remember reading in the paper about President Bush when he was touring the site. A tearful fireman took him by the sleeve and said "Mister President, don't let them get away with this!"

"I won't," answered President Bush. If that doesn't inspire pride in your leadership, I don't know what does.

After "9-11" it was no longer easy to walk onto a military base in this country, and the MP's weren't wearing Class "A" uniforms. They were in full battle dress and there were a lot more of them at the gate. I remember seeing the seriousness in their eyes, every bit as serious as the loaded M 16 sub-machine guns they were carrying. They looked us over, then we were asked to step out of the vehicle. The car was searched and we were directed to the visitors building where, maybe, just maybe, if your reason for being on post was good enough, you would be allowed to carry out your business.

The 11th. Airborne Division had been disbanded in 1958 and the 101st. Airborne Division, the Screaming Eagles of World War II fame, took its place at Fort Campbell. We were there to visit the 11th Airborne Division museum. I had a letter from my congressman. We were allowed to proceed. My wife and I were just getting out of the car in the parking lot, when I heard of Jody again.

"You won't be back 'til the end of the war!" (Sergeant).
"In the year two thousand and forty four!" (Response).
"You march and march 'til your feet are sore!" (Sergeant).
"And ya never ain't gonna see Jody no more!" (Response).
"Sound off" (Sergeant).
"Airborne!" (Response).
"Sound off" (Sergeant).

"Airborne!" (Response).
"Break it on down!" (Sergeant).
"A -I -R -B -0 -R-N-E!" (Response).

I don't know if it was really Jody I was hearing about, maybe her daughter or her granddaughter. It had been a long time, but the "Jody" cadence was one facet of Army life that you take with you when you leave, forget about for a while, then, for one reason or another, you remember. You pick it up in your mind, hum it a bit, and cherish it wherever you go without really knowing why. I had no idea I would be feeling this way many years in the future, when I made my way to Gate Three that Saturday afternoon in the early Fifties.

Chapter 6
MEETING THE MENTOR

Don't ever let anyone tell you Kentucky is warm in the winter months because it is one of our southern states. This is simply not true. During the winter months the north wind whips down highway "41" like it has an evil spirit chasing it, but in springtime it can be beautiful.

I was standing on the shoulder of the highway. I had my thumb in the air. Almost immediately a red Ford convertible pulled up and stopped next to me.

"I thought I recognized you!" I heard the driver say. I recognized the voice and looked up. It was Eddie Colquitt. I hadn't seen him in three or four long years, but he hadn't lost his charm, or his looks. He was handsome, sun tanned, wearing a red and white flowered shirt, white slacks, red socks and sunglasses. His attire almost matched the interior of the car; it also was red and white.

"Eddie Colquitt!" I said

"Live and in color!" he replied. He looked at me and flashed that same smile he always seemed to wear when we were kids at Shabonna Park not too long ago, but long enough.

"Where are you headed?" he asked.

"I thought I'd hitch hike to Chicago." I explained I had a fifteen-day leave.

"Well," he said, "I can't get you that far, but climb on in and I'll get you as far as Hop town! You'll have much better luck there."

So I got in, the seats were white leather, the floor carpeting red, and, as I said the interior of the car, and his clothes looked as if they came from the same factory.

The exterior was fire engine red and had those big white wall tires that were so popular then.

"Pretty automobile," I said.

"Yeah, it's a super vehicle," he said with a sigh, "I only wish it were mine."

I asked to whom it belonged and he started explaining.

"Well, it's mine and it's not." I gave him a quizzical look and he went on.

"I got out of the service a while back. I had a few bucks saved, and with the mustering out pay I got from Uncle Sam, I bought me a half interest in a used car lot, so the car is mine until I can sell it. 'Till then I drive it when I need a car, and the rest of the time it joins its brothers on the lot."

"It seems as if you keep busy" I said.

"I do, I do!" he replied, "The thing is, it keeps me too busy, I'd rather play a lot more golf than I do, a lot more business golf, but with the lot and all I just don't have the time. It's like the man said, ' golf is my profession, work just pays for it' He was looking in the rear view mirror as he drove. He looked as if he wanted to pull off the highway. "And to make matters worse," he went on, "My partner is getting on in years, and soon he'll want to retire and sell me his half, then I'll be busier than ever."

Looking again at the mirror he cut the wheels, drove off the highway and parked on the shoulder of the road. Cars and trucks whizzed by. From the breeze they created it's a good thing it was springtime. "Look," he said looking seriously at me "Is there any special reason you have to be in Chicago right now?"

I told him there was no pressing need, no immediate reason. I did want to see my parents and a few friends, but I was curious. I asked why.

"Well," he went on, "One of my salesmen just called. His wife is in the hospital up north and he won't be around for three or four weeks. How would you like to fill in for him?"

"You're kidding!"

"I'm desperate! I've got a few very important golf games lined up that I have to play. It's business golf. I have to be there and it's part of the job. I'll be so short handed it will really hurt."

"I've never sold a car in my life." I told him.

"Ah, it's nothing," he said "You sell yourself, the rest just happens, besides if you get into trouble there will be two other guys there to help you out. What do you say?"

"I don't know," I said. There was a long pause.

He looked at me, gave me that smile of his, and said, "It pays twenty five a day plus commission." (In the fifties this was good money).

"I'm your Man!"

So I filled in. Soon it became permanent since the other salesman stayed up north. I'm not saying I did well! I did fantastic! They were calling me "Eddie Colquitt's wonder boy."

I spent my fifteen day leave at Eddie's Mobile Madness out on highway "41." After my leave time was over I went back to being a soldier ten hours a day. Six am to four pm.

I would then drive over, (oh yes, I now had a car, *almost new*, but a car none the less), to the lot where I would be a car salesman until ten pm, drive back to the Company and the whole thing would repeat the following day. There was soldiering to do, cars to be sold, beer to drink and money to be made. Life was good.

In the interim between selling cars and playing soldier Eddie and the boys were teaching me a new (to me) card game. At Shabonna Park I had played a lot of blackjack, poker and pinochle, but this game was a horse of a different color. It was called gin rummy. It was a new and different. I found out in a hurry, that in any card game where you are a beginner, a novice, it costs. It takes money to learn the mannerisms of winning. One asks questions, and becomes a student of the game. To avoid being a perpetual loser this is necessary. Gin rummy was costing me a small fortune. I was seeing most of my commissions go right back to Eddie.

"Cross my palm." Eddie would say smiling, extending his hand after another winning session.

"Obscenity your palm!" I would respond, placing money into it.

However, I was a good student. I do learn quickly. Pretty soon I began holding my own, then, slowly, and I do mean slowly, I became a winner. It was exhilarating. I began beating my teacher, my mentor, and the master of all he surveyed! I'll never forget the first time I looked at him and said,

"Eddie, cross my palm." He didn't like it.

Chapter 7
JUMP SCHOOL

"Yo- left, Yo- left, Yo- left- rhat- left." There he was, counting our cadence, all six-foot-six of him, black as the Ace of Spades and built like a Wheaties box. The rank on the sleeves of his fatigue shirt was, what was called in the service at that time, three up and three down. This meant three chevrons on the top of the insignia, and three curved stripes on the bottom. This denoted the rank of Master Sergeant. The nameplate on his shirt read M/S Blevins. Master Sergeant Blevins.

Master Sergeant Blevins is marching, sort of a half walk and half strut. The rest of us, (pieces of shit, as we would soon be accustomed to being called), are walking. We haven't learned, as yet, how to march. The sergeant's eyes are looking straight ahead, but he can still see most of us, so great is his peripheral. The platoon is moving along counting almost the same cadence you read about in the "Jody" chapter.

I had just returned to duty after my fifteen-day leave and my free hours were spent with Eddie and the boys at the dealership. The company I was assigned to was no longer training recruits, it was in the process of being brought up to strength necessary to becoming a regular Army infantry company.

An infantry company trains. Training is its sole purpose. It trains day in and day out. The very same thing you learned in Training, the marching, the rifle, the hand grenade, the bayonet, the field problems you went through in Basic, you do constantly in a regular rifle company.

I had decided to become a paratrooper some weeks before and my name was on a waiting list to attend jump school. My reasoning was simple. I wanted to stay at Fort Campbell in the company I had been assigned to, and at Eddie's Mobile Madness. Most of the people who weren't paratroopers were being shipped out to other outfits and other Army posts. As long as the government had decided I was to be a soldier, I decided I was going to do it my way. To stay there I had to become a paratrooper. I had to enroll in jump school and "Win my wings." So there I was *moving along.*

"I don't know, but I've been told!" (Sergeant).
"I don't know, but I've been told!" (Response).
"Airborne wings are made of gold" (Sergeant).
"Airborne wings are made of gold!" (Response).
"Sound off!" (Sergeant).
"Airborne!" (Response).
"Sound off!" (Sergeant).
"Airborne!" (Response).
"Break it on down!" (Sergeant).
"A -I -R -B -0 -R -N-E!" (Response).

As we are marching I reflect in my mind why I am doing this, and what my options are. Counting cadence becomes second nature, you're moving, you're chanting and your feet are going along, but your mind is a hundred miles away. I'm living at the company and I'm TDY (temporary duty) at jump school. My car (now my very own), is parked near the school facility; so, when we fall out I drive right over to Eddie's. I have weekends off and it's great. It's almost as if the Army is a part time job.

This is almost as nice a deal as a friend of mine had when he was drafted. He was assigned to the United States Army recruiting station in down town Chicago. You talk about a situation made in heaven. This particular recruiting station was about two blocks from where his office was before he was drafted. He kept his civilian job and got there when he could. He lived at home, with a ration and quarters allowance, and was making more money than before he was drafted. Hardly anyone knew he was in the Army.

My schedule was not that different. Now that I am out of basic my routine has changed. I have more time to spend at the car lot. Gone are the days of working to five o'clock, (1700hrs) I now get off at three (1500hrs). And I don't have to pull any details, those cute little jobs the Army finds for a soldier to do such as KP (Kitchen police). KP is working in the mess hall (now called a dining facility). Here a man does such noble things such as washing dishes, mopping floors, cleaning tables etc. I also didn't have to participate in cleaning the barracks or the washrooms (latrines), or the like. All I had to do was get up in the morning, get over to jump school, put in my time, and head for Eddie's

It was great working there. When we weren't selling cars we would sit around and listen to Eddie's philosophy on gin rummy. I tell you, this guy had a king sized bag of tricks, and most of them were based on common sense. Common sense is a trait or attribute most of us seem to lose when we get a deck of cards in our hands.

"*Customer gin!*" Eddie seemed to announce this as if he were a vendor at the ballpark selling hot dogs.

"Customer gin?" asked Larry, one of the salesmen.

"Customer gin!" replied Eddie. "It's also known as losing politely."

"Picture this," he went on, "You have a customer on the line, not your ordinary run of the mill soldier boy, but a real live customer with real money. He can easily afford anything you have to show him. He is interested in a Chevy Bellaire convertible, one of those beauties we brought down from Chicago last week."

Every once in awhile Eddie would drive a few of us up to Chicago. He would buy a few cars and we'd drive them back. This would keep our inventory up plus we all got a fully paid trip home and back.

"This baby," Eddie went on, "has all the bells and whistles, really top of the line. It's barely a year old, a honey, and a real cherry. Your buyer is in love with it."

"So what's keeping him from buying it?" I asked, "What's holding him back?"

"Because," said Eddie, "Jimmy Knight, down the road a piece on '41' has almost the same deal, only it's a Ford Victoria convertible, for almost the same price. The buyer is in love with that one too! The deal is terrific, a real winner because both cars are expensive and the commission is huge."

Eddie paused to pop open a Heinekens. "Both you and Jim's salesman have had this guy out for lunch, He can easily afford to have both of you out, but it doesn't work that way. In your conversations, it turns up he has a fondness for card playing. There's your opening, the other salesman doesn't play cards.

"You mention you are not much of a poker player," he went on, "but you do dabble in gin rummy once in awhile. 'The bait has been cast.' The buyer mentions a modest game; say a friendly game for a nickel a point. After hemming and hawing you both settle on three cents, because, you tell him, you are not much of a player. 'The hook has been set.' The game begins.

"You realize at once he's not much of a gin player at all. In a drunken stupor you could take him to the cleaners, but this is not the object of the game. The real object is to make sure he buys the Chevy Bellaire, so you carry him. You intentionally make a lot of stupid mistakes, not flagrant, but mistakes non-the less. You end up after an afternoon of lunch and cards being out a C- note. A hundred dollars. You lost fifty, the rest was lunch and entertainment, and so you have a hundred invested in him. Your commission if he buys the car will be close to five hundred.

"The next morning he's in my office signing the papers and closing the deal. And what brought all this about my man? Guess what? You made him feel ten feet tall on the card table.

"Customer gin! Learn how to do this, it's worth its weight in gold."

Chapter 8
IT'S ALL ILLUSION

Webster defines an illusion as "something that deceives by creating a false impression"

There once was a man of African American descent who walks into a bar. He has a parrot on his shoulder. Now this is no ordinary parrot, he has a green body, an orange head; green eyes with red pupils the size of silver dollars. He is, from the top of his head to the tip of his toes, some five feet long. The bartender takes one look and says, "Where the hell did you get him?"

The parrot looks at the bartender and says, "On the south side of Chicago, there's a million of them down there."

This is our first day of jump school. I had thought all the "chicken shit" and harassment we had put up with in basic training was completely over. I hadn't lived. Under the bright and hot Kentucky sunlight we stood there and re-lived all those glorious days of what the Army refers to as indoctrination.

"My name is Master Sergeant Aubrey Blevins. YOU will refer to me as Master Sergeant Blevins. Even my *wife* calls me as Master Sergeant Blevins. Not Aubrey, not honey, but *Master* Sergeant Blevins.

" I will be *yo momma, yo Poppa, yo Sistah, yo brothah, and everything* else that is near and dear! *DO YOU UNDERSTAND?*" he bellowed.

I thought this might be a moment for a bit of levity. "Hey, Sarge," I said with a smile on my face, "How 'bout nurse?" The other members of the platoon laughed momentarily, and then looked over at the sergeant to see what his response would be.

"Young trooper!" he yelled. (It seemed this man couldn't say anything in a normal tone of voice). "You have just committed two unpardonable offenses. *One*, you have gotten familiar. *Didn't* I just tell everybody what my name is? *Didn't* I just say, that at all times you will refer to me as *Master Sergeant Blevins*, not Sarge, not Blevins, but, Master Sergeant Blevins. That's number one.

"*Number two*, is you have just interrupted the man I like to hear best. *Me!*" He walked over to where I was standing in the front row of the platoon and put his hands on his hips and his nose about an inch from mine.

"Dick brain!" he said. "You will now drop down and give me some push-ups. You will knock out twenty-five of them, and if they are not absolutely perfect in every manner, shape or form, you will find yourself digging a hole six foot square and six foot deep just so I can take a leak in it, then, you'll find yourself filling it back up again."

I dropped down and began doing the push-ups; believe me, they were perfect.

"Now, just so we understand each other," he said to the rest of the platoon, "The reason I have to be all of those things to you, is because I expect you to master everything, and I do mean master every little bit of material I give you as if your life depended on it, because it might. When Ol' Master Sergeant Aubrey Blevins gets through with your young asses, some of you will be heading off to a place called Korea. And if you learn everything I teach you, and learn it right, you just might make it back to Jody. You won't end up with some gook with a knife in his hand sneaking up in back of you and cutting you to pieces because you forgot one of the tricks of the trade I tried to give you!

"What you *will* be able to do, if you pay attention to me, is take that knife away, stomp the dog shit out of him, and send him to wherever the hell these *friggin gooks* go when they leave this world."

He glanced down at me as I was getting up from doing the push-ups.

"You might just remember that, Dick-brain!" he said.

Second day of jump school: It is bright and sunny out, it has been this way for a week. And hot? The temperature is ninety-five degrees and the humidity is way-way up there. The armpit sections of the fatigue jackets are soaked with sweat. In the evening, when the shirt dries, white rings will form. This is perspiration salt.

We begin this sunny day by putting on parachute harnesses under the watchful eyes of Master Sergeant Aubrey Blevins. This apparatus is comprised of nylon straps that have metal ends with holes, not entirely unlike those you see on the seat belts in your automobile. The back part of the harness is shaped like the letter "H" with the two upright straps above the horizontal member worn over the shoulders. The straps on the bottom of the "H" are worn between the legs. The four straps click into a small metal box (quick release box), with a button in the middle. When this button is hit with the heel of the hand, it causes the straps to fly out of the box. In this way the jumper can exit the harness swiftly.

"No, no, no! Dick-brain." (Guess who he was talking to?) "You wear the straps around your balls, not over them. You want to sound like a soprano the rest of your life? Now get down and knock out twenty-five."

I dropped to the ground and made another contribution to the Sergeant Blevins push-ups collection, all the while thinking I didn't have enough rank to be a Dick brain. The best I could do was to be an asshole.

There is a section of the jump school facility set aside for parachute harness training. There are small towers twelve feet high set ten foot apart. They are made to accommodate ten jumpers in each row. There are ten rows. There is a six-inch wooden beam between each tower. In the center of each beam are two hooks set shoulder width apart. Two nylon straps (risers) are attached to these hooks. The jumper trainee climbs a small ladder and fastens his harness to these risers. The ladder is removed allowing the trainee to swing freely just as he would as if he were wearing the real thing in an actual jump.

There are drills he must perform; the act of wearing the harness while hooked to this wooden beam is a drill in itself. The feeling caused by the tightness of the straps lingers long after the harness has been stepped out of. It is similar to the feeling you got as a kid when you removed your roller skates. In trainee jargon the harness drill is, for obvious reasons, called "*The nutcracker.*"

Sergeant Blevins is ever present, and he issues commands relating to each drill.

"*Normal position!*"

This would be the position a jumper assumes for a normal descent.

"*Moving into trees!*" and "*Moving into wires!*" are among the drills, and the jumper trainee must react in a prescribed manner. Possibly the most important would be:

"*Moving into water!*" When approaching water landing, the jumper must hit the quick release button just prior to entering the water. That same device, the parachute with its canopy and shroud lines (nylon lines running from the harness to the canopy) that was life sustaining during the jump can become life threatening in the water if a jumper becomes tangled up in them. Every drill performed by the trainee is preceded by classroom sessions and movies.

The next item on the agenda is the thirty-four foot tower. At the top of this tower is a platform with a mock-up of a partial side of an airplane. At the middle of this there is a door similar to the actual door a jumper jumps out of. The trainee climbs a ladder on the side of the tower to this platform where he meets an awaiting drill sergeant. He is issued three commands, the first of which is "*Hook up!*"

The trainee hooks his harness to an awaiting pulley that runs on a cable from the top of the mock- up to a point on the ground a hundred yards away.

"*Stand in the door!*"

The trainee moves into the doorway and "Assumes the position," His chin is raised, his eyes are facing forward, the knees are flexed and the palms of his hands are flat on the outside of the mock up just outside the door.

"*Go!*"

The jumper exits the mock-up, falls eight feet, the risers become taught and he rides the cable to the ground where he tumbles into his parachute landing fall (PLF). This fall is executed ideally if the jumper touches ground with the balls of his feet with the knees flexed. The knees are then rotated in one direction or another depending on which direction the jumper was coming in. The weight then shifts to the side of the calf, the knee, the hip and finally the shoulder. At this point the jumper is on his back, his feet are about three feet off the ground and he comes to a rocking halt.

All this happens too fast to be thought out; it's much like sawing a piece of wood, or sweeping a floor, you don't think of the actions involved, they are just done. Relax and fall to one side probably would be the best way to describe it.

Going through the tower is compulsory prior to the trainee making his first jump. There was a general who needed to become a paratrooper prior to receiving his second star. He had frozen in the tower twice. He had stood in the door but couldn't make himself jump. This attempt was to be his final. You only get three. In the first two tries the drill sergeants even went so far as to attempt to shove him out. All to no avail, they couldn't budge him. The desire was there, but the man couldn't make himself do it.

"I can't!" he said

Sergeant Blevins, standing on the platform next to him was a quick thinker.

"Sir!" he said to the general, "what you're looking at is all an illusion. You're only up thirty-four feet. After you fall ten feet you'll be hooked up to the cable and you ride it down to the ground. You've got to be confident. If you do it once, that will be the end of it, you'll never have the problem again."

"Help me," said the general.

"Sir," said the sergeant, "You've got to establish a positive attitude, an illusion of confidence. Place your left hand on the top of your helmet, and the right hand on the seat of your pants. Lift up with the right hand and yell *JUMP*, and you will."

The General gave the sergeant a skeptical look, but went ahead. He placed his left hand on his head; his right on the seat of his pants and yelled, "*JUMP!*"

At that moment Sergeant Blevins put his right foot on the General's butt, gave a little push and another jumper was qualified.

"Illusions," Eddie was saying at the dealership. He popped the cap off another Heinekens and continued. "There are all kinds of them, and it's important you recognize each and every one of them. Not only to use them yourself, but also to spot them when the other guy is trying to lead you down the garden path. Let me give you a few examples:

"A player wants to give the impression he is looking for high cards. This is done by reaching halfway toward the discard pile when a high card turns up, pausing, and then doing it again. He is trying to create the illusion he has a high card combination working. He wants to convey this impression to force you to hold onto high cards you might otherwise get rid of.

"Another way for him to create this illusion is to discard three of four mini's in a row. This usually gives the impression whether true or not you are seeking high cards.

Example: A player is dealt two kings, two queens, two jacks all unrelated, and four small cards. He wants the "Rembrandts" so he discards the minis. This is usually a tip-off of what he is seeking, the high cards. The same illusion is true when the opponent wants you to hold high cards.

"If the game is Oklahoma Gin where the twenty first card is turned up and used as a call card, many people will pick this card up if it is a high card. The idea is to force the opponent to hold high cards around the card that was just picked up as a defensive measure. It's called *tap dancing*. Be alert, many times there will be cards in your hand that will enable you to see through this ploy.

Remember, these illusions are just that, illusions. They are meant to keep an opponent off balance. They are ploys that are meant to be used just once in awhile, and are based on the laws of gullibility (if there are such laws). Watch for the other guy to use them. Or if you're that type of person, use them yourself, however, my advice would be to play it straight. How's that saying go? "You can't cheat an honest man.""

The weekend came, and with it Saturday morning. The early hours were spent on preparation for the weekly Company full field inspection. This in contrast to the outdoor Payday Parade inspection is done in the barracks. Everything is laid out on the soldier's bunk. Class A uniforms are worn. This inspection is usually gotten over with quickly because everyone involved, the people who conduct the inspection, the Platoon Leader, the First Sergeant, the Platoon sergeant, and the troops want to get it over with so the weekend can begin.

This is usually over by 1100 hrs. And then for me, it's off to Eddies. Eddie called me over to one side when I got there.

"Do you know a Sergeant Blevins?" he asked.

"Yeah," I said, "He's my drill, and hand to hand combat instructor in jump school. Why?"

"Well he's going to be with us for awhile. We're going to teach him all we know about cards, and he's going to show us how to handle Negro customers. It's going to be a whole new market for us!"

"Hey," I said, "we don't get along at jump school, how the hell am I going to get along with him here?"

Eddie's desk chair spun around and I was looking into a black smiling face.

"Oh, I think we gonna get along fine, young trooper!"

At least he didn't call me "Dick-brain!"

Chapter 9
THE FIRST JUMP

Dawn: The Jump School Company Street The only time of day when it's really cool. In a half hour or so the sun will be coming up and then it will start getting hot. We hear a mechanized noise. This would be the two and a half ton trucks (deuce and a half's) coming by to take us to the airport. We all look to our left and we can see the blue colored exhaust rising above the trees a few moments before we see the vehicles. They stop in front of the formation and we all pile on, thirty men to a truck. We will be heading for Campbell Air Force Base where we will board airplanes for our first jump. I was impressed. I had been on this post for four months and I was just finding out, not only was it a major Army base, but a major USMC. Base and an Air Force base as well. As we rode along I realized, gone are the days of double timing, the thirty-four foot tower and the nutcracker. This would be the real thing.

The trucks enter the gate, drive almost up to the tarmac and stop. Visible on long bench like structures are the parachutes. Every three feet a parachute has been placed. The 'chutes are in sack like containers, olive drab in color and have been expertly packed by a Company called "Parachute maintenance company." This is an outfit that does nothing but pack and maintain parachutes. I have often been asked if I packed my own 'chute. My answer always has been, "No, never have, never would have."

The parachute assembly consists of the harness itself and two risers that extend upward to a flexible nylon circular device to which nylon cords, (shroud lines) are attached. These lines extend upward to the parachute itself (the canopy). This canopy in the 1950's measured thirty feet across and was called Parachute-T10. OD. US ARMY. To the top of the canopy a braided nylon rope (static line) is attached. This static line when hooked to a cable running the length of the ceiling in the airplane pulls the parachute, which has been intricately folded, out of the sack when the jumper exit's the aircraft.

The parachute itself is worn on the back of the harness. There is another small parachute called a reserve 'chute which is worn on front. There is a nylon loop on the left side of the bag containing the chute. A metal handle (rip cord) is on the right. This ripcord when pulled spills the reserve parachute out of the bag and it deploys. This reserve 'chute is only used in case the main parachute fails.

The jumpers hop down from the trucks and proceed to the benches where they put on their parachutes. Each man assists the man next to him. Once this is done they proceed (shuffle off!) to the nearby airplanes.

The airplanes used at the time were *C-119's* (flying boxcars). The exterior of this airplane is polished aluminum riveted to metal ribs (struts); the interior is quite skeletal in appearance with the metal ribs exposed. There is no sound insulation as there is on a commercial airplane, so when the aircraft speeds down the runway the noise and vibration reach bedlam proportions. The jumpers enter the airplane by means of a ramp and take seats on the long wooded benches that run the length of the cabin.

At *take off* the airplane speeds down the runway and seems to leap into the air. A short time later it has reaches its jumping altitude of one thousand feet. One thousand feet is the prescribed altitude for jumps made in jump school. Training jumps are made from eight hundred feet, while mock-combat and combat jumps are made anywhere from five hundred to seven hundred feet. The explanation for the difference in altitudes is simple. The higher a jumper is, the more time he has to react to a malfunction. They don't happen often, but they are possible. In a combat jump the Army wants the jumper on the ground A.S.A.P. because people may be shooting at him.

Upon reaching one thousand feet the aircraft levels off and zeros in on the drop zone (DZ). At this point it's very peaceful, the noise level is down to a drone, and I allow my mind to wander. I think of the upcoming session at the car lot, of my customers, and my first session of explaining some of Eddie's theories about gin rummy to Sergeant Blevins.

"Do I have to call you Sergeant Blevins while we're here, and not at the school?"

The good sergeant looked at me and smiled. "Rules of the game!" he told me. Even my——."

"Yeah, I know I said, Even your wife." His smile broadened.

"Okay, Sergeant, have it your way. I continued, "You impress me as having a fair amount of card sense. No, better than that. You've played a lot of cards, a lot of gin rummy, 'that right?"

"I've been in the Army ten years." he replied. "You do learn a lot. Playing cards is just a small part of it. What I really want from you people at Eddies is a refined knowledge of the games. I don't really want to beat anybody badly, I just don't want to get crucified myself!"

"Okay, fair enough." I answered.

"Here's one of the first things you're going to run into." I told him. "You happen into a small time game, a penny across, or one-one and two. You have an opponent or a partner who number one is always asking what the call is, or what the count is. Number two, he always has his eye on the discard pile prior to discarding.

"A person who can't keep up with the game, and repeatedly has to ask questions regarding the status, you should avoid at all costs. You certainly don't want him for a partner, and as an opponent he'll drive you crazy. He's a waste of time in a low stakes game, and in a greater valued game he can cost you nothing but money in the long run.

"Glancing at the discard pile is always done, there's no way that I know of how it can be avoided. Studying it every time you are making a discard is considered gross. If you have this habit, I suggest you get rid of it"

"In tournament gin rummy there is a small plastic container (shoe) in which the discards are placed. In a gambling situation this is not the case. Discards are done at random, almost haphazardly, flipped, so to speak, onto the pile. It's a strange situation. A person may reach out and straighten the pile from time to time, but this action if done too often will cause eyebrows to rise. There's no real answer to the problem. This is sociable gin rummy, high stakes or not, and we all have to get along."

"One player, and I don't advocate this, became so distraught watching the other guy repeatedly study the discard pile, picked it up, fanned it out and said 'Here! Take a good look you sonuva bitch!' I got a kick out of it, but I wouldn't advise it!"

"Losing streaks: When you are unfortunate enough to have absolutely nothing in your hand, I mean Milwaukee Avenue all the way, you should avoid the temptation to "Get blood out of a stone." It won't happen. The only move for you in this situation is to reduce the value of the hand. You dive. You pick up every low card that comes along and get rid of the higher ones. First it reduces your deadwood count, second, if you do lose, you won't lose as much and your partners will stand up and notice you did every thing you could to get low. Third. Sometimes these mini's match up, you wind up with a halfway decent hand and are right back in the game."

"The perpetual caller; this guy plays every hand the same way. He will pick up his cards, set all his unrelated high cards off to one side and get rid of them as soon as he can. He is running for the hills, going for the call. There is nothing wrong with this style; in fact, a lot of people play this way. The only thing in question is it's easy to spot, especially if you have scouted this person. If you are in a position of knowing how the other guy is going to play the hand most of the time, you have a marked advantage. More times than not, if you reduce your deadwood total with him, you will be in a good position to undercut him, or at worst, lose very little."

The plane drones on. The noise has subsided. The jumpers look at one another. Not much is said. Some think, some sleep, some pray. It is after all a new and strange experience. I nod my head and try to think of the car lot.

Sergeant Blevins made five more appearances at the car lot and while we taught him a lot about the game he didn't already know. In return, he taught us all a lot about the Negro customer.

"The main thing," he told us repeatedly, " is most of them, be they soldier or civilian, is they have very little cash on hand, so a sizeable down payment or, an outright cash sale is usually out of the question. So, nine times out of ten, it comes down to, not how much the car is going to cost, but how large or small the payments will be. .

"I've been around here a long time. I went to the Philippines and on to Japan when I enlisted in 1944. Then I came back here. I've had two tours of duty in Korea, but I always seem to wind up back here at Fort Campbell. I know a lot of people in Nashville, especially people in the banking business. Most of them are Negro like me and all of them are right on top of how money is loaned out, and where it's going.

"Did you know, right now there is a major civil rights campaign going on. In a few months the government will be bending over backwards to ensure minorities, that's what we are going to be called, get their fair share of *easy money*. What I'm telling you is most minorities, mostly Negroes will be able to buy a lot of items they couldn't afford in the past. A black man will be able to walk into a car lot, pick out a car and put down next to nothing as a down payment.

"The loans will be set up for up to five years and the payments will be quite small. Both of us know most of these loans will be reneged on, but the government will be guaranteeing them. The buyers won't care a bit about paying the car off. That will be the farthest thing in their minds. Uncle Sam will pick up the tab! All they will care about is the super low monthly payment. You will hear it time, and time again, 'How much are them there *notes?*' If you and Eddie are on the ball, you should be able to clean out that car lot two or three times a month." This did come to pass. Not just then, but the practice lasted all over the country for quite a few years.

We got along fine at the dealership, M/S Blevins and myself. We taught him a lot, and he taught us a lot, although at the Jump school, situations remained the same. He was still Master Sergeant Aubrey Blevins, and I was still a "Young trooper!" I think during his short tenure at the dealership he learned probably the most important part of gin rummy, or any card game for that matter, the art of scouting.

Eddie was sharing his philosophies about scouting.

"Scouting," Eddie said, pointing his right index finger at us. "You simply cannot do enough of it. I don't care it its gin rummy, poker, pinochle, or what have you. I would no more play a stranger for a lot of money, without having kibitzed him, than I would enjoy wearing dirty underwear while being taken to the hospital after an accident.

There are basic questions a player must ask himself while kibitzing. Does he get rid of bombs right away? Does he send out salesmen? Often? Does he speculate? Often? In poker, is he a wide-open player, or a percentage player? Does he bluff a lot? These are all questions you have to ask yourself. While you are playing watch your back. Turn around once in awhile and notice if anyone is scouting *you*. If so, play your cards 'close to the vest'. The less someone else knows about you, and your hand, the better.

"Mannerisms," he said, "They are more like little habits, little quirks every one of us has, especially when we come under stress. We scratch our heads; drum our fingers and the like. Many times stress will affect the way we play. It may cause us to run scared. Remember these things, they are often the difference between going home with money in your pocket or going home broke."

"*STAND UP!*" Each jumper stands up.

"*HOOK UP!*" Each jumper hooks his static line to the cable overhead.

"*STAND BY FOR EQUIPMENT CHECK!*" Each jumper checks the packing of the parachute of the man next to him for possible flaws.

"*SOUND OFF FOR EQUIPMENT CHECK!*" Each man in turn issues an affirmative, confirming his buddy's parachute housing has no visible flaws, and the man is properly hooked up.

The response is loud and vocal; "*Nine Okay, - Eight Okay!*" Etc.

In a normal combat or training jump there is one jumpmaster standing by the rear door of the aircraft. There are two twenty-man lines (sticks) of jumpers on each side. The jumpmaster is by the left door. The first man in line by the right door is called the stick leader. Both of them are watching for the first of two lights to come on. The first light is red. When this light is lit it indicated the airplane is approaching the DZ (drop zone). At this moment both men stand in their respective doors and assume the position described in the thirty-four foot tower. There is a highly alert atmosphere present in the airplane at this time.

Drop zones are measured in seconds rather than feet. In other words, how many seconds does it take an airplane flying at eighty knots to clear this drop zone? Therefore it is of the utmost that both twenty men sticks clear the airplane swiftly.

When the light turns green four things happen at once. The jumpmasters' jump, they exit the airplane. The two twentieth men, the last ones on the stick (stick pushers), who have also been watching a similar set of lights, lunge forward. The impact with the man in front of them causes a chain reaction where both twenty man sticks seem to run out of the aircraft all at once.

In jump school the procedure is quite different. There are two ten man sticks and two jumpmasters. Sergeant Blevins is one; the other a carbon copy of him, a sergeant named Bobby Holmes is the other.

The light turns red. The command is *"STAND IN THE DOOR!"* The first jumper stands in the door. The light turns green and he next command is *"GO!"* The jumpmaster whacks the jumper on the butt and out he goes. He jumps. This procedure is repeated for each jumper until the airplane is cleared. This usually takes several passes over the drop zone.

Upon clearing the aircraft the jumper is greeted with an exhilarating feeling. The force of air generated by the propellers (prop blast) throws him clear of the airplane. The static line plays out, pulls the parachute from its housing pack and it pops open. The jumper is now in an inverted position. His feet are facing the sky. As the 'chute blossoms out his feet lower and he is in the same position he was during the Nutcracker drill on the ground three weeks ago. He glances up at the canopy and checks it for damage. The canopy is made of silk and nylon. It is camouflage in color and is very sheer. It is not unlike a pair of lady's panty hose, one can almost see through it, runs and holes can occur.

He then looks down past his boots and gets his first glimpse of what Mother Earth looks like from a thousand feet up. There is no sensation of falling; it's more like a drifting or floating feeling. There is, however what seems to be a slow process of descending. It is, however, not slow by any means, it is quite rapid, it just seems slow. All of a sudden there is an awareness of peripheral movement. This would be ground structure, such as trees, buildings etc., being picked up by his peripheral vision. He is now some eighty or ninety feet from the ground. At this point his chin is raised, knees flexed, and he awaits impact.

He hits hard tumbling into his landing fall. He comes to a stop, and it's over. He almost feels like laughing. Getting to his feet he collapses the parachute by pulling the shroud lines down on one side. The risers and canopy are then *figure-eighted* by rolling them around the forearms. He places the 'package' on the ground and runs off the drop zone. Thirty seconds have elapsed and the first jump is history.

I tell you that first jump came close to being the most remarkable thing in my life; I was scared shitless, but I'll never forget it. As an old jumpmaster once told me, "Jumping out of an airplane is the greatest feeling a man gets in life with his pants on!"

The next four jumps, a trainee makes a total of five, were almost routine, except the night jump. No one ever forgets that one either. You would think while being up a thousand feet floating around, everything would be shrouded in darkness like it is when you look out of an airplane window on a commercial flight at nighttime. It is not. On a commercial flight you are a lot higher. The ground from a night jump, a thousand feet up, seems close and illuminated. It's an eerie feeling difficult to describe. I guess one would have to have been there. I know I'll always remember it.

The first thing I did when I got off the drop zone after the night jump was to pin a set of wings on my shirt. I had bought them at the PX. I heard a voice. It was Sergeant Blevins. He seemed to have materialized from out of nowhere.

"Take them back off Dickbrain!" he told me, "You're still a pooper trooper! Tomorrow morning after the ceremony you can put them back on because then, you'll be a real *live* paratrooper. You think you can wait that long?"

I took a long second to look at him wondering if this guy was for real. I thought of many things I could say, but the best I could come up with was, "I guess I'll have to!"

" You got that right, young trooper, he said. Then he put out his hand. I took it and looked up at his face. He was smiling. He gave me a wink and said; " You'll be an airborne soldier then, and I think you're gonna be a good one."

Master Sergeant Aubrey Blevins made a lasting impression on my life. At the time I would have liked to think he and I had parted as friends. I smiled back at him, and I sincerely hoped I would see him again later on in life. I would, but it would be a long time coming.

So that was jump school. I graduated and earned my wings. I won them. I love them, and I still have them on my key chain. I'm proud of them and I carry them wherever I go.

The rest of my Army career was really nothing exciting. I was working for the government, working for Eddie on the side, and learning a lot about life and card games. In retrospect, I suppose I might have done things differently were I not selling cars at Eddie's Mobile Madness. I did like the Army and I was proud of my physical conditioning. I was proud of the uniform I wore, and proud to be a soldier in the finest Army in the world.

However, a change in my life was in store.

Chapter 10
A SHORT TIMER

The months passed. The Korean War had long since become a thing of the past. I was now a "short timer"—I had two months left to serve in the Army. Eddie was talking of selling the lot and going back to Chicago. With the war over, the draft was cut in half; the used car prospects dwindled. It was time to move on.

My outfit, The 11th Airborne Division, was slated to leave Fort Campbell and relocate in Germany. "Operation Gyroscope!" they were calling it. I had another stripe and a pay hike waiting for me if I went for it and re-enlisted. I didn't. My heart said yes, but my head said no!

In the late fifties, it all came to a head. I left the Army, and went back to Chicago. The card room at Shabonna Park also became history. A lot of things had happened in a very short period of time. I got engaged to a girl I knew in high school. I became a bricklayer and went to work. Shortly afterward, Eddie did sell that car lot and headed back to Chicago where he opened another "Eddie's Mobile Madness!" It was on Cicero Avenue, a Mecca for used car dealers. Did I ever see him again? Sure! But I would have to wait some twenty years or so before our paths crossed again.

I had married and was bringing up my family. I was in a construction business that was doing well. Golf became one of my vices and I joined a country club. I played golf three times a week, sometimes four. Golf was usually followed by gin rummy.

They played partnership gin there. There were two, sometimes three players on a side. The scoring was of the "Hollywood" variety with three games being played at one time, sometimes for a little, sometimes for a lot. It's a friendly club.

One day I walked into the card room, and there he was, the same old Eddie, even though it had been some twenty years. It was summertime, and he had on the white slacks, and yes, the red Hawaiian shirt too. We had a few drinks together, then later dinner with our wives. During the next few years I played a lot of cards with him, gin rummy and different types of poker, and did I learn.

I was now learning about "the other guy." I was learning how to scout him, how to observe his mannerisms, how to spot signs of trouble, and how to watch his eyes to detect emotion

A lot had taken place since the early Fifties; a lot of water had gone over the dam. I thought he had covered a lot of things years ago. He hadn't scratched the surface. Most of what I know about cards today came from Eddie many years ago. I'm just happy to pass it along. It was the beginning of my card playing career, and the end of my Army career.

I had left the service, but I left part of myself there. When I walked away I was under the assumption everything related to the Army was over. *Gone!* I didn't realize it at the time, but when I left Fort Campbell and the Army, a certain part of me, a very important part of Kenny, remained. It stayed there and said— *Goodbye!*

PART TWO:

A CIVILIAN AGAIN!

Chapter 11
OLD MAN KARDS

Did you ever wonder why you could sit down at a car table and win hand after hand after hand? It goes on and on! You can do no wrong. It almost seems there is a light shining from up above. Why, for instance, if you are holding a Jack of a particular suit, and you need the ten you catch it! Either your opponent, "Good old Charlie," throws it, or maybe you just reach out and pluck it from the deck, or the discard pile. Did you ever wonder, how hand after hand, one could be dealt two, maybe three spreads? You reach out and pick up your hand and yep, there they are. You almost yawn it's so easy.

How about the times when you are dealt nothing at all? Milwaukee Avenue it's called, two minutes later after three key picks you're ready for gin. It's almost like magic. Some people talk about mental telepathy. Is there such a thing? Does it really take place? Is it actually possible for one person to place his mind above another's and compel him to act in the way he is directed?

Consider this; you are in need of the seven of spades. You need it to go with the six and eight of spades you are holding. It's an inside catch, a *belly shot*. There is no way in the world you should be considering such a move. Eddie Colquitt would sneer. It goes beyond all the laws of probability. Why are you doing this? It doesn't make sense. Who knows, maybe you read about it somewhere. You look straight at Charlie; he doesn't even know he's being watched. He's concentrating on his hand.

"Seven of spades!" you say to yourself. "Seven of spades, Charlie throw the seven of spades." You say it over and over and over again. Forcing yourself to concentrate you say it again, seven of spades, seven of spades. *Bingo!* Low and behold here it comes. As if by magic it almost jumps out of his hand and into yours

How about this scenario? You go on for weeks, sometimes months, you never lose. Oh sure, there are times you must throw a few crumbs to the wolves, but by and large you don't lose. You are enjoying a winning streak the like of which has never been seen, (of course it has, but basking in your glory, you refuse to believe it).

You look in the mirror. This happens a lot lately. Your vanity knows no bounds. "Hey good looking," you say to the mirror, sometimes even out loud, "Where have you been all my life?" You give yourself a love pat on the cheek. "You have got to be the best, the very best, the finest gin rummy player God created." Everywhere you go you are on cloud nine. It is becoming difficult for you to wait for Wednesday to roll around so you can venture into the card room and survey the victims that are awaiting you there. Many years ago there was a soft porn book (probably tame by today's standards) called "Impatient virgin." Your impatience makes her look like a nun.

It has become an obsession. You find yourself neglecting your business, your family, and your golf game. Your income may be five grand a week after taxes. But what the hell fun is that? True excitement is winning five or six hundred or so, two or three time a week, playing cards. There is this running tab kept in your mind, or maybe it's even put it down on paper. This is the way you keep track of how much you are ahead since January first. This is July so it has to be ten - fifteen grand at least.

Sitting at the bar you look around. You nod at this person, smile at that one. They smile back. You have become a celebrity. You find yourself buying drinks for people you hardly even know. Sitting at a table nearby you see a couple whose acquaintance you made just last week. You call the waitress over and tell her you would like to send a round of drinks to their table.

"Go ahead," you say, making a motion with the back of your hand and your fingers, "Bring Mr. and Mrs. Whatzername a cocktail, and put it on my tab." Moments later the drinks arrive. Mr. And Mrs. Whatzername smile their thanks. You nod pleasantly. You feel proud, and why not? You are a *Bon Vivant*.

"What the hell," you tell yourself" "I wonder whose ten bucks that was?"

This has been going on for quite some time now and it's never going to end. Never-ever, ever, and why should it? You are a *star*. You've had winning periods before that lasted a week or two, but that was all luck This, This latest streak has been the real thing. Every move you've made, every hand you've won, has been based on skill. The skill you've put together. The skill honed with your own intelligence, your own knowledge.

You look at the mirror in back of the bar and smile, you feel like you're in heaven. Life is good; the cards keep coming. What could be better? Then all of a sudden you commit sin! *Bang!* It hits you like a ton of bricks. You have been so God- awful cocky that you say something you should maybe only think, let alone say out loud.

When a player is able to declare gin by the third of fourth card of a new hand being played, it is considered somewhat of a rarity. The term used is "no-brainer," suggesting that there has been no skill or thought involved, merely the task of picking the cards up, arranging them, and laying them back down three plays later, and saying *gin!*

You seem to have made a habit of this lately. One day you again make gin on the third card played. This is the fourth time in a row you have done this. You are not surprised; you're a genius aren't you? You look at your hapless opponent, whom you've been kicking the daylights out of the past eight weeks, and say to him; "My man, you have just been beaten by, not only the finest gin rummy player in the United States, but in the whole wide world."

The words roll off your tongue so easily you don't even realize what you have just said. What's worse, when you do become aware of it, you believe every word .Of course you smile when you are saying these words just so Charlie, or what ever his name is will know you are just joshing, *Ho, Ho, Ho.* But you are not. Deep down inside you know you are not kidding. You're not kidding because it's true. *Of course it's true*; why else would you be such a winner.

Every time you make an appearance at the club you're treated as if you are royalty, a true celebrity. People reach out to shake your hand, to pat you on the back. Everybody wants to be seen with you, everybody wants to be your friend. Everybody wants to be your partner when the next Hollywood rolls around .The bartenders beam at you. The waitresses all but adore you. "Would you like a table by the window sir? *Absolutely*! Right this way!" People look at you with admiration. They nod their heads toward you as you pass and say to one another, "There goes a "Wheeler Dealer!"

You reflect on this while dealing the next hand, then, *Whappo*! The words have been out of your mouth only for a minute or so when lightning strikes. You can almost see the flash and hear the following thunder.

The very first hand you play after uttering those despicable words you get your ears pinned back. And it doesn't stop there. It goes on and on, hand after hand. It lasts days, then into weeks. You cannot believe it can last into months, but it does.

All those key cards you were picking up? *Goodbye!* All those, so clever discards you were making? *Forget it!* Ginning the hand by the third or fourth card? *You've got to be kidding!* Getting dealt two or three spreads every hand? *No way!* You'd be happy just to be dealt a spread every other hand.

Did you ever see the painting called "Dante's Inferno?" This is a portrait of hell. There is an inscription showing through all the fire and brimstone that reads, "ABANDON HOPE ALL YE WHO ENTER HERE!" This is the feeling you get every time you pick up your cards to begin a new hand.

Despair? You feel as if you coined the word. *Getting blitzed?* You feel as if you're in Berlin in 1945.

You think about that nice tab you were running, you know, the one that showed how much money you were ahead since One January. *Shit!* You tear that damn thing up. You were used to walking around with money in your pocket. You know, the money your wife doesn't know about. (You told her you were just breaking even.) Your pockets aren't loaded with it any more.

You think of the good times not so long ago, when you could buy your wife presents and trinkets, and all that. Trinkets don't come cheap anymore do they? Stop into your local jewelry store and you'll see. Treat yourself good? Damn right you did!

"How about a new set of irons?" says the golf professional.

"Sure thing." you say, "Pick them out for me and let me know how much I owe you." All this cash is dwindling away to a point where you now feel like a pauper.

Two or three members at the club are automobile dealers. They have really been patronizing you, really coming on lately. "Get you a cocktail my friend? It would be my pleasure!"

Now they avoid you, almost shun you deny your very existence.

How about your new friends? Do you remember all those nice people you were buying drinks for? Where are they now? Do they ever buy *you* a drink? *Shit!* When the bar tab comes they all head for the men's room.

Now, think about all those guys who couldn't wait to be your partner, and how they would buddy up to you. What happened to them? Look closely and you'll see. They carefully poke their heads around the card room door-jamb. If they see you sitting there at the table waiting for a game, they withdraw, they silently slink away, leave the club, get into their cars and go play gin rummy elsewhere.

How about the bartenders and waitresses? Now even they seem to have their backs turned when you need something. Everybody avoids you as if you had Leprosy.

Julius Rimdzious, to whom this book is dedicated, called it "Pay back time." In other words, you are just paying back a little to all those people you have been beating the crap out of these past three years. I call it *"Old Man Kards"* at work.

In business there are many people employed, busy, busy, busy. Companies prosper, Companies fail, dollars are made, dollars are lost, people are hired, and people get fired. Somewhere, someplace, there is a little man armed with a computer. He locked in a room with no windows, keeping track of all this stuff. Well, I think the same thing holds true for gin rummy.

I believe there is some kind of a spirit floating around over each and every card table sorting everything out. Making sure the status-quo is maintained. I believe this is necessary because there are so many variables in the game that are, at best, left unexplained. There are things such as no-brainers for instance, winning hands that required no skill at all. Just luck.

How about times where your team needs only one point to go out and end the game, and you can't get it. In fact you never do, then the other team comes out of nowhere and wins. There is no sane reason for this. There are more of these so-called variables in gin rummy than in any other game. Who is responsible for this? I think it's this spirit I just mentioned. I call him *Old Man Kards*.

Some people say "Lady Luck" I don't. Everybody pictures "Lady Luck" as a beautiful sophisticated lady. A lady who could walk into Tiffany's, demand everything in sight and walk out of the store not paying for a thing. She's that kind of lady. When she smiles at you, things become rosy, but when she turns her back things can become dismal. But she is always a lady. *Old Man Kards* on the other hand doesn't fall into that category. He is distantly related to Lady Luck, but it ends there. Where she is beautiful and sophisticated, he is the opposite. I picture him as a wrinkled old fart that is basically sadistic by nature and enjoys grief whenever the fancy takes him.

There are other times however, when he can be a good old Joe. This happens when he decides he likes you. Then again there are times when it seems he isn't even around. These are times when normalcy seems to be descending onto the gin rummy table. When this occurs one can get by with talent alone. If one is the better player he will win more than his share of hands.

These are known as favorable conditions, but, and that short word but, can become a big one if one does something out of the ordinary. Maybe a great play, or possibly something happening that is completely out of line. This would be something that is said or done. When this happens *Old Man Kards* will turn around, raise his eyebrows, and take notice.

This can be good, or bad. If you are observing the proprieties of the game he will probably ignore you, leave you alone, or maybe even help you a little. At times like this, one should just float along, smile, and enjoy all the good fortune that comes, and avoid doing anything to aggravate him. Aggravating him is like waving a red flag in front of a bull.

If you can abide by this simple rule, you will enjoy a fair amount of success at this game and make money. Be a gentleman, be amiable, congenial, and you will get your share of no-brainers.

Read all the gin rummy percentage charts you can get your hands on. These are usually buried in the archives at the public library. Locate the volumes of instruction written by the old masters of the game. Read the sections on discarding and strategy. Pay close attention to the rules put down in these encyclopedias of the game and obey them. Keep saying to yourself, or even out loud, "The book says to do this," or "The book says to do that." If the book says do it, then do it! Many times it will hurt to do the correct thing, but remember the road to success is sometimes a rocky one. The road to success may well be keeping *Old Man Kards* off your back.

In the Good book it says; "It is better to be cast into the water with a millstone tied to your neck, than it is to lead your neighbor into sin!" Well, in gin rummy it's almost the same. "It is better for a man to get into his mother in law's new Cadillac with dog do-do on his shoes, than it is to irritate *Old Man Kards*.

What I am saying is DO NOT VIOLATE! That same old loveable guy who once was your good buddy, who rewarded your every move, will suddenly turn upon you like an angry tiger. He will punish you for every mistake you make no matter how minute. He can become very much like the con man of old. The man who will pat you on the back with one hand, and pick your pocket with the other.

In the construction business there is this proverb, "A bent nail on a new deck will soon be noticed and pounded down." Do not become that nail, because, *Old Man Kards* is waiting around the corner with a hammer.

While we're on the subject of proverbs, try this one on for size: "Hell hath no fury than that of a woman scorned!" *BALONEY!* Whoever said that has never seen *Old Man Kards* when he's pissed off.

Chapter 12
WHY DO THEY CALL IT GIN RUMMY?

Eddie and me were sitting at the bar at Itasca after a session at gin rummy. After a few drinks and a half hour or so of solving the world's problems, we got into discussing more important things in life. Items such as the naming of the game. During the time spent waiting for the other players in the game to finish up their hands, Eddie asked me if I ever wondered how gin rummy got it's name. The waitress came by and I ordered a cheeseburger and fries for him, and the same for myself. These two items work well with a bottle or two of Heinekens, so I got those too!

"It's like this," he said, "I've been playing this game since I was a kid, and one of the things I always wondered about it was how it got its name.

"There are many reference books that deal with the subject, and I decided to do a little research. Believe it or not, there has been much written on the subject, some of it good, some of it not so good. I actually read where one author went so far as to trace the game back to the early Egyptians." I looked at Eddie and considered this for a moment.

"What did they do?" I asked, " Use papyrus for cards, and keep score in hieroglyphics?"

He looked at me and laughed.

"Can you just see King Tut playing a few games with the Pharaohs?" he said. "I wonder how you say, 'Get rid of the Bombs!' in Egyptian?"

We let it lie there for a few minutes while we attacked the cheeseburgers and beer that had just arrived. After a few mouthfuls Eddie went on. "There are books that mention 'rum poker,' 'whiskey poker' and 'gin poker.'"

"I noticed that," I said. Then I thought about it for a moment. Some researchers try to make the point these games were the forerunners of gin rummy. This may or may not be true. One thing you may notice is the names of all the games in question, have alcoholic beverages in their content. Keeping this in mind, is it not possible for one to make the assumption that card games and drink go hand in hand? Of course it is. By the same token, do not cards, drink, and good times relate? Certainly! I also firmly believe, through most of this historic research, these so-called historians had, as I do every day, a deck of cards in one hand, and a cocktail in the other. I explained my thoughts to Eddie.

"Exactly!" he said. "They were putting their time to good use. Naming a new game. Man seems to take his pleasures in many different ways."

"You know if you examine all this," I said after a mouthful of beer, "You can draw these conclusions and they make about as much sense as anything I have read or heard.

"WAS IT BECAUSE: Anne Boleyn, who said to her husband, King Henry the Eighth, 'Any man who would leave his wife and mistresses alone in the castle, so he can go out with his buddies and play cards and drink gin all night must be a rummy.' *Maybe!* Old Henry, of course had her be-headed. Now, could this also be the reason a number of his future wives met with a similar fate? Gin rummy widows, beware.

"WAS IT BECAUSE: The settlers who came over on the Mayflower, and founded this great country of ours, had a taste for gin, and learned the game from the pirates who drank rum? It could be! With a little stretch of the imagination, one can almost visualize John Alden and Miles Standish discussing the fate of the beautiful Priscilla while playing a few hands of gin rummy on a tree stump.

"HOW ABOUT: The gladiators and soldiers who, the night before those glorious contests in the coliseum, played cards and drank anything that was wet? *We're getting closer!* Do you remember those historic scores? LIONS- 27, CHRISTIANS- 0.

"OR WAS IT BECAUSE? Of Eli Whitney, who in 1793 invented a machine he called *The Cotton Gin*. This machine separated the desirable parts of the cotton ball from the un-desirable. This action is not unlike the same motions ones hands make when the game of rummy is played.

"Eli and his wife loved rummy and played it every night. They were always experimenting.

"What if we did this," or "What if we did that?"

One night they discovered a form of rummy they really adored. From that moment on it was the only game they played. Other forms of rummy were now unimportant.

"Eli," his wife said, "We love this game so much, we really should give it a name!"

Eli thought for a moment, raised his right forefinger, and exclaimed "I think I'll name it after my invention!" *AND A STAR WAS BORN!"*

Eddie smiled, and thanked me for the sandwiches and beer, then handed me the check to make sure I picked up the tab. I paid it. Some things, my friends, never change!

Chapter 13
DO YOU BELIEVE IN MIRACLES?

Recently I saw a movie called *Miracle on Ice*. it was a true story about the 1980 American Olympic Hockey team. A team that was very much the underdog when it took on a star studded Russian team and beat them, then went on to win the 1980 Olympic Gold Medal for ice hockey.

With only seconds remaining in the game, when it was apparent the American team would come out on top, sports broadcaster Al Michaels said the words that launched his career, "Do you believe in miracles?"

One day two nuns were driving through the business part of town when the right front tire of their automobile went flat

Obviously they were in no position to fend for themselves. This would entail rummaging through the trunk, locating the spare tire and the jack, and removing them from the far corner of the trunk where they are secured, and I do mean secured. (When the people in Detroit take it upon themselves to secure a spare tire and jack assembly to the inside of a trunk, they secure a spare tire and jack assembly to the inside of the trunk in no uncertain terms). All this involves the twisting and turning, (not without pain) of getting the human torso into position to remove the one wing nut (usually over tightened) that holds this entire assembly in place.

If all this sounds difficult, consider performing the same operation in reverse after the tire has been changed. Everything is to be put back in its proper position, or so it would seem. At this point, most people simply surrender and just throw everything involved back into the corner where it lies in repose until the next time it is needed, or until the vehicle is sold. The latter is usually true.

To say these two nuns with clean hands and faces, (mandatory for teaching grammar school) and dressed in their freshly pressed habits were in no position to change a tire is putting it mildly. To their good fortune, it would seem, a truck driver happened by, observed their plight, and offered his assistance. In no time at all, (twenty-five minutes) he had the spare tire and jack assembly removed. Swiftly, (another twenty) he had the lug wrench removed. Our hero then had the jack placed underneath the front bumper. He took a deep breath and began to pump the handle furiously. In his haste he had forgotten to position the bumper jack properly, and it slipped from the bumper and lay prone on the pavement.

"*Shit!*" exclaimed the truck driver.

"*Language!*" cried Mother Superior.

Repositioning the jack, (properly now), the slightly overwrought truck driver again began pumping the jack handle. At this point, the jack handle refused to cooperate. It slipped from the socket and dove for the pavement taking the driver's hand, and oh yes, his knuckles, down where they met the road surface with a resounding force.

"*Bastard, asshole, sonuva bitch!*"

"My good man," said the second nun, "we are ladies of the cloth! Please conduct yourself properly."

After apologizing profusely, the truck driver again began to operate the jack.

A brief pause in our story while we mention, prior to beginning the tire-changing procedure, it is highly recommended the transmission selector, (gearshift handle,) be placed in the park (P) position and the emergency brake set to immobilize the vehicle.

This procedure was apparently overlooked, as upon reaching its prescribed height the jack shifted its position and everything, the jack, the jack handle, and the car collapsed onto the street.

"*Goddammit!*" yelled the truck driver.

"Young man," said the nun, "if you cannot keep a civil tongue in your head, we will be forced to seek assistance elsewhere!"

"Well, what the hell do you want me to say?"

"Try God help me!"

"*God help me!*" yelled the truck driver.

At this moment, the front of the car, in lieu of any assistance from the bumper jack, began to rise from the pavement to its prescribed altitude.

Mother Superior observing all this said, "*Holy Shit!*"

So do you believe in miracles? Maybe yes, maybe no, eh? Here's my point. Any daydream believer card player knows, in his own mind, he can beat any man alive if he just gets the cards. In football it's the same, look at your kick off return man, or the punt return man. He's thinking, "Wow, if I can just get a few blocks, it's 'Goodbye Charlie!' I can take this thing all the way. In baseball there's the story of the hitter who's been out of action most of the season with a dislocated shoulder and a broken wrist. The very first time he comes to bat he knocks it out of the park.

So I'll ask you again, "Do you believe in miracles?" It does give one something to think about, wouldn't you agree? Let me tell you about a real miracle.

Chapter 14
THE BLOOD BATH
(A real miracle)

One afternoon not too long ago, Eddie Colquitt walked into the card room at Itasca Country Club. He didn't have a game.

"Anyone looking for a player?" he asked.

Well here I am, sitting there, all by myself, and I think, *Why not? Life's been good. I've had a good run of luck, and I've been playing well lately.*

"Sit down Eddie," I say. "Make yourself comfortable, I'll get some cards, a score pad and some pencils." I returned with all this. We each ordered a drink, got some popcorn, and began playing gin rummy.

In the next three hours I had me some hands that were simply unbelievable. The cards were flying into my hand as if by magic. If I needed an eight between a seven and a nine, I'd draw it. If I were dealt a pair of kings the first card to come up on the discard pile would be a king. If I were dealt a pair of kings, a pair of queens, and a pair of jacks, my first three picks would be a king, a queen and a jack. To top it off, after my three successful picks, Eddie would throw one of these cards and I would gin! All this would happen by the fourth card. At one point I was actually becoming disappointed if I wasn't dealt three spreads.

Talk about your no-brainers, hell, I was getting hands the monkeys in Lincoln Park Zoo could play.

One old player I once knew had this philosophy; "If your cards are on top of the deck, you're gonna win! If they're on the bottom, you're gonna lose!" Sometimes, though this is the gist of the game. What could be simpler? At this point it's blind luck. Is all this far fetched? Nope, happens all the time.

Well, that's the way it went. In every hand there are key card situations, the third king, a seven that will fit between a six and an eight, a low card that gives you the call. The expert knows how to position his hand so he is able to get his share of these key cards. Sometimes it's skill, most of the time this is the case, but sometimess it's simply *"Old Man Kards"* at work.

At any rate, was I getting key cards? Wow! Was I ever? If I needed a five of hearts I'd pick it. If I needed a third king, he'd throw it. Talk about being open-holed, there I was! When you're hot, you're hot!

Eddie, on the other hand, had none of this good fortune. There's an old saying regarding an expert playing an average player. If the expert gets by the third card played, without getting into trouble, he's got the average player beat. This is because, by that time, judging by the six cards in the discard pile, and the ten cards in his own hand, the expert has a good idea of where the hand is going, and can play his own hand accordingly. This is called 'tap dancing.' However, one can tap dance all he wants, but if the other guy is catching cards from the pile, one after another, it will do nothing. He might as well have two left feet.

Well, Eddie couldn't get anywhere near the third card. I was usually down with a call or a gin by then. If not the third card, certainly it would happen by the fourth. This and the fact, Eddie was being dealt "Milwaukee Avenue" all day.

The term Milwaukee Avenue is a Chicago gin rummy expression. It stems from Chicago history. In the late 1870's shortly after the fire that destroyed most of the city, the citizens began to rebuild. The logical place to start was Milwaukee Avenue. Milwaukee Avenue is one of the principal thoroughfares in the city. It has its start in the northern part of the downtown area, and heads northwest into and through what is now known as the northwest suburbs.

Because of its length and locality, this was one of the main roads where the rebuilding and construction work was taking place. This was where it all began.

"Get the housing started, get the stores and factories built. Get the city back in business! Slam bam thank you *ma'm*!"

Unfortunately, all this was done with little regard for zoning. One would see a house being built next to a store, a theatre being built next to a church, and a factory on the other side. All this, with the elevated tracks just ten feet to the rear of the lot lines. This condition is still in existence today. Everything is incongruous, nothing matches. There is no relationship from one building to another.

Further compounding the issue, there are six different languages with corresponding dialects spoken along the way. Is it any wonder that a gin rummy hand where nothing is in agreement is called "Milwaukee Avenue?" This enigma was what Eddie was encountering hand after hand.

One famous gin rummy instructor has stated; when one man has a great hand, his opponent will probably have one too! Well, "It ain't necessarily so!" and it wasn't that afternoon when I took Eddie to the cleaners.

So, do I believe in miracles? You bet your bottom dollar. There it was, I beat him. I broke him. But I didn't break him beyond repair, for the next time we played *head to head* I got my ears pinned back.

After the blood bath was mercifully over Eddie retired to the bar for a well-deserved vodka martini and a Marlboro.

"You know," he said to the bartender, "there are three things a man should keep in mind after having his brains beat out all afternoon. You still have your dignity, you still have your pride, and if he wishes, a gentleman always leaves the room to pass wind!"

Chapter 15
RULES ARE RULES

Eddie and me were driving to Indiana to take a look at a couple of cars he had heard about. Interstate 65 just north of Indianapolis becomes quite wide open, and it's possible for two people to carry on a long conversation without worrying about other cars. Traffic, except for a few trucks was almost non-existent. I was driving, and Eddie was sitting with one leg, his left kind of draped over the seat. We were in a convertible, had the top down and it was a very pleasant ride.

"You know," he said to me, "it is next to impossible to find a game, where there are not, certain conditions that apply governing the actions of the participants."

"Wow!" I said, "What the hell brought that on?" He ignored me; sometimes he liked to show off how articulate he is. He should have been an English major in college prior to his entering the service.

"These conditions are called rules," he went on.

"It's strange you should mention that," I said. "I was thinking about it, just last week' The rules, by the way, do vary from location to location. Wouldn't you agree?"

"Certainly," he said, "and the variations are endless because there really are no official rules for gin rummy.

"There aren't?" I said glancing at him.

"Of course not!" he replied. "In any new game, gin rummy included, some of these rules were, and had to be made up on the spot. It is somewhat amazing to me, that some of these rules are still in practice to this day." I thought about it for a few minutes.

There is a basic set up which we all know, ten cards to each hand, a pile of cards referred to as the stock, (the pile), etc., another stack of cards known as the discard pile. The ten cards, put down on the table, with all cards matching is called gin. Ten cards laid down with most of the cards matching is called a call, or knock. This is basic rummy. In gin rummy there are variations in the scoring such as Hollywood scoring where three hands are scored at the same time, variations in dealing, such as Oklahoma gin, where the twenty first card is turned over to designate the call, penalties for improper play and so on. I made mention of this to Eddie to get his views because I knew he was about to get on a roll, and when this happens, there's no telling what he will come up with.

"It is highly recommended you know the conditions of play," he began. "And where you are. Consider this." He shifted his position on the seat and went on.

"There is a man, the subject of this interlude, who we'll call George." I rolled my eyes. "George is on a business trip. His company being quite successful enables him to mix business with a little pleasure. He is a golf fanatic. He knows the area has many golf resorts, so, he consults the yellow pages. He finds a resort that seems appealing, gets into his car, and heads over there. The size of the place is awe-inspiring. A huge building, four stories high, a tree lined driveway, huge putting green to the right, a fleet of golf carts to the left, with the verdant green of the golf course and white sand traps to the rear. The landscaping is unbelievable. George has never seen so many beautiful rock and flower gardens in his entire life"

"Entering the lobby, one is greeted by the atrium with the immense polished reception desk, and the waterfall behind. Almost afraid to ask, George inquires about the overnight price of the rooms."

'Our best accommodation,' says the reservations clerk, peering over his glasses, 'Is the penthouse, five dollars a night.'

'You mean, five hundred dollars.' says George.

'Young man,' replies the clerk, 'I said five dollars a night!'

'Do you mind if I see the room?" George asks.

The clerk, signaling a bellman says, 'Not at all.'

George is led to an elevator. The accompanying bellman is well groomed, good looking and personable, sort of a younger version of Tom Cruise.

Reaching the top floor, they proceed to a set of double doors, which the bellman opens, and there it is! Spacious living room, master bedroom suite every bit as big, a huge bathroom complete with whirlpool bath, a kitchenette, and of course the balcony overlooking the golf course and swimming pool.

"'I'll take it!' says George returning to the desk.

"'Splendid!' replies the clerk placing the registration form in front of him. George inquires about a restaurant and is led to one of the finest he has ever laid eyes on. Everything is as it should be, beautiful décor; linen, polished wine glasses, genuine silverware, and a table by the window overlooking a rock and flower garden.

"Again with an apprehensive eye, George looks at the menu. He can't believe it. Shrimp cocktail, seventy-five cents, filet mignon, a dollar and a half, the finest bottle of cabernet, a dollar a bottle. He wishes he could have dinner here every night of the week. The next morning, after a great nights sleep in the king sized bed he decides to play some golf. After a fantastic breakfast, (he is wondering how the hell he could be hungry after last night's dinner, but who could resist those prices) ? He decides to play some golf. Stopping off at the pro shop, he inquires about green fees.

"'Complimentary.' says the golf professional, 'It's covered in your room charge.'

"'Wow!' George says to himself. Looking at the pro, George says 'Let me have three Titleist golf balls. Charge them to my room, and point me toward the first tee.'

"After a very enjoyable round of golf, George returns to his room and prepares to check out. He takes a quick shower, changes his clothes and heads downstairs. Standing at the reservations desk he examines his bill.

"'Yes, yes,' he says to himself. 'Everything seems to be in order, hold on! What the hell is this? A three thousand dollar charge for golf balls?' 'Hey!' he says to the same clerk who checked him in, 'What's this three thousand dollar charge for golf balls? I only bought three, not a carload.'

"'Yes sir' said the clerk, again peering over his glasses at George, 'Some hotels get you by the *rooms!*'"

"What's the moral of the story?" I asked.

Eddie gave me that quick grin of his, shook his blond hair, laughed and said, *"Know where you are, and know the conditions, they do vary!"*

At the same time Leon and Anton Sitkowitz were driving on Interstate 290 on their way to a golf tournament in Lemont Illinois. Lemont is the site of the Joe Jemsek golf course *Dubsdread*, which hosts the Western Open golf tournament.

For many years The Western was held at revolving locations much like tournaments such as the US. Open or the PGA. Some of these site locations were as far east as Pittsburgh. In the late 1970's the USGA decided it wanted the Western played at the same course every year on a trial basis. They decided on Butler National near Aurora Ill.

The clubhouse was huge and the parking more than adequate. The problem was the golf course itself. While being lush and beautiful the course is demanding and brutal. There are golf courses that allow a player to recover from a mistake by hitting a brilliant shot; and, there are courses that fall into the punitive category. Butler fell into this realm. Make a mistake and you pay dearly. Most touring golf pros welcome the opportunity to hit a magnificent recovery shot because they are capable. At Butler there was none of this. *"You made your bed now lie in it!"*

Realizing these conditions most of the touring pros refused to play it after it had been held there three years. Joe Jemsek, a man who had been in the golf course business all his adult life saw a possibility. His company owned, in addition to other courses in the area, a golf course he named *Dubsdread*. It was not an overly long course but loaded with trouble and sand traps, hence the name *Dubsdread*. The possibility he saw was bringing *Dubsdread* up to PGA standards and convincing the USGA to hold the Western there on a permanent basis. Joe Jemsek had been in the golf business for many years and he had quite a few friends at the USGA. A committee came out to Lemont, looked over the golf course and told Joe what he would have to do.

In a few years the course was lengthened new trees planted and the rough allowed to grow. The sand traps were left alone. No course in the Midwest has as much sand per hole as *Dubsdread*. The committee from the USGA came back for a look and Joe Jemsek had his wish. The Western would be held at *Dubsdread* on a permanent basis.

The touring pros loved it. The course was everything they wanted in a championship layout. It was tough but fair. *Dubsdread* gives every touring golf professional all they can handle. That is, with the exception of Tiger Woods. He tears it apart every time he plays it.

Anton was smiling. This was July and the course was being readied for the tournament. There was no way the public would be allowed to play the course at this time. But Leon found a way. He had a Golf Digest connection, an old drinking buddy who bent a rule or two and got Leon and Anton on the course. Anton continued to beam. Leon always found a way. This was the famous Sitkowitz edge at work.

Leon also had a smile on his face, but his was for another reason. He had just made a great deal on an eight month old Buick Rondevous. It was his first SUV since the mishap at Lake Geneva. This was, of course, not the reason for the smile. The reason was the great deal he had just made on the purchase of the car. He had wanted another Rondevous since the incident and he had scouted Eddie's Mobile Madness late at night until he saw one he liked. His method of buying a pre-owned vehicle, (he had never owned a new one), was to buy either a program car from a new car dealer or buy what he wanted at a reputable used car lot.

A program car is a demonstration vehicle owned by the manufacturer and lent to a dealership. The salesmen have these cars for personal use and use them when showing the vehicle. These cars usually go on sale eight to ten months after the dealership has had them while they still have most of their value. Eddie's Mobile Madness was a reputable dealership and at times bought program cars from the manufacturer or from the used car auction. He kept a sharp eye on Eddie's until he noticed an over abundance of cars on the lot. This overcrowding meant the line of credit from the bank Eddie dealt with would become strained and something would have to be unloaded.

"For Crissake!" he yelled at Eddie, waving his arms. "Ya want to make *all* the money in the world?"

He turned his head sideways and kicked at the gravel surface of the used car lot. It was July and hadn't rained in two weeks and his kicking raised a cloud of dust that began to settle on the sparkling surfaces of the like new cars lined up. He knew Eddie took a dim view of this. Too bad he thought. A man has to have some kind of an edge. "God knows you're about forty-fifty grand up on the Gin tables, you and that *kapusta guova* buddy of yours Kenny Allen "For Crissake give the rest of the world a break We all have to live!"

"Leon!" cried Eddie. "Please keep your voice down a bit." He gestured right and left to the various people on the lot. " Other people are watching and listening."

" So let them watch and listen. What the hell do I care? What're you, the champion of other people all of a sudden? For Crissake! You ought to be ashamed of yourself, you god-dam bandit, asking *nineteen five* for that piece of shit! Hell, I'll bet if I walked around it a few times I'd find all kinds of nicks and scratches!" His voice rose considerably as he went on and as he spoke he managed to raise more dust from the gravel.

" That's if you or anyone else could see them with all that dust you're kicking up." Eddie told him "Now please keep your voice down, this is a respectable place of business."

" Hey, screw my voice and screw you! Maybe I should go over there to that nice lady and gentleman," he pointed to a couple standing twenty feet away talking to a salesman, "and tell them what a crook you are. And don't give me that 'respectable business' crap. I've been thrown out of better places than this! *Fifteen grand*, fifteen grand and not a penny more will I pay for that bucket of bolts. What is it, made of gold!"

" It does everything but float." Eddie was aware of the Lake Geneva debacle.

"Ho-ho, that's rich you bastard."

Eddie put his arm around Leon's shoulder. What did Leon think; that he was the first customer to try to brow beat him. It was time for soft soap 101.

"Leon, It's a bargain at *nineteen five!*"

It was. Eddie had just marked it down from twenty two thousand, which was more than a fair price. A fact Leon had researched and knew.

" Maybe I'll go sixteen."

" No way!"

" *Cash!*"

"Let's go into the office and talk." Eddie said. He figured once he got Leon into the air-conditioned office he could reason with him a bit. He did have to move the car.

"Nineteen two fifty!"

"Sixteen!"

"Nineteen one" and you're driving a hard bargain!"

"Take sixteen two fifty and be happy I'm such an easy going guy!"

"Nineteen!"

"Not today!" Leon said and started to walk away.

Leon reflected back on those two words "Not today." He smiled and said them half aloud.

"What was that?" Anton said.

"Oh nothing," Leon replied, "Nothing at all."

He allowed his smile to broaden. The deal had been made at seventeen thousand. Leon had bought a car worth over twenty thousand dollars for seventeen thousand The Sitkowitz edge was still intact. "It's nice doing business with friends." Leon had told Eddie when he picked up the car.

"Yeah, tell me about it!" said Eddie. He had just about broken even on the deal.

"Hey Leon said," Let's get together and play cards sometime. Me, you, my brother and Kenny.

"Sounds good." Eddie replied. Maybe he'd get some of his money back.

"Great!" Leon told him." I'll give you a call."

Leon and Anton began their card playing careers in the card room of Shabonna Park. It was there they first met Eddie Colquitt and later Kenny Allen. The two of them excelled at pinochle and bridge, not only because they were so quick witted and sharp, but because they had the ability to speak Polish across the table.

Leon was the youngest and smartest. He was the best dancer, the sharpest dresser, and very fast on his feet while talking with the girls.

Picture this scenario; Leon a construction worker at the time, was working on a high-rise apartment building in one of the northern suburbs of Chicago. One day right around Christmas time, he was making his way back to his car after quitting for the day. On the way to his car there was a post office with a big blue and red mailbox in front.

Standing by the mailbox was a very pretty young lady attempting to put her packages into the box. She was having difficulty and one of the packages fell to the sidewalk. Leon was *Johnny on the spot*. He bent over, scooped up the fallen package, and with a flourish, presented it to her.

"There you go, Young Lady!" he said.

"Well thank you." she said, "That was nice of you!"

"No," answered Leon, it's I who should be thanking you." The lady gave him a bewildered look.

"Whatever for?" she asked.

"Well," said Leon," It's like this, you look stunning, very beautiful, and I don't think it's any accident. I think you worked very hard on your appearance, the dress, the make-up, and the hairdo. You are indeed a joy to behold. We see you every day me and my buddies, so on behalf of every man working on that building right over there, he gestured with his hand, I want to say Thank you very much!"

The young lady, a bit taken back, started to walk away. She then stopped, turned around and looked at Leon.

"You know," she said, "That's the worst line of bullshit I've ever heard," Then she smiled, and said," But I enjoyed every second of it. Thank you!"

Anton, on the other hand, was not so suave or sophisticated; he got by being big and tough. He was not as shrewd as Leon, but he was bigger than a horse and tougher than *Oh Shit!* People used to say he was big enough to eat hay, and crap on the pavement.

I remember years before discovering the benefits of the card table, Leon and Anton honed their skills by trading comic books, a very popular pastime in those days. Where Leon would use his wits at negotiating the best deals in the world in comic book trading, Anton would not.

Me stoop to that! He would tell himself, there are better ways!

"My action comics are twice as thick as your Marvel Comics. He would say. " I think I should get two, maybe three for one." He would then expand his chest, flex his biceps, and glare.

"Hell yes," I would tell him. "*Shit!* Take three, take four, and take five! What the hell!"

They began playing pinochle for money when they got into high school, and it became a joke. They would line up unsuspecting players and converse in Polish across the table. The repartee would sound something like this:

Anton: (in Polish) "Hey, I've got a great hand, a lot of high cards, so I can take a lot of tricks, but I've nothing to make trump!" Leon (in Polish) Not a problem, I've got a lot of spades including the ace, ten, king queen. I'll take the bid, make Spades trump, and that will be that!"

The other players who were partners would complain loudly.

"Oh," Leon would say nonchalantly, "We were just discussing baseball, I asked him how he thought the Cubs would do tonight, and he said he thought they would do fine, depending upon who was pitching."

"Well ask him in English," would be the reply. It would happen again, and again the protests would be heard, but, if they got too loud, there was Anton and his biceps to consider.

Chapter 16
THE HISTORY OF THE RULES

Just north of town there is a Comfort Inn where we decided to stay the night. It is in a super location, with other motels, plenty of quality restaurants, and an equal number of major chain fast food establishments. We decided to bring in a couple bottles of Meridian Chardonnay, a couple of entrees from a nearby Red Lobster, and have dinner in the room.

From his overnight bag Eddie produced two decks of Bicycles and suggested we play some cards—gin rummy, what else? There is always some chatter going on during a gin game, and this was no exception. Being relatively new to the game I asked Eddie about its recent popularity.

"It is quite amazing," he began, "that most of the people who play the game today were either themselves, or had ties with people who learned the game while in the service.

"Since the end of World War II the popularity of gin rummy has increased from where it was an east coast game distantly related to some other forms of rummy, and maybe mahjong, to where it is now played throughout the country.

"During the war, which became a melting pot for every ethnic and cultural background in the country, the popularity of the game virtually exploded. I've heard of fighter pilots, who after completing their missions would pick up their cards, and complete a game they were playing just prior to being called up. When I was in Korea, in almost every duffle bag, shoulder pack or sea bag there was a deck of cards. The game was played in airplane hangars, mess halls, troopships, and foxholes and of course the barracks. Thus it could be said, the popularity of the game, as we now know it, had its true beginning during World War II and Korea."

"How about before then?" I asked.

Eddie polished off the last of the shrimp from his dinner, took a sip of the Chardonnay, and smiled at me. "You make me out to be older than I am." I couldn't believe it, the great Eddie Colquitt giving me an opening like that.

"Well," I said looking him straight in the eye, "you're not as old as you look." I didn't have long to savor my remark

"And you're not a dumb as you look!" he said.

He then started in on how things were in this country prior to the Second World War.

"When I was a kid, nobody had any money. For the very unfortunate there were bread lines. These were food stations where people had to line up to receive, for lack of a better word, nourishment. This was the depression at its most ugly form. There was no money for the barest necessities, let alone money for card games. But, in this great country of ours people always found a way. It wasn't much, but the card game of choice was a game called 'Penny-Ante Poker.' True to its name, it was played for pennies, because pennies were all people could afford.

"A night out was going to a friend's house. The drink of the day was, for most people, a popular drink called 'Pepsi-Cola'. It was sad, but comical in a way, that the few people who were putting in overtime were Pepsi-Cola drivers and mechanics.

Then along came World War II. Suddenly people were back at work. Most of the work force was absent, they were in the Army, Navy or Marine Corps. Overtime was prevalent. The Government wanted production and wanted it now and somehow was able and willing to pay for it.

Draw your own conclusions as to whether all this was good or bad, but, all of a sudden people had money. There wasn't a lot a person could do with it because everything was rationed. So other things, things like recreation and leisure did well. My dad always told me, there are three things people in this world are going to do if they could afford it, and maybe even if they couldn't. They were going to drink, gamble and have sex. All three of these were popular, but gambling flourished. Poker, blackjack and craps regained their popularity, and a lot of money was won and lost. But the true game for the skilled card player, the sharpie, the hustler if you will, was gin rummy. There is no game in the world that flaunts the human frailty for gullibility than gin. The novice firmly believes; if the cards come, he will be successful; it is only a matter of luck. The expert is of the solid opinion; percentages are the determining factor. He still finds ways to lose, although not frequently.

"Many of the people who learned the game in the service, have since gone on to join country clubs, or fraternal organizations. At these places, the game has propagated.

Gin rummy is played for fun, or for various amounts of money. It is played under rules that vary and change from one locale to another. Most of these rules were invented because of the circumstances involved."

I was really becoming interested in Eddie's analogy and I had a ton of questions.

"There is no need for me to go into the many variations and conditions," he said in answer to some of the questions I put to him. These were times where people had money all of a sudden and they wanted to play. They touched on a few basics and took it from there. I'd be a genius if I could dwell on them all, but, Ill try to touch on a few of the more important ones."

As he spoke, I realized he was speaking about basics of the game that I came to treat as gospel, but as he went on I became aware these rules, so to speak, were there because of necessity, and could be changed, or altered if need be. When we got back to Itasca I sat down and wrote down everything he had dwelled upon as best as memory could serve me Most of these were basics, but a lot were not, I had a few surprises coming.

THE DEAL: After the shuffle there are two popular ways to dealing a gin rummy hand. Both involve twenty-one cards. One of the most popular methods throughout the country is to deal ten cards to each player and turn over the twenty- first card. This becomes the call card. In a partnership game, each dealer deals ten cards to each player, and turns over the twenty -first card; the lower of the two cards turned over takes precedence and becomes the call card. Play begins with the non-dealer either taking the card turned up, or drawing from the pile. This is known as "Oklahoma gin."

Another popular method, and some would argue this is the best way, involves the use of a "Call deck." When this method is used, a new deck is opened, shuffled, cut and placed face down on the table. Sometimes it is placed back into the box. As each hand is begun, the top card, either from the pile on the table, or from the box is turned over. This becomes the call value of the hand, (call card). When this method is used

Eleven cards are dealt to the non-dealer. He then begins play by discarding.

The procedures for drawing a card, making a discard, or playing the hand are basic throughout the country, so there is no need to get into them here. Let's move on to a rule that does vary a lot, and it should be ironed out prior to starting play.

THE CARDS CALL RULE:

This rule states; if a player knocks with a call value of, say six, and it is discovered by his partners, or himself, that by rearranging the cards he actually has a call value of four, he is entitled to make the correction, further, his partners are entitled in this respect, to help him because it is also their money that is being played with. By the same token, the player being called upon has the same option. You may agree or disagree with this rule, there are views pro and con. Suffice to say, it should be brought up and ironed out prior to starting play.

THE MIS-DEAL:

This can happen in a number of ways. Too many cards being dealt, too few, a card exposed during the deal, a card or cards from Team A's deck that is mixed in with Team B's deck showing up either when the hand is being dealt, or in play. All of these conditions mandate a re-deal when discovered. This is both fair and unfair, and yes, I grant you it can be done intentionally, and it is entirely possible one could make a play out of this. There are also complicated rules in tournament gin rummy that deal with this but, we are dealing with country club gin, and we all have to get along. Think of the many arguments and discussions that would come about were we to do otherwise.

THE MIS-CALL. I always enjoy thinking about this one. Eddie likes to preface it by telling a little story:

"The year is 1886. Jesse James and his band of outlaws are robbing a train. Jesse rides his horse along side of the train, pauses, and then vaults from the saddle onto the platform of the railroad car.

"He bursts through the door and draws a pair of six shooters. 'All right!' he bellows, 'We're going to rape all the men, and rob all the women!' The passengers in the car are terrified, but not all of them.

"'Jesse,' says a little old lady, looking up with expectant eyes, 'Haven't you got that backwards? Don't you mean you're going to rape all the women?' A little fag sitting in the corner, jumps up on his seat and exclaims in a loud voice:

"'Say, who's robbing this train? You or Mister James?'"

Eddie is trying to get the point across that a mis-call is simply thinking one thing, and saying another. Example: The call value is five. Charlie calls, but upon laying his hand down it is discovered he has a deadwood total of six, not five or under.

"There is a penalty involved!" Eddie states. "Some of these include horsewhipping, or burning at the stake." I think he said this last bit to see if I was paying attention.

"One penalty, and only one makes sense." he went on. "That penalty is the player making the mis-call loses twenty-five points plus whatever deadwood he has in his hand. He is allowed to put down his spreads and runs. In Charlie's case he called with five, he actually had six; he loses twenty-five pints plus the six points in his hand, a total of thirty-one."

"I've heard of other penalties," I said. " Is this true?"

I picked up my glass and drained the last of the Chardonnay and waited for his answer.

"The penalty for a mis-call varies throughout the country" he told me, "And most of them do not make sense. There are some locations where the player guilty of a mis-call must lay his hand down and play an open hand. The opponent is entitled to study this open hand and play his own hand accordingly. The player playing this open hand must continue to expose every card he picks, although in some locales he is entitled to hide these cards.

"In my opinion, the concept of playing an open hand is ridiculous. This is no penalty at all. I have seen games with the open hand rule in effect where the guilty player made a few lucky picks and went on to gin the hand, so where is the penalty?

"I have also seen games, where a sharp player, hustler, as it were, playing a tough hand was faced with two alternatives, play a discard he was sure would gin the other guy, or intentionally mis-call and hope he could get away with it. He figured if his mis-call were caught he would take his chances with the open hand. Later, when I would question this player, he told me a play like this works out more often or not.

"No," Eddie told me, and he emphasized this by hitting the table with the heel of his hand,

"The only true penalty is the twenty five points plus deadwood penalty. However this rule, as any other rule should be discussed at the beginning of the game."

"Remember the mis-call must be observed and brought to everyone's attention, immediately, on the spot, not after the hand has been completed and the scorekeeper has recorded the tally. By that time it is too late"

"How about a mis-call caused by laying down an incorrect call card by mistake." I asked.

"Well," Eddie replied, this is a very controversial situation, and it happened just last week. Charlie has an ace and a three in his hand. The call is two. He wants to call with one, but inadvertently turns over the ace and lays down the three. He hasn't said a word, uttered a sound, something like '*I call with one point*, he just lays down the hand, then realizing his error, he takes the three back, turns it over and exposes the ace. Is this play allowed to stand? Think back to the Jesse James story. A miscall is saying one thing and meaning another. The situation here could be called a dilemma. Webster defines a dilemma as a situation where there is a choice between two unpleasant items. Some people would say a dilemma is seeing your mother in law drive your new Cadillac over a cliff. In most country club gin games, the play is allowed to stand. In a big money game, I would think not. Once again, this a ground rule and should be straightened out at the beginning of the game."

We were playing cards while this conversation was taking place, and I was losing, not much, but losing non the less, and the conversation wasn't bothering me, but I bring this up because, if it were affecting my play, I would do the most sensible thing to do, and that would be to refuse to take part in the conversation. The person doing all the chatter would soon get the message.

"Eddie," I said, while laying down my cards for a Gin (one of the few times this evening). "There's one rule that has always bothers me, and that's the rule that says you are not allowed to use the 51st and 52nd cards in the deck."

'I don't know where this rule got started, or whether or not it makes sense. For that matter, nobody else I know does either. In essence it is a rule that has been handed down through the years and basically says this; you may not use the last two cards in the deck. Further, the opponent must use the fiftieth card played to gin with, or as a discard. He may not call with it. It's one of the hard fast rules in the game that apparently has no variables. Everyone seems to know about it, and it seems to work admirably so I don't question it, however it would be wise to bring it up as a ground rule if you are playing in a game with strangers."

I did by the way; when I got home I looked up Eli Whitney in the encyclopedia, to see if possibly he had something to say about it. But no.

Chapter 17
VARIABLES

"A word to the wise!" Eddie came out with. I looked at him. It was the next morning. He was driving now. He had seen ten cars, bought five, and wanted them all in the lot in the morning. He decided to have them shipped to Chicago. We were just coming into the Chicago area where Interstate 65 meets Interstate 80. Traffic there, day or night is horrendous, but that didn't stop Eddie.

"A word to the wide," he continued. "By this time you should have become aware that there are no hard fast rules in the game of gin rummy. The rules have been made up out of necessity from the inception of the game, and they still continue to be made up on the spot. How many times have you been in card games and questions pop up. Questions about this rule, or that one. Somebody is sure to speak up and say, "Well at our club we do it this way." There is then a brief discussion, and a decision is made. This is what is called an 'on the spot rule.' It happens all the time.'

"What are you getting at?" I asked.

"Well," he said, "I only bring this up, and I realize I am being redundant in doing so, to make you fully aware of what has gone on in gin games since people began playing the game

An old friend of mine, Tom Kelly, a very astute gin player said many times when he was still with us, 'I would never play this game for any serious money at all, because there are too many variables, both in the rules, the scoring and the actual playing of the hands. The same holds true for poker, pinochle, or blackjack. It really holds true for any card game for that matter. The rules vary, no matter where you go. The scoring always varies, and everyone plays their hands differently. But that was Tom's philosophy.

I myself prey upon this. I study every player I am up against no matter what card game I am playing. I size up any opponent just to try to see if I can find out what makes him tick. Once I determine this, I play the man rather than the cards."

"What do you mean," I said, "You play the man?

We had just turned onto The Chicago Skyway. If that doesn't turn your hair gray, nothing will. Traffic was bumper to bumper at sixty-five miles an hour. Eddie didn't seem to notice. The top was now up so we seemed a bit self contained.

"If I'm playing poker, and I've determined one man in the game, or maybe two, do a lot of bluffing, I play the game one way. If I notice a player who is never heard from in the game unless he is certain he has a winning hand, I play him a bit differently. The same holds true with gin rummy. If I'm playing a speculator, I pay little attention to most of his moves. If I can't tell if he is speculating I avoid making discards close to the cards I think he is taking from the pile. Most of the time I can tell, to a certain degree where he's at. All these things are called variables. There are also many variables in how the games are played. You have to make decisions about how you are to play your opponent or opponents. The rules he has been playing under may differ from your accepted rules and you may have to treat them a little bit differently. What's that saying, "'We're all different?' Well so are card games."

Chapter 18
DIFFERENT STROKES

We had gotten back to Itasca, and Eddie dropped me off at my house. I had a few things to do, a few errands to run. When I returned I reflected on a few things Eddie had mentioned on our trip back.

There are two distinct ways of dealing a hand. One involves dealing ten cards to each player, and turning the next card over. This becomes the call card. The other is to deal ten cards to one player, and eleven to the other. A separate deck, which is shuffled, replaced in the box, determines the call and one card at a time is drawn out at the start of each hand. This then, becomes the call card.

There are those who believe there are advantages and disadvantages to each system One faction believes accepting or refusing an exposed call card gives way information about the hand, and they would prefer the call deck

Players who prefer the call deck are players who enjoy as much secrecy as possible. They don't really feel they are gaining anything by using the call deck, they just feel they would be giving up too much in the exposed call card method. Players of this nature can be quite adamant regarding this opinion, and are usually tight lipped, play 'em close to the vest, conservative individuals.

When encountering players of this nature, it is generally wise to reduce the deadwood count in your hand to low card combinations, as they have a tendency to quick call. In contrast to the speculative player who attempts to force you to hold onto high cards, these individuals attempt to force you to retain low valued cards that have no merit in your hand. Be careful!

One more thing to watch out for while playing in a game that uses a call deck is sixty percent of the call values will be cards of seven and above, usually the latter. This encourages a lot of quick calls and in reality is more of a no-brainer type of a game. The smart player, or expert, is of the opinion one must learn to play both "sides of the coin," that is the high call and the low call. A player must be shrewd and on his toes to be continuously successful in hands having a low call value. Most of country club gin rummy players do not fall into this category.

They think they do, and many times they are correct, but in the long run accomplished players are few and far between.

Let's spend a few minutes with this.

The weaker player, because of the greater amount of high call cards would tend to prefer the call deck. It is far easier to *"dive for the sewer"* and end the hand with a call. If *Old Man Kards* is smiling at them they sometimes catch the opponent with a good count, twenty points or so. Most of the time this would not be the case as the expert recognizes what type of player he is up against and acts accordingly, seven or eight points lost would tend to be the norm. Strong players enjoy capitalizing on the weaknesses of other players, backing them into a corner and playing the hand for gin. Most of the time this would prove successful. The low call would give them more of an opportunity to do this. Strong players are usually extroverts, always aggressive, hardly ever throwing a hot card, and tend to play most hands for gin. They are very dangerous.

Eddie Colquitt once looked back at a long winning streak and discovered most of the winning hands he played were hands with knock values of four or less. He felt this gave him a tremendous advantage, where he could discard high cards without his opponent picking them up and spoiling his hand with a high call. On the other hand, there is nothing wrong with calling, say on the third or fourth card and punishing the other guy.

If you are an accomplished strong player, the best advice I could give you is to get away from the call deck as much as possible and opt for the exposed call card the odds favor this. It says so in the laws of probability. Conversely, if you are not such a strong player, you should insist on the call deck, you would be in a much better position to use the call card as a weapon.

There is another method of determining the call value. This is the "Call sheet." It is a chart showing five or six call cards, one high, one around seven or eight, two middle cards two low cards and one gin card, an ace. These call values are used in succession this method is used a lot in country club gin rummy tournaments and is being experimented with at some professional events. Some feel the advantages of the system is it tends to keep things moving along faster by ensuring an equitable amount of call values.

Many players do not go along with this as, they feel a truly sharp player will know what kind of call cards are on the way and will be able to play his hands to that purpose. This would, I guess be like a pitcher in baseball pitching around a strong hitter, not giving him anything good to swing at, even to the extent of walking him because he knows a weak hitter is due at the plate next. So too in gin rummy a lot of players are of the opinion the expert could play in advance, when he would be calling, or when he would play the hand for gin.

Myself, I don't think it makes any difference one way or the other, however if you fall into this category I'd suggest avoid giving people like Eddie Colquitt your cell phone number, because they're going to want to talk to you.

Chapter 19
ANNOUNCING YOUR GIN

An old man in his nineties walked into a Roman Catholic Church one day. He made his way to a confessional box, opened the door, stepped inside, closed the door and knelt down in the darkness. The small rectangular door in the partition between the confessor and the person making the confession slid open.

"Yes, my son," said the priest.

"Father," the old man said, "Last Saturday night while I was standing at the corner of Harlem and Addison. A late model convertible pulled up. There were two very attractive young ladies in the car. The necklines on their dresses were very low and the breeze from the openness of the vehicle had pushed their hemlines well above their knees. Despite my age, my interest zoomed from being a gem like flame to a raging inferno!"

"'Hop in, Pops,' one of them said. 'We'll show you a good time.' So I got into the car, and off we went to a motel where we made mad passionate love for three days and three nights!"

"How old are you?" asked the priest.

"Ninety-two," was the reply.

The priest thought for a moment. This must be some kind of a fantasy. I'll humor the old man. "My son," said the priest, "for your penance, say three Our Fathers and three Hail Mary's.

"I'd love to," the old man said, "But you see, I'm not Catholic."

"Well, if you're not Catholic!" exclaimed the priest "Why are telling *me* all this"?

"I'M TELLING EVERYBODY!" the old man said jubilantly.

Ginning a hand is the ultimate way of winning. It is the name of the game, the purpose in playing it. Few things in this game are as satisfying as laying down your cards and saying *"Gin"*! There are many ways to do this. Some people don't say anything; they just lay the cards down and look at you. Some just say *"Gin"*!

In many games at the club, as the evening wears on, and a few cocktails are put away, the methods become more flamboyant, more extreme. For Example:

"Oh you sweet thing!" (*Sweet thang* is the way it's pronounced south of the Mason Dixon line).

"What did Eli Whitney's wife drink?"

"Well bless your little heart."

"What do they make in Peoria."

"What did the old lady put in the stew?"

"It ain't *no* sin to go ginny-gin-gin."

"What do they make martinis with?"

"What time is it "? (Looks at watch) "Gin time."

"What's the name of this game?"

"Ginny boo!"

"What goes with vermouth?"

"1 don't know what you got, but I got gin."

"Get *a* count, *Pard!*"

"*Yes suh*, that's my baby!"

"Well, what do you know? The last train from Peoria!" (This is usually said when there is only one card left in the deck that can complete gin for a player)!

"*Ringa-ding-ding!*"

"I got *Ringy!*"

"Dixie Belle!"

"Bingo!"

Watch out for this last one, it can cause trouble;

"Well, if I put this one here, this one here, and that one there, *and the Camp town ladies sing this song!*" All this is done with the shifting of the cards, picking up the opponent's discard, and with a flourish, placing it in the hand and tamping it down with an elbow.

It is highly recommended for you not to attempt this while playing opposite an ill-tempered scorekeeper who has had a rough evening. You could find yourself on the way to the men's room to extract a pencil point from your eyeball!

Chapter 20
THE GREAT SASECASEWICZ TOOL COMPANY

Leon and Anton were bricklayers by trade. They worked for their father. One day on the job there was an accident. A steel beam fell and landed on the handle of Leon's brick hammer.

"What the hell was that?" Leon shrieked.

He looked at the beam; one end was on the edge of the scaffolding, the other jamming the handle of the hammer into the ground. He bent over for a better look, *Yep!* The handle was broken. He moved the steel beam, bent over, picked up the hammer and looked at it. He had purchased the tool at a major department store in the Chicago area, and they had a slogan in their tool department. This slogan said in effect, "If one of our tools breaks, for any reason, any reason at all, we will replace it!" This slogan was printed on a big sign on the wall in plain sight of everyone who was thinking of buying tools.

That evening after work Leon made an appearance at the store. He explained the situation to the clerk, and pointed to the sign. The clerk told him to go get another hammer. Leon walked over to the hammer section, chose a new hammer and was about to leave the store when the clerk called him back.

"You forgot this!" he said, gesturing at the remains of the brick-hammer.

"Don't you want it?" asked Leon

"What the hell am I going to do with it?" replied the clerk "Take it with you! Get it the hell out of here! If my boss ever found out I were crazy enough to be so easy on you he'd ream my ass raw. I'm supposed to make out a full report. But it's late!" He flicked the back of his hands at Leon. "*Go——Go!*"

As Leon was leaving the store an idea was forming in his head. By the time he reached his truck, parked a half block away, it had become a full-blown reality.

The new hammer had a price tag of ten dollars ($10.00). The hardware store across the street from where Leon had parked carried hammer handles that sold for one dollar ($1.00). Why not, he thought, buy a new handle, repair the hammer and keep it for his own use, and sell the newly acquired hammer, to any one of the many bricklayers he knew, for six bucks. Overall he would have a profit of five dollars ($5.00). What could be simpler?

He thought further. The department store where he bought the hammer had seven stores in the Chicago area. If the situation were repeated he would have more new hammers to sell for six dollars, and more repaired hammers to sell for three dollars. The possibilities were endless. Soon handsaws power saws and all different kinds of power tools wrenches, pumps generators, etc. became additions to Leon's stock of tools and equipment.

The only fly in the ointment was, it could not continue to be a one-man operation for too long; soon, suspicion in the eyes of the clerks would rear its ugly head. No matter how Leon would try to juggle his appearances at the stores, playing one clerk's off duty hours against another's, he was certain to be noticed. If two people were doing this, it could stretch the operation out a bit. Leon took Anton in as a partner.

The tenure of "The great Sasecasewicz tool company" lasted for five months; by that time the managers of all the tool departments demanded receipts and inspections. The damaged piece of equipment or tool had to be surrendered. This was all right with Leon. The revenue taken in was fifteen hundred dollars ($1500), a thousand for Leon, five hundred for Anton. This was tax-free income and compared with the average yearly income for bricklayers, ten thousand dollars ($10,000) in 1960, when all of this took place. This gave Leon the kind of an edge he enjoyed.

He had even figured out a way to get the tools they had to return back in stock. This could be done through a cousin who worked in the tool division of the department store chain, but enough was enough!

Chapter 21
DISHONESTY
(Intentional and otherwise)

Many tears ago I was closing the deal on the very first house I ever bought. Not having been in this situation before, I was concerned. Concerned about everything that was going on. I wasn't represented by counsel therefore I was insecure about everything. I was watching everything like a hawk. I was told not to worry by the closing officer, she assured me she was competent and would make sure everything went the way it was supposed to happen. I still remember her words, "Most people are basically honest." This proved to be true, not only in this closing, but many times in the future.

Let's look at the other side of the coin. A man I worked for, a very long time ago, put it this way, "There's a little larceny in the best of us!" This may be true, but I had a sneaking suspicion he was talking about himself!

Let's discuss the word "Honesty." Thorndike defines it, as "being fair, truthful and upright." This would seem to lay it right on the line.

Eddie Colquitt has what I consider the best definition of honesty, as it would pertain to gin rummy. "When you are seated across the table from the other guy, and he looks at you, what type of player do you want him to see? What kind of an opinion would you like him to form of you, an honest, or a dishonest player? Play your gin rummy the way you would answer that question. I once knew a man who was caught being dishonest. He now has trouble finding a game.

We were at Itasca on a Tuesday evening, Eddie our wives and myself. They have a special there called *two for one*. This is where when you buy certain items on the menu you can get two dinners for the price of one. Not really a bad deal because it's a win-win situation. It gives the club a chance to get rid of some items that are not moving too well, and it gives the member a chance to have a rather economical night out. They do, however, kick up the drink prices to cover themselves a bit, but our wives don't drink that much anyway. Years ago, when they were in their late twenties they were two-fisted drinkers and could drink most of the twenty-two- and twenty-three-year-olds of today under the table.

Now, they've scaled it down a bit, and it's a glass of wine here, and a glass of wine there.

After dinner, Eddie held the floor as usual and he was talking about one of his favorite subjects. "Unintentional cheating." Whenever he dwells on a subject he likes to preface it with a bit of levity. Tonight was no exception.

"There was a man who, while crossing the street, a major thoroughfare, became a hit and run victim. The paramedics came and soon he was taken to a hospital.

"This was a Catholic hospital. After being in the hospital for some ten days, he was ready to leave, to check out. It was time to settle the bill. The person responsible for checking patients out of the hospital was, of course, a Nun.

"'Do you have any money'? The Nun inquired.

"'No, no money.'

"'Well, how about a credit card, do you have one of those'?

"'No, no credit cards,' was the reply.

"'Well', said the Nun, becoming a little distraught, 'Do you have any relatives, you know, some relative with money or funds sufficient to settle this account?'

"'Lady', replied the patient, 'The only relative I have is my sister, who is a Nun. She is a spinster like yourself.'

"The Nun drew herself up, 'My good man,' she said, 'A Nun, is a lady of the cloth, she is not a spinster. She is married to the Lord'.

"'Terrific!' said the patient, 'Send the bill to my brother-in-law!'"

We all got a kick out of the story, and then leaned back and listened to Eddie. Eddie's wisdom:

The man dealing the cards, the party of the first part, who placed his opponent in an occasion of sin, as it were, usually causes unintentional dishonesty. This can happen at the beginning of each hand, and is brought about by:

The shuffle.

Careless cutting.

Sloppy dealing.

(1.) The shuffle: Highly important, not highly regarded. How often do you see a player, whose turn it is to deal, pick up a deck of cards and carelessly go through the motions of shuffling. This causes four or five cards stick together, plop-plop-plop! Nothing seems to be mixed; it would almost remind one of a bunch of ping-pong balls being picked up while wearing boxing gloves.

Look at some of the people you play with and you'll see what I mean. They make a feeble attempt at mixing the cards while filling the air with gossip, "*Blah-Blah-Blah!*"

This is a mistake, and a serious one. Cards, after ten or fifteen minutes of use tend to stick together, and there is a strong possibility for every other card to be related and wind up in your hand or the other guy's. This can cause an abnormal amount of spreads to be dealt to one player or another, or both.

There is an expression; "Well, it's the same for everyone!" This is not true, it is simply not true, because an extremely sharp player will pick up on this in a heartbeat. Learn how to shuffle properly. Insist that your opponent does the same.

"What's the problem?" you may hear, "don't you trust me?' It is not a matter of trust it's common sense. If the situation arises, explain as nicely as you can, you don't want to be taking unfair advantage of anyone, and you certainly don't want anyone taking unfair advantage of you.

Even experts, spread the cards out and mix them up. This is done every hand, every hand! Take a little pride in the game. Mix and shuffle the deck.

(2:) Cutting the cards:

Great care must be taken not to expose the bottom card while cutting. Doing this can give your opponent a distinct advantage." Eddie says, "Up to five per cent." He will know a card you do not, and he will know just about where it is. Suppose, just suppose, after the last hand has just been completed there is a lot of idle conversation going on. The cards are now in the process of being shuffled. The deck is offered for a cut. The non-dealer reaches out and gives the deck a haphazard cut, and the chatter goes on until each player have picked up and sorted their hands.

Eddie continued; "But, what really happened?—— "Bill is dealing to Charlie. After finishing, he offers the cards to Charlie for a cut. You can almost see Charlie reaching out his hand. Charlie reaches out and cuts the cards. This is to say he moves the top portion of the deck to one side, picks up the bottom portion and places it on top of the first portion now lying to one side. If in doing so, Charlie bends his wrist a bit and exposes the bottom card of the deck, he gives Bill an opportunity to observe this card. This can happen very easily, and needless to say it's unintentional, but it happens, and why should it? Why should Bill be given this advantage?"

"Aren't you supposed to avert your eyes, refuse to look?" My wife Jeanette asked. Eddie brushed some lint off his sleeve and looked at her.

"That's right," he said. "But put it this way, the road to hell is paved with good intentions. Mother Superior would look."

"Look Jeanette," I cut in, "Bill is dealt a seven and eight of hearts. When Charlie cut the deck Bill noticed the bottom card was the nine. He also know a card he needs, the nine, is fairly close to the middle top of the deck and he can play his hand accordingly.

Jeanette gave me a look like I was out of my mind. "Bill would never do this," she said. "True!" I replied, "But consider this, we are playing friendly gin rummy, and are making the assumption that we are gentlemen and honesty shall prevail, but why tempt Bill? Why chance giving him this advantage." I emphasized three rules for her.

Cut the cards carefully.

Do not always cut the cards in the same place.

Do not always cut thick or thin.

Eddie added onto this, " Try not to incriminate yourself! When you cut the deck, keep the cards flat, by this I mean pick up the portion of the deck you wish to place on top, and move it sideways, keeping the cards flat. If you are right handed, and rotate your wrist clockwise, from, say the nine o'clock position to three o'clock, you are running the risk of exposing the bottom card to your opponent. Worse you are running the risk of exposing this card to yourself."

Jeanette looked at him and said "But you are not really doing this."

"True!" Eddie replied. "You may have no intention of viewing this bottom card. Most of the time this motion you make while cutting the deck will go unnoticed, however if your opponent does notice it, he will probably let it pass the first time or two. If it is done repeatedly he may not say anything, but he sure as hell will think plenty. Be careful when you cut the deck."

"Another method of cutting is to pull the middle portion of the deck toward yourself, place it on top of the deck, on top of then place the bottom portion on top of that. This is all done with the left hand. This amounts to a partial shuffle, however if the left wrist is rotated improperly, the bottom card will be exposed. We are trying to avoid this. This is country club gin, and we are all there to have a good time, and we all wish to walk into the card room and be able to find a game. This is why we go there. Keep the cards flat!

I agreed whole-heartedly with what Eddie was saying and I decided to take the floor and *entertain* the ladies for a bit.

"There will be times when you offer the deck to the other guy for a cut, and he refuses. If he doesn't, simply reach out and do it for him. This is fair. Hoyle gives you this option. The rule states: 'The non dealer may have one turn at the shuffle, with the proviso, the dealer shuffles last.' If this situation presents itself, you are entitled, by the rules, to protect yourself. The other guy may have seen the bottom card during shuffling, or maybe you may have seen it. If the opponent refuses the cut, reach out and cut the deck yourself. Hoyle does give you this option. You may cut with the proviso the opponent may re-cut or re-shuffle."

"Boy!" you'll get arguments if you try that." Jeanette said.

"You're right." I told her. "I have seen objections to this and also the non dealer cutting the deck, or re-shuffling the cards, but you are not trying to do anything illegal, all you are trying to do is prevent anyone, yourself included from seeing the bottom cards when the deck is being cut."

We left the club and walked to the car. It was a beautiful autumn evening. The leaves were turning but most of them were still on their branches. A hint of smoke was in the air, probably from a few distant leaf fires and again probably from some pre-mature fireplace embers. There was an absence of urgency so we walked slowly, but that didn't stop Eddie. He was on another roll.

"Suppose you are in the process of dealing the cards," he was saying as we got to the car. "And in doing so you tilt your left hand, the one holding the deck, to the left or right." He demonstrated with his left hand. "You are, in effect, running the risk of exposing every card you deal. Not only the ones you deal to your opponent (he could care less, he's going to see those cards anyway), but the cards you deal yourself. Those are the cards a sharp player would be interested in."

"Most country club players would tend to ignore all this, however a hustler or sharpie will only not ignore it, he will remember it, and the cards you are exposing. You may say, 'No Way!' don't bet on it. Think of the advantage you may be giving away by careless dealing. Think about what a sharp player would be able to do if he knew most of the cards in your hand before things even got started.

I call this next one, the Laurel and Hardy trick. Charlie says, "What time is it? I have to make a phone call!"

Lou turns his left hand over to look at his watch, and in doing so exposes two or three cards in his hand. Far fetched? Tell me about it!

Look around you and see if you can spot this. Try to see how many players you can see who hold their cards down so the other guy can, with no trouble at all, see every card in the opponent's hand. How many times have you reached out, and with the back of your hand pushed his cards upward. The opponent smiles his thanks, but within two minutes he is again doing the same thing. Don't fall into this category. *Be careful.*

Chapter 22
HONESTY

At Itasca Country club in Illinois there is a huge pond next to the sixth green. It is on the left side and catches many balls that are hooked. It is plentiful with lily pads and in late summer abounds with frogs.

A golfer, playing by himself, knocks his approach shot into the pond where it comes to rest on a lily pad about two feet from the outside perimeter of the water.

The golfer, muttering words not to be mentioned here, bends over and reaches for the ball. A frog sitting on a lily pad interrupts his reaching.

The frog, looking at the golfer says,

"How would you like to shoot the rest of this round in even par?" What the hell is going on here? the golfer thinks. He looks around, doesn't see anybody. "Maybe it's the heat," he says to himself. He looks around for a moment, then thinks again. "No," he tells himself, the frog spoke.

"How would you like to play the rest of this round in even par?" the frog asks again.

"I'd love to?"

"Pick me up and put me in your pocket, and we'll be on our way."

The golfer picks up the frog, puts him in his pocket and proceeds to shoot the remaining twelve holes in even par. He finishes with a smooth 135. This gives you an indication of what a can of worms the first five holes were.

"Take me to your garage," says the frog. They get there and when the golfer opens the overhead door he sees the garage is filled with bright shiny gold bars. They are almost pure. "One thousand fine," it is called. He is rich.

"You've been so nice to me," says the golfer, "I'd like to do something nice for you, is there anything you would like?"

"There is," says the frog, "Take off your clothes and get into the back seat of your car with me."

Our hero looks at the frog; He can't believe what he's just heard. *I will not* he thinks. This is ridiculous, there's no way in the world I will do such a stupid thing. But wait a minute, this small creature has done so much for me, he's got me playing par golf, he's made me rich, one would have to be completely inhuman to refuse him anything! So he hops into the back seat and removes his clothes. Now what? He wonders.

"Kiss Me," says the frog"! The golfer puckers up and kisses the frog, and the frog immediately turns into a beautiful, voluptuous, gorgeous fifteen-year-old girl. "*And so help me your honor, that's exactly the way it happened!*"

Chapter 23
HONESTY IS THE BEST POLICY??

"There is honesty, being ethical or unethical, and downright dishonesty; cheating."

Eddie was talking over a few beers in Kentucky years ago. It had been a busy day; a lot of cars had been sold. It was payday at Fort Campbell. Later in the month we'd probably be seeing a lot of these cars back on the lot as repossessions. Right now we were closed, and were unwinding. He spoke on and off for about an hour. I tell you the guy was fascinating. He was speaking of honesty, and the gist of the matter went something like this:

"When you're growing up, the Nuns in grammar school speak of nothing but fair play and the golden rule. 'Do unto others as you would have them do unto you.' and, 'Always give the underdog a break.' All this sounds great, but when graduation day has come and gone, you come to grips with society, and if you allow it, society will kick you right in the teeth.

"No,' you may say, then tell me this, if the Nuns were correct, if honesty really is the best policy, why do your friends salute you when you announce you have found a way to make the *IRS.* for a few pennies on last years return?

"How about this, you managed to get a few trumped up estimates on the front of your car so you could make a few bucks at the insurance company's expense.

"*Way to go Charlie, stick it to those bureaucratic bastards*" Your friends would say.

"Honesty is the best policy" Eddie continued. "Or is it? If this is really the way to go, why are colored lights shining down at the steaks and pork chops when you see them at the supermarket? I'll bet you always wondered why they never looked the same when you got them home, or, why are the choicest strawberries always on the top?

"Many years ago, there was a sports palace in Chicago called The Chicago Stadium. It was, by today's standards a small building. It held 16,666 spectators for a hockey game. This number was all the fire code allowed, however they used to cram twenty three thousand into the place when the Montreal Canadiens came to town. *More honesty!* You could not buy a decent seat at any price. The standard repartee between ticket buyer, and ticket scalper went something like this:

"Buyer: "I just *got* to see this game!"

"Scalper: "How bad do you *got* to see it?"

"There were times that didn't even work. The only way to see a game of this magnitude was to purchase tickets for seats with a partially obstructed view, like behind pillars. One would then make his way down to the choice seats, the boxes. Here one would encounter an usher.

"Hey, my man," you would say, "A friend of mine sent me down here to find out if there were any no *shows tonight*." (A *no show* was a season ticket holder, who for one reason or another didn't show up for every game).

"Maybe yes, maybe no," the usher would say, "What's your friend's name?"

"Alexander Hamilton!" you would say, flashing a ten spot.

The usher would look at you, let a frown creep over his face, and say, "And what's your name?"

You would then flash a twenty and say "Andrew Jackson." Hamilton's and Jackson's *business cards* would quickly disappear, and the usher would say;

"Mister Hamilton, why don't you and Mister Jackson take those two seats right over there, and I guarantee you no one will bother you."

Some one once wrote a song similar to this, it was called "Hamilton and Jackson side by side."

"So," continued Eddie, "One would ask if all this business with Mister Hamilton and Mister Jackson was honest or dishonest? I would answer half your question this way; Is it honest? Well, not entirely, but is it dishonest? I would think not, it would be just a simple business deal one would encounter in life many times during the course of a week." Eddie hoisted another green bottle of Heinekens, popped the cap, and continued.

"Is there a finely divided line between honesty and dishonesty, good and evil, right and wrong, like there is between black and white? Or is there a bit of gray matter there? If you accept the gray matter aspect, as I do, then honesty and dishonesty disappear; they do not come into play. Your conscience must be your guide.

"How about ethical and unethical? Thorndike, and Webster equate ethical and unethical with right and wrong. Really! How about fair and unfair? Two new fish in the water.

"Now, is it right to offer the usher thirty dollars, to look the other way while you and your friend use two seats, that otherwise would have gone unused that night? If it were not right in your mind, why would it be wrong? Is it fair or unfair? To who?

"Look at it this way, the usher has a living to make, a family to support. You and your friend want better seats and are willing to pay for them. If 'Hamilton and Jackson' don't use the seats that night, they will sit empty, and everybody loses.

"So, honest or dishonest, ethical or unethical, right or wrong, fair or unfair, what harm does it do? The whole point here is not honesty or dishonesty it's gray matter. Do you see what I mean?"

I raised my hand, "What does all this have to do with gin gummy?" I asked.

"Glad you asked the question." Eddie said, "Let's look at this scenario. "You are involved in a Hollywood game. Your team is close to going out. If you can call and win fifteen points, you can put your team out across the board. Your team will win all three games. The other team is not on board. They have a score of zero at this point. To compound the matter, your team has been getting it's brains beat out all day. If you are successful with this call, or knock, not only will your team go out in all three games, but the other team will be blitzed (glossary) across the board.

"Your call is successful. You win more than the points needed. Terrific! Your team goes out across the board. The other guys are blitzed.——*"Tunt-tah-dah!"*— All previous losses are going to be wiped out. "Rags to riches!" You and your partners are not going to have to reach for your wallets. It's going to be the other way around. After the call, your partners are all over you. They are jubilant, they slap you on the back, and they offer high fives. The scorekeeper records the tally, the cards have long since been turned over, but what is this? The call value was five you realize. You called with six. 'Horrors!' You look around. Your partners are still in a high state of euphoria. Your opponents look as if they wish they could slip out to the parking lot and let the air out of your tires. Not one person has noticed your miscall. Do you accept the accolades of your partners?"

" *'Way to go! You da man! Yes suh!'*"

Or, do you spill the beans and accept their solace? " 'Don't worry about a thing Charlie, anyone can make a stupid idiot moronic mistake!'"

"I will leave this answer up to you, and give you my views in a moment.

"How about a card dropped on the floor? or a card falling from the other guy's hand? Is it fair to look, or should the eyes be averted?

"But that's not the question here. The question deals with being fair or unfair. If one sneaks a peek, is one committing sin? I don't think there is a correct answer. Some would say it depends! Depends on what? Eddie would say it depends on how much money you have with you, if you are winning or losing and how much. It's easy to be philosophical when you are ahead, and condemning when you're not.

It may depend on whether or not your wife gave you a rough time when you left the house.

"Are you going out to play that silly game again?"

'So, some would say, 'It depends!' others would say 'Absolutely not!'

"My views are, and please keep this in mind. This is country club gin; we all have to get along. Be fair, be ethical, but be practical. Above all leave your conscience at home. Accept what life hands you, pleasant or unpleasant. You'll enjoy the game a lot more."

Chapter 24
CHEATING

I was playing the eighteenth hole at Itasca and about to hit my second shot, when I noticed a golf cart coming my way. One of the bag boys from the cart shed was driving it. He pulled up to me and handed me a note. I handed him a fin and took the sheet of paper from him. The note read, *"Call me a.s.a.p. Eddie.* I walked back to my cart, grabbed the cell phone and dialed his number.

"Hey sport!" he began, "Get home, start packing, and grab Jeanette, we're heading for Las Vegas!"

I looked around, the weather here was balmy, and there was plenty of action around, why in the world would he want to go to Las Vegas?

"What the hell are you talking about?" I asked him.

"I just got us invited to a big time gin gummy Tournament at the Twentieth Century."

"Don't we get enough gin time here?"

"Not like this, now get home and get packing!" he hung up.

He had just gotten us invited to a gin tournament in Vegas that usually costs five grand to participate in, plus your expenses. We go compliments of the head of security of the hotel. There had been a rash of cheating at the casino the security department was more than able to handle, but they were not as adept of handling it at a gin gummy tournament as they would like to be, so they called, in the security chief's mind, the country's foremost expert in that field, one Eddie Colquitt.

"They're up on all kinds of cheating," he said. "But they're kind of lax on gin gummy. The deal is we go out there, get them straightened out, they pay our way, us and the ladies, pick up the tab for everything, and put up our entry fee for the tournament if we care to play in it. How you like them apples?"

I didn't think of asking him how he knew the security chief. At the time I didn't care. But I was in for a surprise.

The gin gummy tournament was part of a junket. A player could pay his own transportation, pay his own expenses while there and pay his own entry fee, or

108

if his name in the game were big enough all transportation and expenses were compliments of the hotel). People are allowed to walk around and watch the gin games while they are in progress, and it is a drawing card for the hotel much in the same way boxing matches and the like are draws. They get people into the casino. There are also gambling junkets run in which the tournament is part of. A player comes to Las Vegas, puts twenty five thousand dollars up front as gambling money and plays against it. For this consideration, the hotel picks up the tab for everything, in this case also the gin gummy tournament.

The idea of going for free really appealed to me, and I didn't have to try to hard to persuade Jeanette to go along. You go out there in a chartered jet from O'Hare Field. Shortly after the plane gets airborne the extremely attractive flight attendants disappear into the galley section of the airplane, and when they re-appear they are wearing bikinis. Drinks and steaks are served and everything is first class, well worth the $20.00 per man the people who were running the junket collected as tips for the flight attendants.

When the airplane lands everybody is taken by limousine to the hotel. The rooms we are quartered in are more like palaces. We check in, have lunch and a few cocktails and Eddie takes me to the business offices of the hotel. We stop by the security office and the chief's secretary tells us with a wave of her hand to go right in.

As we entered the office the man's chair was facing away from us. He was looking out the window as he was talking on the phone. I thought I vaguely recalled the voice, but at the time I couldn't place it. He hung up the phone and spun the chair around.

"How you doing' young trooper?" asked the smiling black face."

"*Master Sergeant Aubrey Blevins*" I said.

"United States Army Retired." he replied as he came around the desk to shake hands with Eddie and myself.

"What the hell—" I said looking at the man. It had been forty years and he didn't really look like he had changed that much. You know the old saying? *I haven't changed, it's just everybody else.* Well, the person responsible for that comment must have had Aubrey in mind.

"What brought you here?" I asked.

"Well, when I retired from the Army, I was a thirty year man, and I figured I'd better get out before they threw me out," he said with a grin. "I went through the discharge center at Fort Campbell with another old fart like myself, Bobby Holmes. He was retiring as a military police master sergeant and he was heading for Las Vegas because things were ripe for men who knew security, and they were hiring. It sounded like a good thing to me, the weather here is nicer than in Kentucky, so I talked my wife into it and out here we came. We been here for a few years and we like it fine. Why don't the six of us have dinner tonight, and I'll explain what I got in mind for you guys."

On the way back to the room we passed through the casino. In Europe, it's said; all roads lead to Rome. Well in Las Vegas all paths go through the casino. I watched Eddie sit down at a blackjack table, and he got a taste of what keeps Las Vegas in business. In ten straight hands he had eighteen or better and got beat when the dealer either blackjacked, or pulled twenty. "They live in trees," he said. "A bunch of god-dam monkeys."

The crap table proved to be no better. I handled the dice, while Eddie handled the chips. One of the big secrets in winning at a casino is money management, knowing what to bet and when to bet it. Even with a sharpie like Eddie handling the finances we went through five hundred bucks in about a half hour. Five hundred dollars was all the cash the two of us had on us, our wives had the rest. We weren't signed onto the junket as yet, so we were for all practical purposes, broke.

I tell you, being broke anywhere is no fun, but in Vegas it's miserable. All this action going on, and you've got to just sit there and watch. We had some pocket change on us so we ended up playing Keno so we could get free drinks until the ladies returned from shopping. All this confirmed Eddie's philosophy on cards. Playing cards, in a casino is not even gambling. It's organized losing.

"Well, some people win," I said, feeling like an asshole the minutes the words were out of my mouth.

"Hell yes they do." retorted Eddie, and they keep on returning. Then they give every cent they won right back, plus. Take a look around, you think the promoters built these casinos and hotels, hell no, the losers did. And don't ever forget it."

We continued this conversation at the dinner table. With Aubrey Blevins' clout, (I was now permitted to call him Aubrey, or Sarge as most of his friends did). We were having dinner at Mandalay Bay.

"Look at blackjack" Eddie was saying. No matter how sharp you are, and I'm pretty sharp, the best you can do with the odds is get them one and one half percent against you. So unless you run into a really great run of luck over the long run, you're just another loser. That's why I like gin rummy."

"Isn't gin gummy a form of gambling?" Jeanette asked, looking up from her drink. I had convinced here to have a few Manhattans, and forsake the Chardonnay for a while."

"What the hell," I had told her... "got to have some fun in this town."

Eddie looked at Jeanette and took a sip from the Heinekens he was holding. He was off the hard stuff for now, as he was going back to the blackjack tables in a while. "Gin rummy to me, as Kenny here will tell you, is really a business to me. I win maybe eighty percent of the time, and Kenny isn't far behind. And out of that eighty percent, maybe five to ten percent is throwing a few crumbs to the wolves to keep them coming back for more.

"Let's get back to blackjack. The big thing that makes you a loser is the mostly overlooked fact that *the dealer hits last!* Were it not for that, it would be a pretty even game and they wouldn't be holding these games in palaces like the one we're in right now. We would be playing cards in a tent.

"In spite of the odds against them, people love the game. The action is fast, and the game is fun. On the other side of the casinos are the crap tables. The odds you get there are a lot better, but it moves along a lot slower, but when a shooter is on a roll, it's the noisiest place in the world. Every time a shooter makes one point after another there is hooting and hollering like you wouldn't believe. It's like you were in another world."

"That's right!" We heard a voice from the side of the dinner table. Our hosts Aubrey Blevins, and his wife Julia had just arrived. Julia was sort of a chunky woman with black hair straightened and done in bangs. She had, we would find out later, a dynamic personality. Being married to Aubrey, she would have to have one; it would be her main line of defense. After introductions, and sitting down and ordering cocktails Aubrey continued.

"The crap table, when all the hooting and hollering is going on is where most of the professional, and by the same token, amateur cheating is going on." he looked at Eddie and me and said "Tomorrow morning we'll be in my office, and I'll let you watch some closed circuit TV"

That being said, there was nothing to do but to dig in and enjoy the magnificent dinner the Mandalay Bay had prepared for us. I'll tell you right now, you might get a few arguments, but the best steak, or the best seafood dinner you can get in the country is served in Las Vegas.

The following morning at ten o'clock sharp we were in Aubrey's office. We met him, and he took us into an anteroom. There on all four walls were closed circuit television monitors, one right next to another. Each camera serving the monitors was located at various points in the casino. Each crap table had one overhead, each blackjack table. There were cameras surveying the slot machine area, the hallways and the entrances to the casino. No area was left un-watched.

"This is our spy system." Aubrey said proudly. We can see everybody and anybody we want."

" It's almost like wartime." I remarked. Aubrey looked at me and said
"It is wartime. It's us against the cheats.

"He's right." Eddie said. "With all that money floating around in the casino
the management has to take every step it deems necessary to protect itself.

"There can't be that much cheating, or attempted cheating going on," I said
looking at the two of them." Aubrey pointed to one of the TV screens.

"There can't? He cried. "Look at this," he said " This is a movie taken
yesterday of one of the crap tables."

The table shown on the screen was a typical crap table standing a little over
waist high with a cushioned armrest running across the top. Just below there
were individual racks for players to put their chips. The screen showed a view of
the side of the table, and the picture was taken from up above. The shooter was
in plain sight, and the stick man was pushing a set of dice toward him. The
shooter selected two of the dice, blew on them, shook them and sent them
cascading across the length of the table. Everybody standing around the table
stretched and leaned toward the rolling dice.

"Seven!" Cried the dealer.

This had been the shooter's fifth pass. The box men immediately began
paying successful bets and collecting chips from unsuccessful wagers. There was
a lot of noise; a lot of frivolity, and all attention was directed to the action at the
table.—Almost all of the attention!

A short man wearing blue jeans, Levis they looked like, and a white golf shirt
with horizontal black stripes moved from a place just adjacent to the table
toward the table, to his right where he was slightly to the rear and just to the
shooter's left. As the shooter leaned forward to collect his bet, the short man's
right arm reached out toward the rack of chips just under the shooters belt
buckle. He then turned to his left, seemed to bump into another man standing
behind the people gathered at the table. He excused himself and started to walk
away. The screen showed him being encountered by two casino security agents
and being whisked across the casino floor.

"Ya see that little *sumbitch*? Ya know who that is, the little bastard?" Aubrey
was pointing at one of the television monitors. He then answered his own
question. "No play on names," he said, "but that's Fast Eddie Trelevan. We
been trying to get the goods on that little son of a bitch for years."

I looked at our black friend, and then used his given name for the first time
in forty-five years. "Aubrey," I said, "It would appear you've done just that!"

"Nah!" Aubrey said, looking at the TV screen with disgust. "When we got
him to the security office he was clean. What he did is, what he always seems to

do, is make a hand-off to his partner standing just to the left. We can't call the cops. We can't even call the gaming commission and make a complaint regarding theft. He has no stolen goods on him."

Eddie was starring at the television monitor. "I take it this has happened before" he said.

"Damn Right."

"Well, in spite of the fact he has no stolen money on his person, how does he explain his right hand moving toward the rack with the chips on it?"

"Most of the time he just says he stumbled. There was one time he even said he was queer and was just trying to *cop a feel* during the excitement."

"No!"

"Yeah! And I can see where you're going with this. How come we don't bar him from the casino?"

"Yes, the thought did cross my mind," said Eddie.

"Well, it's like this," Aubrey said, There are what maybe three, four thousand casinos in and around Vegas, not counting other nearby towns. We don't see Fast Eddie all that often, when he does show, we pick him up on the surveillance cameras at the hotel entrances. Most of the time he just shows up, meanders around a little, and leaves, probably for another casino. He works with a partner, sometimes the same one, sometimes not. This is what he does for a living. He's a thief, he steals."

"He does this for a living Sarge?" I said. (Notice how brave I had become, calling him Sarge, once the ice was broken)." How much money can he make doing this?"

"Well, Aubrey said, " Think about how many chips he can get, with a fast grab. Now bear in mind he's grabbing '*blackies*'. The black one hundred dollar chips."

"How does he know where these chips are at on the rack, giving that he has to make a fast grab?" I asked. Aubrey didn't have to answer the question. Eddie did. He pointed at a rack on another table, the camera had a close up of it. The black chips were in the middle, flanked by the 'greenie' twenty-five dollar chips. The red ones, five-dollar chips, were on both ends.

"Kenny," he said to me as he was pointing, do you see how the chips are aligned in the rack? How the more expensive ones are stashed in the middle. This is because if some *light fingered son of a bitch* is standing next to you and he wants to try to take a chance and grab a chip or two, he'll get five, maybe ten bucks. He'll have to work a little harder to get the ones in the middle. This is why people stash their chips that way. I do the same thing myself.

Aubrey came back into the conversation. "People like fast Eddie come into a casino and immediately case the crowded crap tables. They're not hard to spot. You can hear them. They look for high rollers at the table."

"Do they know them all?" I asked.

"They don't have to, they all fit into the same category: a lot of chips in the rack, a lot of chips on the table in front of them, and big bets. Fast Eddie and his crew can almost smell them. A lot of the time they recognize them, they've seen them before."

"What do you mean crew?" I asked.

"Well, he moves into place to make the grab himself because he's small and quick handed. He'll have the hand-off man close by so he can slip him the goods. He will also have at least three other people creating a screen, just standing in the way so Casino security can't spot them. Most of the time when we spot Fast Eddie and company on the overhead cameras, he's already made his grab and handed it off. By that time it's too late."—I was wondering how much money they could make on a scam like this. I asked Aubrey.

"A grabber like Fast Eddie," Aubrey replied, "can average six or seven chips and be gone in the wink of an eye.—— Then it's off to another casino and the situation repeats itself. They average thirty five hundred a night. Fast Eddie holds onto a grand for himself, and the other four or five guys split the rest. They work four or five nights a week all year 'round. Do the math! Its pretty good pay."

"And if you or one of the other casinos catch them, what happens?"

"They get a slap on the wrists from the cops, or the gaming commission police, a tiny fine and a couple of nights later they're right back in business."

"Well," I asked, "Why is it your concern, they're not robbing you, they're robbing the high roller.'

"Here's the thing, Aubrey said to answer my question. If word spreads that things like this are happening in your casino, it's goodbye high roller, he'll just go next door, or someplace else where he feels safe. You don't want to run the risk of losing him. He's too valuable. You've got too much money invested in him to let him go and gamble at your competitor's place. So we kind of soft-pedal it. Get by with doing' the best you can.

"You have to have it down pat, with documentary proof, such as the camera catching his hand with a few chips showing. Then we can press charges and make it stick. Then he's not looking at a slap on the wrists. And he's not looking at us barring him from the casino so he can go to the god-dam ACLU and bitch about how we have abused him and his constitutional rights. He's looking at jail time. Sooner or later he'll make a big mistake and we'll have him."

"Well can't you kind of lean on him? You know, a broken leg here, a couple of broken fingers there?" I asked.

"Hey! That's all television bullshit." Aubrey said. "They can do anything there. We have a lot of money invested in this gold mine, and that's what it is. Like I said, sooner or later his ass will be ours!"

Chapter 25
CHEATING PART TWO

We took a break at four o'clock and went to the hotel bar. There one could get any kind of drink imaginable, plus all types of hor d'oeuvres were available. When we went back to Aubrey's office. He pointed to the monitors where the crap tables were under surveillance. He began talking about mechanical cheating. He began explaining how cheaters using loaded dice on the crap table operate.

"Here's the concept," he said. The stick man pushes a set of dice to the shooter. The shooter already has a pair of dice palmed in his hand. He then goes into the motions of his pass, holds onto the dice given him by the stick man, and rolls the loaded dice. They are either dice with rounded corners, or dice that had been treated with metal in the eyes of the dice so seven or eleven would come up.

"You see," said Aubrey, the dice with the rounded corners will come up seven or eleven most of the time when rolled, so they can be used for a few profitable passes from time to time, and then be withdrawn."

"That is, if you don't get caught," I said.

"That's if you don't get caught," Aubrey continued. "Now the dice with the metal in the eyes need to be operated by an accomplice using a magnet. Now, look at this screen here," he pointed at one of the monitors on the end. We walked over and stood in front of it. Aubrey picked up a hand held control and pressed a button freezing the screen.

"This is a tape of a couple we filmed some time ago. We keep it around for instruction purposes. You know, when we hire a new agent. When a new agent is hired we put him through sort of a school, sort of a training program, and he gets to see what you're seeing today."

He pointed to another bank of monitors. I tell you, I almost thought I was right there in the NASA space center in Houston, with all the technology present." This is part of our training program." He continued.

"Now look at the lady in that little vehicle," He pointed at a woman in one of those little battery-operated carts disabled people use in supermarkets. "Watch her he said, she'll come right up to the crap table where the dice are landing.

"Look!" he went on "People even step aside and make way for her."—— Sure enough, people were being super nice and stepping aside so this woman could get right up to the table.

"She's the other part of the team," Aubrey went on. "She has a magnet in that little buggy. All she has to do is press a button, and it activates a series of magnets, and she can make those dice do pretty much what she wants them to do, depending upon how they're programmed."

"It looks easy, I commented."

"Well it's not. She has to time it just right to make it look like a natural roll. If she hit's the button too soon, the dice will slide, a dead give away. Too late, and the dice will turn over after they stop."

"It's almost like learning a trade," I said.

"That's right," said Aubrey. You have no idea as to what lengths people will go to, to rip us off."

"To make a few bucks!" I said.

"Well," Aubrey said, it's more than a few bucks, we're talking about a lot of money here, especially at the crap table. A person betting increments of five big ones (five black chips, $500.) spread around the table, you know, playing the numbers, the pass line, the come line, if he holds the dice for say ten minutes, can really clean up.

I had a sudden thought. "How," I began, "does the cheater know which dice to pick up when the dealer pushes a number of dice to him for his second roll? I mean, in most casinos the dealer pushes three or four sets of dice to the shooter for every roll?"

Aubrey smiled, and then he continued "The eyes of the loaded dice are treated with a special dye so the cheater, wearing special contact lenses, or glasses can identify them, so this way, when the sets of dice are presented to him, he can identify them, and use them again for his next roll.— The cheater would then attempt to re-palm the dice and substitute the legal dice. All this would be tried under the watchful eye of the boss of the dice pit.

"Mark my words," Aubrey said, "At any time the pit boss can reach out and check the dice. If they are found to be illegal, and this doesn't happen too often, the pit boss nods to a nearby security agent, and the cheater is escorted to the casino office. Another agent confiscates the chips the cheater had, and brings them along. And this time, depending on the seriousness of the offense, the cheater may be asked to leave the premises, and never return. His chips may then be confiscated, and he may be roughed up a bit, or all three. All this is reported to the authorities, and it does no good for the cheat to get a lawyer and appeal to the courts or the ACLU, for nobody sympathizes with a proven cheat!"

"How did you catch this couple?" I asked.

"Aubrey laughed. "Actually we didn't. We got word the scam with the handicapped person wheel chair was used one time in Atlantic City, and again in Biloxi the next night. It's only good for a very short period of time before the word spreads. Then it's no good because everybody's alert and it's too easy to get caught.

What we did do is buy one of those carts, hire a couple of people, train them, and send them into the casino to see if they could get away with it with our dealers, pit bosses, and security. The guy is a song and dance man from one of our shows. The woman is a lady named Melissa. She's one of our showgirls."

"What happened? Did they get away with it? Asked Eddie.

"Well almost," Aubrey said, "We had a bunch of new people at the first table they tried, but, the pit boss, an old pro picked up on it right away. Don't forget, our people learn their trades too! Like I said, it's a war! *Us'ns agin them uns.*"

Eddie suggested we call it a night, and *hit the hay.* I agreed, Jeanette and I hadn't had a moment alone for two days, and I wanted to make up for lost time. I learned a long time ago, if there ever was a town to make a man horny, Las Vegas was it! Eddie, on the other hand had a mission. His mission was to play the tables in the casino.

He had twenty thousand dollars of credit. This is the amount he had to put up to play on credit in the casino. We had left Aubrey at eight thirty. At eleven thirty, he came up to me at the crap table. He asked me to sign a marker (a promissory note drawn against the balance in your account with the casino) for him in the amount of fifteen thousand dollars. He was broke. I signed the marker, and went to bed. At four thirty am he was knocking on my door. He had been playing blackjack most of the night, and was now down over thirty thousand dollars.

Jeanette went down and signed a marker for him in the amount of twenty thousand dollars. When she came back up, she remarked, " He'll probably lose that too!" *No Way!* When we met for breakfast at 9:00 a.m. He was ahead. "Some people are born to it!" Jeanette told me over her coffee.

Chapter 26
BUDDIES

Captain James R. Heavey III, "Heavy Heavey," as his friends called him, sat in the control tower at Miramar Naval Air Station, just South of San Diego California. Jim Heavey was a captain in the United States Naval Reserve. He was probably the reigning expert for take offs and landings for naval fighter planes in the United States.

Being sixty-one years of age, he was long past the age of normal retirement. However his expertise required the Navy to keep him on, and put up with his *bullshit*. Few people in the world knew more about co-coordinated take offs and landings than the Captain. One could say he wrote the book on the subject, but this would be incorrect. He had written several. Every year, to satisfy his contract with the Navy, he was obligated to revert to active duty for several months at Miramar and teach classes on quick landings and take-offs, *touch and goes* as they are called.

Putting up with his *bullshit* meant; his frequent absences from the air station. Regulations demanded, that at no time was a senior officer to be more than fifty miles from the Naval Air Station.

Interstate 15 is just west of San Diego and the Station. This would be the same Interstate that becomes the famous, or infamous *Strip* in Las Vegas Nevada, it runs right through the city. Every weekend, or so, sometimes even during the week, whenever he thought he could get away with it, *Ol' Heavy Heavey* would be on that famous *Strip*, in that famous city.

He was well known. He was on a first name basis with the politicians. The dealers knew him passionately. The cocktail waitresses knew him intimately, and the "B" girls knew him better than that.

"Down, down!" he said half aloud——. He was watching a twenty five year old kid, a Lieutenant Commander, by rank, bringing several million dollars worth of Naval aircraft down for a quick landing, and then a quick take-off. This was the famous touch and go drill that all Naval pilots had to master. The drill is simple. The wheels just barely touch the landing surface. This is the *touch*. The pilot then puts the aircraft into full throttle and the plane rapidly takes off again. This is the *go*. The secret was the timing.

"Slowly, softly, you dumb son of a bitch," he mentally said to the pilot. "Make those wheels touch the ground the same way you'd touch a lady's boobs for the first time."

He watched in horror as the pilot bounced the plane into the ground, almost collapsing the landing gear.

"*Softly I said*!" He yelled over the microphone.——"Now take her back up, you dumb shit, and try it again!"

His cell phone rang. ——"Heavey!" he said into the instrument. He heard a familiar voice on the other end of the line.

"Heavy Heavey, you old fart, how ya doing? This here's Big Time Blevins!"

Many years ago, before Aubrey retired from the military and came to Las Vegas, he drove a red Cadillac Convertible, purchased from partial proceeds of his mustering out pay. The words "BIG TIME BLEVINS" were emblazoned in white on each side of the automobile.

Once he got the job in the Security Department,the lettering had to go. His bosses just didn't understand. But it was fun while it lasted. Aubrey always craved attention, and nothing provided it quite like that car. Now he still drove a Cadillac, but it was a black Deville sedan. Gone also were the flashy clothes. He now wore conservative business suits; he was, after all an executive.

" Are you busy right now?" Aubrey asked.

"*Am I busy right now?*" Heavey retorted with feigned disgust. "Hell no I'm not busy, I'm *never* busy." then, "Of course I'm busy you idiot. I'm teaching kid pilots to fly so they can defend your black ass, since you're no longer able to do it yourself."

"Never you mind about my ass," Aubrey said, " I rang you up to talk to you about your ass! What I would like you to do is trot that fat behind of yours out here to Vegas. We got a problem, and some people need to talk to you."

James Heavey in his thirty years at Miramar, got to the town of Las Vegas, the Las Vegas Strip, and adjoining areas three or four times a week. San Diego by plane is not that far away and is relatively inexpensive He knew most of the gambling casinos like the back of his hand, and what's more, he knew a lot of the gambling sharks by sight, and was on a first name basis with most of them.

Whenever Aubrey had a problem with cheats invading his casino, Jim was the man he called to point out the culprits, more than likely responsible, for the cheating, or potential cheating going on in his casino. They went way back, having met when they were partners in a golf game at the old Desert Inn. The golf game led to a high roller Gin game, and they became lifelong friends.

Jim was instrumental in Aubrey being named Head of Security at The Twentieth Century Hotel and Casino. He knew all the important people in town, and most of the not so important. A Captain in the United States Navy was a man to be looked up to.

"The telephone is a marvelous invention," he told Aubrey. "You know, all a body has to do is pick one up, punch in the proper set of numbers, and just like magic he's talking to another person miles away. Did you ever think of asking your people to try doing that?"

"A favor I need, *bullshit* I get!" Aubrey came back with. "When you got your tit in the wringer because you couldn't control yourself when the good looking show girls threw themselves at the big handsome naval officer, was it your priest who got you out of trouble? Hell no! It was 'Big time Blevins.' (The Captain was known as a ladies man).

"And how 'bout the time you couldn't get a flight back to Dago cause you were too drunk to get to the airport?" (The Captain was also noted for *taking a drink or two*). "Who poured you into the Cadillac and drove two and a half hours so you could make reveille? Ol' Aubrey, that's who." (They had good-natured conversations such as this many times throughout the years). "An' how 'bout the time—!"

"Ok, Ok, you talked me into it! But I'll tell you one thing right now, Master Sergeant Aubrey Blevins!" That was the tip off that fun and games were over, when one or the other addressed his buddy by his military rank.

"Talk to me Captain!"

"How soon do you need me there?"

"How's noon tomorrow?"

"You got it!"

Chapter 27
THE VIEW FROM ABOVE

"Leonard Harvey, or is it Harvey Leonard?" Jim Heavey asked, pointing to a man at a blackjack table. Jim, Aubrey, Eddie and myself were sitting in Aubrey's office at the Twentieth Century, looking at a TV monitor. Heavey shook his head in disbelief. "I haven't seen him in years, what the hell is he doing here? Don't tell me he's a cheating suspect."

"Well, not at blackjack, that's kind of risky for the likes of him." Aubrey told us, "People who get caught in an out and out cheat situation are in for a rough time. They run the risk of getting roughed up a bit, all the chips in their possession are confiscated, and they wind up being barred from every casino in the vicinity."

"How do the other casinos know?" I asked.

"Well, there are ways, but the main one is photographs are circulated via computer, and if they attempt to enter a casino, they are automatically picked up by the surveillance cameras at the entrances. Now Leonard, up there on the monitor is suspected of doing slightly underhanded things in gin rummy.

He used to pal around with another shark they called "The Boomer." Now he's working solo. We're really trying to promote this tournament, so we want to make sure, a hundred per cent sure, that everything is on the up and up. Eddie, and Kenny that's why you guys are here. Jim, I invited you, because, I believe that between the four of us we'll get to be a hundred per cent."

We switched over to another set of monitors. These were showing re-plays of last years gin rummy tournament. There were twenty monitors in all, each with split screen capable of showing forty hands being played. The four of us concentrated for a while making notes. While this was going on we chatted on the various ways cheating could be possible in a gin tournament.

"There is mechanical cheating." Eddie was saying. " These methods are primarily used by gambling professionals." He took a moment to look at the three of us. " All four of us are aware of this. Aubrey, you and I more so probably, than Kenny and Jim."

"That's right." said Aubrey, "Kenny, you're here listen to the two of us and try to pick up on anything we might have missed, Like I said, we want to be one hundred percent."

"How about me?" Jim asked. Aubrey looked at him and smiled.

"Well outside of seeing your happy smiling face, I wanted you here to look at people and see if there's anyone you would recognize. We want to keep everything on the level." He reached up and hit a switch and ten monitors on each side of the gin rummy tables were panning back and forth showing action from last years gin tournament.

"Now, there's your old buddy Leonard." Aubrey was pointing at a screen. "He just looks like he's just playing his hands," he said. "Nothing out of the ordinary."

I took a look at the player they were referring to. "He looks normal to me," I said. "He does seem to brush his hair back and scratch a lot. What's he nervous or something?" There was a lot of silence. No one said anything.

Eddie laughed. "Nervous my ass!" he said, "Can't anyone here see what he's doing?" More silence. "Watch how he shifts his cards around, the way he does it doesn't make sense from a gin stand point. He'll take an ace out of a spread and place it so it's the top card in his hand if he were to lay the cards down, then he brushes his hair, hesitates, and then runs his fingers across the back of the ace he just put on top."

"He's marking the cards!" Aubrey said pointing at the monitor.

"I don't understand," I said.

"He's got some kind of dye in his hair. When he gets an ace, he'll place it on the top part of the hand, run his fingers through his hair, and mark the back of the Ace so he'll be able to see it in a future hand when it's the top card in the pile, or when it's in his opponent's hand. He'll mark other cards in the same fashion, only with a different mark."

"Well, how does he see the mark?" I asked. I still didn't see what was going on.

"His glasses!" cried Heavey. "His glasses. He's wearing a special type of glasses that enable him to pick up the markings on the cards. I've known Leonard a long time, and I've never known him to wear glasses or contacts. This has to be the first time. He's got perfect eyesight. The little devil, he's marking the cards." All of a sudden it became clear to me. Leonard would shift a card to a position in the hand, run his fingers through his hair and place a mark on the ace, king, or whatever card value he would want to identify.

"He could, if he wanted to, mark the whole deck, couldn't he?" I said.

"Yeah, he could." said Eddie, but most accomplished cheats wouldn't have to. Just the aces, and a few picture cards would do the trick. It would be enough of an edge to turn the tables in their favor."

"Can this be done in other games, like blackjack for instance? I asked.

"Not really," Aubrey said, "In blackjack the player only touches the back of one of the cards in most cases, and the rest of the cards are turned up and not handled by the player. This and the fact that we use four decks of cards dealt out of a plastic device known as a shoe would make any wholesale marking by Leonard's method very obvious. We also change decks of cards periodically, so this fashion of marking would be kind of unproductive. In Blackjack it would be a waste of time, but in gin knowing a few cards, and where they're at can be a marked advantage."

"I don't think you'll see a lot of cheating in your gin tournament," said Eddie, "These events are usually pretty honest. People like Leonard are few and far between."

"That's right," said Aubrey, but just one could give the tournament a bad name. I just want to know what we'd be looking for so we can nip it in the bud if it happens. If Leonard shows up again this year, I'll have somebody give him the old heave ho!"

Aubrey looked at the three of us, and then settled on Eddie. "Eddie, tell us, in a nutshell all you know about mechanical cheating.

"Well let me point a few things out" Eddie said, "You don't see a lot of mechanical cheating in casinos as a rule, security is too tight, and it's too easy to get caught, and if you do get caught, well, a man could get hurt. This isn't exactly kindergarten. There are a few devices, but you're more likely to see them in big money private games.

"There's a device sometimes called a pin prick. It's used for marking, pricking or scratching the cards. It's usually palmed, or worn on a ring or a watch. Certain cards in the deck are defaced, cards such as kings, sevens or aces. The concept is, when the cheat deals the cards he will be able to feel where these cards are going. He will be able to know if those cards are in your hand. There are cheaters who wear rings equipped with the same type of ink Leonard was wearing on his hair. When your attention is elsewhere, or if you leave the table, the cards are marked.

"The cheat will then be able to pretty much know what cards you are holding just by looking at the backs of them. This is the most popular gimmick. There are also pre-marked cards. These are available in magic or novelty shops, they usually keep them in the back. You have to know somebody, and naturally, they are expensive.

"Also available, if you know where to look for them, are reflectors. These are usually worn on watches. These devices enable a cheat to have a good idea of what he is dealing you. Look out for the guy who wears his watch with the face on the same side of the hand his palm is." It should be remembered, these devices are costly and the technique involved is difficult and takes a long time to master. There are also different ways of dealing the cards. These are methods mentioned in any card playing manual One very seldom sees anything like this at the country club level because most of the players know one another, but beware of strangers."

He glanced at the three of to see if we were following him. "In you tournament here, you should be watching for people who tilt the cards one way or another while dealing. If this happens, look for a person standing behind the person being dealt to. He may be 'reading the deal' and somehow signaling the person who has just dealt.

"The cheating you will see from time to time in private clubs, and you would have to watch out for it here, is on the score card. Mistakes, intentional or un-intentional can be made. Someone on your team should either be keeping the score, or watching it.

Example: A player on one team has knocked and won twelve points. When giving his report to the scorekeeper he announces twelve, then in a lower voice barely audible, he says thirty seven, giving the impression he has just won twelve plus gin. With the commotion and jibber jabber at the end of a gin rummy hand, this action almost went unnoticed. Imagine if a scorekeeper with loose morals was on the same team. Check the addition every hand. When the points are awarded and the arithmetic is going on, everyone should be observant. Many experts have advocated the use of two scorekeepers. This works sometimes, sometimes not.

One year when we tried it we had a scorekeeper who was terrific. The problem was he didn't hear too well, so we tried the two-scorekeeper method. The problem was the other guy couldn't add."

Eddie laughed. "So nothing is foolproof. Probably the best method is to have one competent scorekeeper on one team, and someone on the other team should be watching him.'

"Here's one you might see," Eddie said, and it's so simple I'm surprised it's not seen more often, or maybe it is, and it's almost impossible to detect. The deck: Make sure all the cards are there. One unscrupulous character would remove one card at his convenience and avoid building his hand around it. Now, this would be a distinct advantage. Think about it, a card could be palmed, be hidden, and placed back in the deck at any time. New decks should be introduced often."

We broke for lunch and took a stroll up the *Strip* just north of where the major casinos were. Here one would find the "hole in the wall casinos" These were nice places, good gambling, but not major hotels. Some have small lounge shows most do not. The main attraction there, outside of the small casino, is Breakfast or lunch for a Dollar. We stopped in at one of them played blackjack for awhile, lost about fifty dollars apiece, and then had lunch for a buck, and thought we were saving money.

On the way back, we walked past Caesar's Palace. I remember my first time in Las Vegas. It was about thirty years ago, and we stayed there. I was just a magnificent then as it is now, maybe a little bit smaller. We walked through the massive entrance, and up to the reservations desk.

Jeanette looked at me and asked where the casino was. I remember turning my head to see if I could see it, and, yes there it was. We were in the lobby in which was located the reservations and check out desks. About fifty feet away, on the other side of a three-foot high partition with flowers and plants on top, was a room that seemed to sprawl out in all directions. This was the casino. You could see it much more than hear it, in spite of the rather low ceiling. Talk about your major job of soundproofing that was it.

We were young then. We made it a point to see a dinner show every night. A show at eleven o'clock, all with top Hollywood or recording stars. Then we would hit the midnight snack featuring steak, shrimp, lobster, cold cuts, and any kind of desert imaginable. The next morning we would be up at seven, have a huge breakfast, and then go out to the golf course.

The afternoons would be spent either in the casino, or at the pool. At six p.m. It would be back to the room to get ready for, what else? The dinner show, the late show and the midnight snack.

We did this for a week. It's a wonder that, after seven days of this we didn't weigh four hundred pounds apiece, or worse yet, be dead from exhaustion!

As we walked back into "The Twentieth Century" Eddie was talking about gin rummy as it's played in country Clubs.

"Make sure all the cards present. Spread them out and mentally make sure they are all there, it doesn't take too much effort for someone to palm a card and get rid of it. Whenever you are in doubt, introduce new decks into the game.

"You know, I've seen people using used decks when starting a game. This doesn't make a lot of sense. They can be ragged, dog-eared, or even marked. They tend to stick together during shuffling; mixing the cards properly becomes next to impossible. A sharpie can pick this up very quickly.

"Back at Shabonna Park, when we were kids, we used talcum powder to make the cards slide easier, but we weren't playing for any kind of money then. It just seemed that way. I always find it amusing that in this day and age one could easily lose fifty to a hundred bucks in a card game and be reluctant to spend a few dollars for a couple of new decks."

We spent our evenings at the Twentieth Century because everything was complimentary, courtesy of the security department, with one exception. We went over to The Bellagio to see a dinner show. I was amazed. Years ago, a dinner show at a major hotel in Las Vegas, didn't cost a hell of a lot. The casino picked up most of the tab. They were happy to get you into the place.

To get to the dinner and show room one had to pass through the casino. Human nature being what it is, there was always a stop at one of the tables, and more times than not, the money lost at one of the tables more than covered the cost of the dinner and the show being put on.

Today, with the high price that Hollywood performers and Recording stars command, the money taken in from gambling doesn't begin to cover the cost of the dinner, the overhead, the stars and the supporting cast. For this reason, dinner shows can get quite expensive. The same holds true for the late shows.

In years gone by there was a two-drink minimum. Ten dollars a drink was the norm. Now there is a two drink minimum, plus a cover charge. Neither comes cheap. Of course, if you are on a gambling junket, the hotel and casino pick up the tab for everything, air fare, lodging, meals, drinks, shows, green fees and the like. That's their obligation. The gambler's obligation is to put twenty five thousand dollars on deposit with the casino cashier, sometimes fifty, and gamble against it. Four hours a day must be spent gambling in the casino.

It was a nice gesture on the part of the "Twentieth Century" to allow us to play in the tournament, and make everything complimentary, but Eddie, the wives and me had to decline. Eddie had action back in Illinois, and I had a business to get back to. We were all sitting at the bar adjacent to the casino. The four of us and Aubrey were just killing time before we had to go to McCarran Field, the airport in Las Vegas.

We had just finished our drink, and were about to order another when I happened to glance out at the casino floor. I was so surprised I almost dropped the glass I was holding. I was staring straight at two people I knew way back in the fifties in Chicago. Two people who were not above bending the rules a bit. I was looking straight at Leon and Anton, the Sitkowitz brothers.

Chapter 28
ANTON AND LEON

"I don't want this to come as a shock to you," I said to Aubrey. "But I know those two guys at that table where the waitress is standing." I was pointing to a good-looking young lady standing at a blackjack table. She was wearing a tight white blouse, a skimpy black vest, tight black shorts, fishnet stockings and black high heels. She had an apron around her waist and a tray balanced on the palm of her left hand. She was serving drinks to the people at the Blackjack table. She had tired eyes. Most cocktail waitresses in Vegas have tired eyes.

"I know them too," said Aubrey, "Or rather, I know of them. They're on camera right now. We've been watching them for days, every time they come in." Eddie had just returned from the men's room and had overheard us. Looking out to the casino he pointed.

"That's Leon and Anton Sasecasewicz," he said. We call them Sitkowitz for short. What the hell are they doing here?" Looking at Aubrey he said, "We knew them many years ago back in Chicago. Why are you watching them?

"We think they're switching aces!"

"What does switching aces mean?" I asked.

"Well, said Aubrey, continuing to look at them, it's an old scam, and kind of a stupid one now, because it's so easy to get caught. Two people sit next to each other at the dealer's extreme right, last two seats at the table. The cards are dealt one up and one down. If one of the players is dealt a k.q.j.or10 for an up card, and his partner is dealt an ace, or a face card, the move is to attempt to palm the two down cards and switch them below the table. This move gives the one with the ten value card an ace and blackjack."

"You've got to be kidding!" I said.

"No, with a lot of practice some people can get quite good at it."

"Isn't it easy to get caught?"

"Yes and no, first of all, if they get caught, we can get them put in jail, but even so it's still tried once in a while. Is it easy to get caught? Well a sharp dealer will catch it every time, so they try to pick a tired, or sleepy dealer near the end of his shift, and their odds improve. They do, do a lot of scouting of dealers before selecting the, in their estimation, correct one.

"Then there's the TV camera, and the pit boss, so, yeah the odds favor them to get caught. What they do is lean forward and cough or sneeze, or makes any move that will allow them to get both hands over the cards when the dealer is working the other end of the table. The cards are palmed, brought down below the surface of the table, they are switched, brought back, still palmed, and replaced on the table." Aubrey spread his hands, "Voila! Blackjack."

"Seems far fetched," I said. I had been watching Leon and Anton on tape while the conversation was going on, and I didn't see anything out of the ordinary, and I said so.

"Well it's not," said Aubrey, following my gaze. "Competent ace switchers put in a lot of practice, and every move they make appears to be perfectly natural, also they usually have a good looking girl with a low cut blouse as an accomplice, who engages the dealer in conversation, *'How do I play this hand?'* and the like.

"Can't you stop them?" I asked. I was still bewildered that they could do this and get away with it, and I couldn't spot it even though I was watching for it.

"I could walk over to their table right now." Aubrey told me, "Right this instant!— I could walk over and ask them to leave. And they would! But they'd be back, either here or somewhere else. I want to catch them in the act. Get one hundred per cent proof, take them to the office, and threaten them with jail, then, and only then, I'd be sure. I'd be sure I'd never see them again."

"How do you do that?" I asked.

"Well, we've been kind of stringing them along, allowing them to get away with a few moves that were suspect while they were making small bets, giving them just enough rope to hang themselves, all the while knowing, that sooner or later, when they got overconfident, they'd try it when they started to make the big bets." Aubrey pointed to a little old lady standing just to the rear of Leon and Anton.

"Do you see that woman with the blonde hair?" He gestured toward the table. "Well that's Melissa. She's one of my newer agents. She has a camera, and it's aimed at a point just about where the two hands would meet when making the switch. When she thinks the time is right, she'll take the picture, and that will be that!"

"You mean jail?" I asked.

"Maybe! To tell you the truth, stuff like this pisses me off."

Eddie had been listening to the conversation. He tugged Aubrey's sleeve. "Look," he said, "Why not do it this way. I've known these guys for a long time.

Many years! They're, not real crooks, just a couple of bumblers who like to tip the odds their way once in awhile. If they did this for a year, they couldn't hurt you; they're not smart enough. Some times they remind me of the "Three Stooges" except there's only two of them. Why not let Melissa take her picture. Then you can make a big *to-do* in hauling them to your office. Get them in there and scare the living shit out of them. I'll make a chance appearance. I'll act like I'm surprised to see them. I'll have a little talk with them. You can act like you're doing me a big favor by not pressing charges, and I guarantee you'll never see them again."

And that's the way it went down! I sat on the airplane on the way back to Chicago and thought about this, tried to re-hash it. From what Eddie told me he and Aubrey put on academy award performances. Eddie acting as if he was the Great Benefactor in getting his two old buddies sprung, and Aubrey taking the part of the outraged, but forgiving innkeeper. Leon and Anton must have looked like two whipped puppy dogs with their tails between their legs, all the while promising they would never set foot in Aubrey's casino, or for that matter, the town of Las Vegas again

It was difficult to think about all this. Gambling junket airplane rides *from* Las Vegas are strange to begin with. The people who have won a lot of money are partying. There is happiness and revelry about. There's a lot of merriment, a lot of noise. The people who were unsuccessful just sit there and watch, and wish the flight were over. "The winners laugh and tell jokes, the losers say deal." Would I ever see Leon and Anton again? Yep, sooner than I thought. I put my head back on the headrest of the airline chair, and tried to relax. I wanted to think about the Sitkowitz Brothers.

Chapter 29
THE TWO STOOGES

Anton drove his Dodge Caravan up to the drive up menu at the McDonalds on Irving Park Road in Itasca.

"Welcome to McDonalds!" the voice in the speaker said. "May I take your order?"

"Two double cheeseburgers, two fries and two Cokes. Extra ketchup for the fries."

"Thank you!" said the voice. "Thank you for coming to McDonalds. That will be five–fifty. Please pull up to window two."

Anton put the car in drive and reached across the seat for his wallet . His hand hit the seat surface. The wallet was not there. Anton stopped the van. He looked under the seat. He looked between the seat and the passenger side door. No wallet! What to do? Putting the car back in drive he drove right past window number two and accelerated onto Irving Park Road.

He looked in the rear view mirror. There he saw a young lady leaning out of a window. She had a white bag in her hand and she was looking at the backside of Anton's Caravan . He thought he saw her yell *'Hey!'* but by this time he had turned the corner and was long gone.

I must have left the damn thing at home! he thought. *I was going to bring lunch for Leon, but what he doesn't know won't hurt him I guess.*

Leon laughed when Anton told him what had just transpired. Anton had decided to tell him about the escapade at McDonalds.

"It sounds like something I would do. One of my angles."

Anton looked at his brother and smiled. Leon was *never* without an angle. Anton had no idea where Leon got it all, the thinking, the scheming, the conning, and the gift of gab!

It couldn't have come from the "Old man" because if it did, Anton would have had it too!

It almost reminded him of the original street corner flim-flam man one used to see on television years ago, you know the guy with the fold up stand with a little money box on top. The guy with the ten wrist watches on each sleeve. The guy with the baggy coat, that when opened would display an array of necklaces and bracelets. The entire inventory could be carried on the man's person. Anton could almost hear the dialogue, the chatter, that kind of rhythmic prater that went on and on until the victim smiled, and then almost started to speak the same way himself.

"What's that you say, m' friend, you say your not satisfied, you say you want *mo-wah* for your money,"— then the slapping of both hands together. "Tell you what I'm *gonna* do! For just five bucks more, five small dollars, five simoleans, five clams, fifty percent of a ten spot, a fin, an Abraham Lincoln, I'm gonna throw in, at great personal expense, a genuine Swiss watch imported from Indo-China with a genuine Bavarian movement etc.— Leon wasn't exactly like that, but he came close.

Anton was familiar with this type of talk because Leon used it during gin gummy Games. He was full of chatter, most of it meaningless, but chatter non-the less! The words were different, but the message was the same designed to keep the opponent off balance. The term for it is "Coffee Housing." Not illegal, but annoying "*The song had ended, but the melody lingered on!* "

I tried to sleep. No way! I thought some more about The Sitkowitz Brothers, and one of the first little tricks they liked to pull. I looked over at Jeanette; she was sleeping. She was out like a light. Eddie and Cathy, his wife were sleeping also. We were about three quarters of the way to Chicago, Kansas City, I think The pilot had us flying over the edge of a giant thunderstorm. We were high enough where the turbulence didn't affect us, and the view was terrific. I called the stewardess over, asked her to bring me a Chardonnay. When she returned I thanked her, and sat back and smiled and remembered, and remembered.

Back in Kentucky, years ago when I was working for Eddie I got a seventy-two hour pass. If done correctly one could parlay this into five days. A man could sign out on a weekend pass, have a buddy sign him back in at the end of the weekend, then an hour later, when the seventy two hour pass would take effect, he would sign him back out. When this happened, Eddie and me would drive up to Chicago and pick up a car. Most of the cars in Eddie's lot originated in Chicago and were brought down to Kentucky in this fashion: He would take one or two of us up there on a weekend and we'd bring one or two cars back On this particular Saturday while we were on our way there, Eddie was talking about various forms of cheating.

"One way," he said, "is a trick called *missing the meeting*. Do you remember the Sitkowitz Brothers?"

132

"Sure," I said. "Anton and Leon."

"Well, they would get one of their cousins, usually cousin Wally, to help out, and they would meet in the parking lot and plan their strategy. They would get some klutz into a game and he would be the only loser."

"How's that?" I asked.

"Well," Eddie continued, "the four of you would be playing a round robin. You would each have the opportunity to have every other player for a partner. You would lose, and lose big with each partner because no matter how well you played, your partner would see to it your team lost When all was said and done, they would meet again in the parking lot and *divvy up' the winnings*. The trick got it's name, when a player after losing, with each

Partner in a round robin, said he was going to arrive early next time; he didn't want to miss the meeting."

"But it can backfire" Eddie went on, "There were four of them playing a round robin. There were Leon, Anton, and two cousins who had at one time or another been accomplices in a 'Miss the meeting' venture. Leon and cousin Wally were t partners. Wally had just won enough points to take him and Leon out in the first game. Getting up from his chair, Wally looked at the other three and said, 'I think I'll go and drain the dragon,' and he headed for the men's room.

When he returned, the other team was shuffling the cards. Leon had lost, not just enough for the hand, but enough where they failed to go out. The wheels began turning inside of Wally's head. "What the hell was that all about?" Wally thought. Looking at Leon he asked, "What'd I do miss the meeting?" The end result was the four of them sitting there, playing cards, each having to pee like wild stallions, and each one of them afraid to leave the table.

"We all go together'! Anton finally said."

Chapter 30
KIBITZING

About a week later after we returned from the desert we were at Itasca to play cards. I had just walked into the card room and I noticed Eddie standing about five feet behind a man playing gin. He was concentrating so hard he didn't even notice me when I walked up and stood beside him.

"Cat got your tongue?" I asked. Eddie smiled sheepishly. He walked away and motioned me to follow. We went to the bar, sat down, ordered our drinks, I had a Meridian Chardonnay and he ordered a Heinekens. I looked at him.

"What the hell was that all about?" I asked.

"I was kibitzing."

"You were what?"

"Kibitzing! If you learn nothing else from being around me, learn this. It's called the art of Kibitzing. In short, it's scouting. Learn it, because it describes one of the easiest ways to gather information about an opponent, to get into his head, and it is really an art when done properly. You maybe have seen it done, and you maybe have done it many times yourself, most of the time incorrectly and without realizing you were doing it."

I nodded in agreement. Saying "*Skol*"! I touched my glass of Chardonnay against the neck of his Heinekens bottle. We drank, and I waited for him to go on.

"Webster defines a kibitzer as: *A spectator at a card game, who looks at players' cards, over their shoulder!* Thorndike describes it much better: *One who looks on as an outsider.* It is important for us to recognize the difference between the two.

"Most knowledgeable gin players become uncomfortable when someone standing or sitting close by observes their style of play. They feel crowded. The wise thing for one to do, if he is really being observant, and wishes to be courteous, is to give the player a little room.

"Why not?" he went on, "Place yourself in a position where you could *look on as an outsider.* This would be five feet to the rear and about three feet to one side. Do it this way and number one, you won't be a bother, and number two, you will remain inconspicuous."

I thought about what he had just said; why people kibitz, and why is it done mostly improperly. The answer came instantly, It's idle curiosity, it's a way of killing time while waiting for a new hand to begin, maybe waiting for a game, or just plain old killing time. What Eddie was talking about was kibitzing with a purpose.

Much time is spent in professional sports, and some college sports, analyzing the other team. What this team, or further, what one particular player is likely to do in any given situation. This is called scouting. For instance, there will be reports on what does this team like to do when it's *third and long*, or how do they defense you in the same situation.

Does the coach like to gamble? Who is the quarterback's favorite target?—In baseball, it might be; what is a particular player's favorite pitch when the count is two and two, his least favorite.—All this information is relayed to the field, and the players act accordingly.

When you are kibitzing, you are in an excellent position to do a little scouting. This, in all reality is what you should be doing. Kibitzing, just to be killing time is exactly that, killing time, wasting it! So, stand back, off to one side, and watch a man you will be playing in the near future, and ask yourself questions regarding his style of play.

1.Does he discard wisely?

2.Is he an aggressive or defensive player?

3.Does he play his hand in the same fashion for the entire hand, or is he aggressive for a while, then if things do not go his way, does he push the panic button?

4. How does he react if he has a count to get under? Does he get jittery? These are all primary questions you should mentally be asking while watching him play. There are questions that run deep, questions that will tend to make you a winner if you can find the answers!

I pondered all of this while Eddie spoke, and I tried to let it sink in. Later after we had finished our drinks he went over to another table and began playing cards. My game had fallen apart so I sat at the bar, ordered another Meridian's, and thought about one of the few times I had *looked on as an outsider*.

I was once watching a player, and admiring his style of play. Card after card he played and I could not find fault with any move he made. His discarding rhythm was brilliant. Draw; place a card in the hand, pause, and discard. Beautiful. This rhythm stems from thinking two or three plays ahead. All the greater gin players do it!

All of a sudden this music like cadence was broken for no apparent reason.

I couldn't figure it out. Then, all of a sudden it became clear to me. I seen Eddie Colquitt do this same thing many times. It was a ploy. It was make believe. He pretended to be in trouble to mislead the other guy. He would hesitate, for instance on, say an eight of hearts, pause, then hesitate again.

Eddie's reputation as a sharp gin rummy player would cause the wheels to turn in the other guy's head. He would begin to question himself. Eddie's reasoning dealt with disrupting the normal train of thought in the opponent. If you can cause him to think in an abnormal fashion, you may have an easier time in defeating him. And you will never know if this play will be successful unless you have watched this player for a while, after you have scouted him. Most of the time, a hesitation is caused by self-doubt, and that's the message Eddie was trying to send.

Back to the art of kibitzing; Eddie's point and the point I am trying to get across is, it *is* paramount for you to question, in your own mind, another players motives in the playing of a hand.

Sometimes you can even ask the player after the hand is over, "Hey Charlie, how come you—." On occasion you might get a valid answer, one you can believe. Then again, you may just get a shrug of the shoulders, indicating he doesn't know, or care! If this would be the case, jot his name down in your book so you can scout him again, it could prove useful.

Speaking of books, you should be making a mental book on every player you scout. It helps, it really does. It is a distinct advantage for you to know the styles of play for every player you come across. Keep all this in your memory, or better still, put them down on paper, and file them away.

Consider this; Just the other day I was kibitzing. I was standing well behind a fellow I have always had a tough time with. I didn't really consider him a gin player of any consequence, but the situation was there. He has always been a thorn in my side. I decided to invest an hour of my time in an endeavor to find out why.

In the short time I watched him I discovered one unusual, or glaring trait or habit he had. I noticed, quite often, he would have a four-card spread, a three-card spread, and a half combination, say a three and four of the same suit or maybe a high pair. The tenth card would be a useless piece of deadwood. He would hang around with this, no matter what the call card was. Sometimes his opponent would call, or gin and beat him, but more times than not he would get away with this, and draw a card to one end or the other of this half combination. I refer to it as a half combination, because there are only two cards in the deck that can put this hand across.

He was so successful with this strategy so many times; I came to consider it his style. The first time I noticed it, I let it pass, but when the same thing happened time after time, I thought maybe he knew something I wasn't aware of. The only thing I could think of was, maybe he had an inkling one of those cards was in the opponent's hand, and he was *tap dancing* waiting for a break. I broke a rule. I casually walked around the table, slowly so as not to attract attention, and snuck a look at the other guy's hand. Nothing! He was, indeed, waiting for *Old Man Kards* to go and get one of those two cards for him. I immediately put him down in my book, because I knew, sooner or later this strategy would jump up and kick him right in the Titleists.

At this point you should be making plans to kibitz for a purpose the next time you have a little bit of time to kill. Keep track of how the other guys react when they are in difficult situations. Believe me the game becomes a lot easier when you have this information at your fingertips. What you have done is, you have allowed yourself to get into the other guys head. Eddie, at the drop of a hat, would tell you to keep in mind these three very important tips:

1. Be unobtrusive while you are kibitzing, while you are doing your scouting. You want to be as inconspicuous as possible. Watch one man's hand, then, turn to another table and watch a player there. The impression you are just killing time, is the one you wish to give.

2. Don't, *do not*, scout one player's hand, then during the same hand, walk around the table to see how the other guy is doing. In the first place you are calling attention to yourself. In the second place, it's annoying. Remember, you are not a participant in the game you are an observer. For instance, if you notice a player does not have the proper amount of cards in his hand, too many, or too few, keep it to yourself. If you notice an error, it's none of your business. By speaking up you will just be calling attention to yourself, and you are bound to annoy someone. Sometimes, silence is golden.

One thing that may creep into your mind is, isn't all this a bit dramatic, a little diabolical? Isn't this game supposed to be fun? Well, most country club gin rummy is played for various amounts of money, and most of the time you will find yourself in a position where you can win or lose a hundred or two of your hard earned dollars. You are guarding against being a loser, and trying very hard to be a winner. Winning is *fun!*

The Japanese have a saying, "Business is war!" Well, so are games of chance!

Chapter 31
BAIT CARDS

(Fishing————Advertising————Sending out salesmen.)

The codfish lays a thousand eggs, the cackling hen but one.
The codfish doesn't cackle, to prove that she is done.
We scorn the modest codfish, the cackling hen we prize.
For proving that beyond all doubt, it pays to advertise. (Anonymous)

Eddie's Thoughts: Fishing, advertising, sending out a bait card, or salesman, are all terms to describe a technique where your discard is intended to lure a certain card from the other guy's hand.

An example of this would be, you are holding an 8 and 9 of clubs, and you need the 10 to complete the combination. Also in your hand is the 10 of hearts. The procedure, if you think you can get away with is, first, to discard that 10 of hearts, giving the impression 10's are safe. If the other guy falls for this ploy, and he has the 10 you need in his hand, he may give it to you on the next one or two discards. Sometimes this works, sometimes not.

He may not have it in his hand, not now, maybe never, this is the gamble you are taking. The card you need may even be one of the last two cards in the deck. How long should you wait for your opponent to fill your open hole combination, or until you maybe draw it yourself? Not too long, my friend, remember you have two useless pieces of deadwood in your hand you have to consider. You should also consider this scenario: The 10 of hearts you sent out as a salesman may fit into his hand perfectly, giving him a heart run, or three eights. Sometimes, salesmen get hired!

How do you spot a bait card? There are different ways. Here are a few. Louis usually plays very methodically. This is one of his characteristics. He goes to the deck, and draws a card. The card is placed into his hand. There is a brief pause, then that card, or another is placed onto the discard pile. All of a sudden the methodical discarding process disappears, and with a very wristy motion he 'flips' a card onto the discard pile, sometimes it even spins. This is all done very nonchalantly, with the eyes rolling toward the ceiling. "Take great notice of this card!" he is almost saying.

At this point, red lights should be flashing in the other guy's head and mental sirens should be screaming. "There's a barracuda in the water." Another sign of a bait card is that same eight of hearts discarded very early in the hand, say the very first discard. Right off the bat, bingo! The other guy looks at it, the 10 of hearts, why so soon, aren't there much better discards available this early?

The other guy can almost see the hook and smell the bait.

There are a few ways a bait card can be sent verbally. Here are two of them. The first is the old reverse psychology trick. Bill sends out a salesman, looks at Louis and says, "Maybe, I'll bait you!" giving the impression the card, say the four of spades, may or may not be a bait card, at any rate, he is calling attention to the card value. *Welcome to my parlor, said the spider to the fly.*

The other verbal bait happens when after a long frustrating afternoon, where nothing has gone right and you feel like the star performer at a firing squad, you look at the other guy and say, "I need the seven of spades, you son of a bitch."

The most successful salesmen are sent out on the fourth of fifth card. This is when the hand is being set up and the normally safe (sometimes) discards having been played. These would be unrelated kings, queens and the like. At that time, an advertisement in the middle of the deck, say a seven or eight, can be very successful. Be on guard!

Eddie is only touching the surface here. There's more. Remember the following tricks. They're important and you won't read about anywhere else. The reverse bait: I have seen Eddie Colquitt pull this stunt many times, but seldom in the same month, and very seldom with the same group of players. Eddie is holding 6 and 7 of clubs; he is also holding the 7, 9 and 10 of hearts. The jack of hearts has been played, as has the 9 of clubs, both are visible in the discard pile. It is Charlie's turn to discard, he hesitates, scratches head, pauses, and then discards the eight of clubs. Eddie says "Thank you so much," and places it in his hand.

"I thought that one would be safe," Charlie mutters, "How the hell are you using it?" Usually when this remark is made, the other guy just smiles, and ignores it. Not Eddie, he still needs another eight to complete his heart combination. Charlie's seemingly innocent remark about the 8 of clubs being safe convinced Eddie, that Charlie broke a pair of 8's when he discarded. He decides he will gamble. He thinks Charlie has the 8 of hearts and decides to bait him for it.

He takes the three-card club run, the one with the 8, out of his hand and shows it to Charlie. "Be my guest," he says.

At that point Charlie didn't know if Eddie had made a club run, or if he had made three eights. Eddie showing him the club run convinced Charlie the other 8 he was holding, the 8 of hearts, would be a safe discard in a future play. Shortly afterward, Charlie needs a safe discard .He discards the 8 of hearts, Eddie picks it up, places it between the 7, 9 and 10 of hearts, and says, "What do they make in Peoria?"

Does this seem far-fetched, Eddie showing Charlie his club run? Don't bet on it! Consider another version of the same trick. Instead of showing Charlie the club run, Eddie just, 'kind of' lets it slide from his hand where it lands on the table face up. Then the hasty, but *unsuccessful* attempt to retrieve the cards before Charlie could see them., would come

"I'm not looking!" Charlie exclaims.

Ha- ha- ha, don't bet on it this either; Mother Superior would look! At that point Eddie would have to do nothing else to convince Charlie another 8 would be safe. Charlie would do this all by himself.

How about this? The first card on the discard pile is the queen of clubs. Charlie picks it up. From that moment on, Eddie is in defense; he is building part of his hand around that queen. He is *tap dancing.* He draws the 10 of clubs, which he keeps for awhile. He is still *tap dancing.* Moments later he draws the jack. He now knows Charlie has queens, but how many? Play progresses past the midway point. No more queens have shown,

also no kings. Eddie decides to gamble. He assumes Charlie has the four queens.

Let's take a look at Charlie's hand. He does have the four queens, also a pair of kings. He is in a little bit of trouble, and would like to reduce the deadwood in his hand. He would like to come off the kings, but which one? Eddie has seen him pick up the queen of clubs; this should make the king of clubs safe. He throws it. Eddie picks it up. Damn, he thinks, Eddie has made kings.

Back to Eddie. He now holds ten-jack king of clubs, a middle three card run and three very low cards.

Charlie draws a card he considers very hot, too hot to take a chance on throwing at this moment. He needs safe discard. He is convinced Eddie has three kings, hadn't he just seen Eddie pick up the king of clubs. He decides to come off his four queens; the queen of clubs should be safe. He throws it; Eddie picks it up and knocks.

There are many forms of bait cards, or salesmen or advertisements put forth. It can become quite comical. In many cases body language is used, a roll of the eyes, a nonchalant whistle, a shrug of the shoulders while discarding. Some people base almost fifty per cent of their game on one form of baiting or another. *Be careful.*

The major part of this chapter is not really an instruction forum on advertising. You will discover many forms of sending out salesmen completely on your own. What I'm trying to do is make you aware of what's going on, and how to defend against it.

Defense: the only safe, tried and true method of defending yourself against bait cards can be summed up in two words. *Ignore it.* That's right, just ignore it. I have discussed this strategy with Julius Rimdzious and Eddie Colquitt, two masters of the game, and they both told me the same thing. "Bait cards are based on the laws of gullibility! Ignore the bait."

Consider this; a player sending out a bait card has two pieces of deadwood in his hand which will become a spread if the bait card is successful. If this ploy is unsuccessful, sooner or later he will have to come off these two cards. Tap dance around the bait card and play your hand for a little time before you assume any card is 100%safe.

If you can remember these two words, *Ignore it,* and play your hand seeking more information before you bite, you will have mastered most of the defense you will need regarding advertisements.

Chapter 32
MANNERISMS

A wino wanders into a Roman Catholic Church, stumbles into a confessional and stands there in the darkness. The priest on the other side of the confessional realizes someone has entered. He slides the door open and clears his throat rather loudly to acknowledge the other person's presence. There is no response. He repeats the action, anything to get the ball rolling. Still nothing. Finally in desperation he hit's the partition of the confessional with the heel of his hand.

"'Ain't no use banging' on the wall buddy', he hears, 'They ain't no paper on this side neither!'

Did you ever play cards with a person, who would draw from the deck, place the card in his hand, pause briefly then discard? I mean draw, place, pause, and discard. One two three four. Slam Bam, Thank you M'am. You watch him while you're kibitzing, scouting. He's like a machine, as regular as one becomes after prunes and oatmeal for breakfast every day. Then lightning strikes, he gets into trouble, gone is slam bam thank you *ma'm*, coffee and donuts take over. Regularity becomes a thing of the past. Hesitation is introduced. Think about it, regularity ambushed by self-doubt. Self-doubt breeds uncertainty, uncertainty breeds indecision, and what does indecision breed, boys and girls? A-hah! *Mistakes.*

In a previous chapter you were shown how Eddie Colquitt won gin rummy hands by using a few ingenious ploys. Remember? He was playing Charlie. There is no way he could have been as tricky as he was, unless he had a few things going for him.

1.) Indecision on Charlie's part,

2.) Having a working knowledge of what Charlie would do in certain situations. He had in the not too distant past, thoroughly scouted Charlie.

Eddie's thoughts on mannerisms.

There are many types of mannerisms, and we will get to those in a moment. First let's discuss mannerisms themselves, and why they are present in, not only games we play, such as gin rummy, but also in problems we encounter in life every day. There are times where things just don't go the way they are supposed to. I'm talking about your job, whatever it may be, and your business if you have one, your home life or the games you play.

Let's look at a job. You're a bricklayer by trade. You're supposed to be an expert at this trade, and every move you make is supposed to be somewhat attuned to some degree of perfection. Let me tell you my friend, it doesn't happen all of the time! There are days where your wrist doesn't work the same way it did yesterday, when things went so well.

In business, every move you, or your employees make is geared to your company turning a profit. Does it happen day in, day out, every day of the week? If it does, your company is one in a million. There are good days and bad days. What about your home life? Is your wife always pleasant, does she always smile at you no matter what *idiotic thing* you came up with this time! Is she in every way the same dynamic sexy person she was the first few weeks before you 'tied the knot?' If she is, find a way to bottle it, and put it on the market, you'll make a fortune, because sometimes things don't always work out that way.

How about golf, aren't there days where the putts just don't seem to fall. How about the tee shot that finished twelve inches out of bounds. Couldn't it have taken a more fortunate bounce and finished that one foot in bounds?

Let's talk about gin rummy. One is sitting there with a six way hit, after only three cards have been played, and none of the six cards that would complete the gin show up. Why not? Maybe the other guy has four of them tied up, and the other two are the last two are on the bottom of the deck. These little idiosyncrasies that happen, that go on every day are part of life. Nobody is perfect. Nothing in this world is perfect. You know it, and I know it. They all can cause anger, desperation, and the last three things we spoke of a moment ago. Self doubt, uncertainty and indecision.

Let's get back to mannerisms, and note a few.

1.) Hesitations, (these are more than mere pauses.)

2.) Whistling under one's breath.

3.) Exhaling vigorously through the lips, causing them to vibrate is another. (There probably is a name for this, but it escapes me right now.)

4.) Scratching ones head.

5). Repeated shifting in one's chair.

6.) Running fingers through the hair.

7.) Pulling one's ear lobe.

8.) Clenching one's teeth. (Usually in anger). There are probably a lot more you could come up with. Study your self and others and see what you come up with.

When you do have a problem, do you find yourself doing any of the things we just mentioned? It's like I said, we all have these little quirks to one extent or another. The goal is to correct each and every one of them as much as possible, because they become signals to sharp players such as me, for example, and we pick them up in a heartbeat.

Let's go back to a prior chapter and look at that little number Eddie did on Charlie. There is no way he could have pulled this off without knowing trouble and indecision were about to creep into Charlie's mind. Self-doubt was rearing its ugly head. Charlie had a halfway decent hand. He would have liked nothing better than to have hung around and played it. He draws the 8 of clubs; he has another 8, the 8 of hearts. He also has two other pretty good possibilities, much better that hanging around with the 8's and hoping. He would like to throw it, he would like to hold it, the game is early, he is playing a master, and all sorts of things go through his mind. He hesitates, yes he does, and here comes Mister Self Doubt. The discard rhythm is gone. He scratches his head. *Hello, Indecision!* Eddie can sense a good hand gone sour just like a wolf can sense a wounded deer. Hasn't he scouted Charlie many times in the past? Of course he has. Charlie is in trouble, and Eddie picks up on this.

Let's look at Eddie's hand, 6- 7 of clubs, 7- 9 and 10 of hearts, four very low cards. He has a deadwood total of, say forty-six. The call card is ten; Charlie had picked up the queen of clubs. This is far too much deadwood to hang on to for any length of time with out a break.

Eddies break comes when Charlie's mannerisms take over. He scratches his head, pulls his ear lobe, does everything but fart, then he comes off the eights, he throws the eight of clubs. We all know what happened then!

Had Charlie maintained his cool, kept his head, and realized the itch was the least of his problems, the hand maybe would have had a different outcome.

So, how do we overcome the mannerisms, these silly little quirks? Well, these silly little quirks are just nervous reactions. They are quite normal. We are all creatures of habit, and these nervous reactions to uncomfortable situations are merely little habits, and habits can be controlled, if not eliminated.

First of all think slow. Breath slow, and without making it noticeable, deeply. The inclination, when you get the feeling of 'impending doom' is to speed up, to draw fast, and to discard quickly. Resist this, and control this impulse. This does not mean become a slow player, there is a difference.

There are basic remedies for slowing everything down a bit. These can be used for hiding the fact that you are in trouble, or, you're trying to buy a little thinking time. Some people use them while waiting for a partner to complete the play he is involved in, before discarding themselves.

Consider this scenario; you think you are in trouble. You are trying to buy time to sort things out. Instead of resorting to a mannerism (scratching your head, pulling on your ear lobe), and coming to a complete halt (all engines stop), try this it works. The other guy has just discarded. You have an interest in the card, but, if you pick it up, discarding might be a problem— Maybe a card you have just drawn from the deck, it looks hot. Do you discard it and run the risk of improving your opponent's hand, or do you hold onto it and break up a possibility of you own?

Indecision is creeping in and you want to hide it. Try this. Perform little tasks. All of them are meaningless, but if you are thinking when you are doing them, they sure buy time! First, put your cards down on the table. Rub your hands together, smile and look at the other guys at the table. Pick your cards back up, spread them out a bit. Bunch them all together and fan them out again. Now your play starts.

Notice you've bought a little time already. Put your hand toward the card, stop halfway, then do it again, only this time get a little closer, while doing this you should have had ample time to make your decision.

Now, let's talk about a card you have just drawn from the pile, and you have that same decision to make. Place the card in your hand, look at it keeping both hands on your cards, then move this card around a bit, move it from position to position three or four times. This should give you time enough to make your decision, plus, it will keep your hands busy. The time it took to read the last paragraph or two, slowly, would give you a good idea of how much time should go by from the time you first see the troublesome card, to the time you finish your play. It doesn't sound like very much does it?

Consider this: Did you ever hear of subjunctive time? Webster describes it this way: "The mood of a verb that is dependant, rather than actual." In real life it goes like this: You have met a girl at a party. You are crazy about her. She agrees to allow you to drive her home. You park the car in front of her house, and you spend maybe forty-five minutes with her. It probably seemed like five. You look at your watch, where did the time go? Spend that same forty-five minutes waiting for a bus and you'll have an idea of what subjunctive time is.

The point is, that little bit of time you bought by going through a few motions, is really quite adequate, and can make all the difference in the world in winning or losing a hand. While you are doing this physically, concentrate mentally on what you are trying to accomplish. It will help you resist the impulse, the temptation to scratch that nervous little itch, or run your fingers through your hair, or tug at your earlobe.

One major thing to concentrate on is your basis strategy; how are you going to play this hand? Which direction are you going to go? Are you going to go with the high end, the low end or the middle, or use a combination of, say two possibilities high, and one low. Once this has been decided, and it may change, try to think three plays ahead. What will I do if I don't fill this combination? Or how long am I prepared to wait for the key card I need? On discards, what does the book say to throw?

If you can train yourself to plan ahead this way, to slow down your breathing, your method of play, to use the delaying tactics I've just described, you will not find yourself hesitating and breaking the rhythm of your discard nor submitting yourself to itches and the like.

The Chinese have a saying, "Few things in life are worse than a severe itch that cannot be reached, and few things feel better than when that itch is scratched" Keep your cool, avoid hesitations, and most of all, when that itch shows up, keep your hands on your cards.

"So, what is all this crap Kenny is talking about? Train yourself to do this, train yourself to do that, breathe slowly, and slow down the pace and all of that bullshit! I'll just bump along, hope for my share of no-brainers, and let the chips fall where they may! It's only a game."

Well, my friend, if you are playing cards, and could lose fifty or sixty bucks in a one hour setting, that itch is the least of your worries. It is a signal that can be noticed by *the other guy*. People like Eddie Colquitt make a lot of money at this game. You may be enough of a gin player to handle players such as this day in and day out but, if you're going to give them signals, you'll become just another addition to their pigeon coop.

Chapter 33
WHEN YOU'RE HOT, YOU'RE HOT!

Eddie was talking about *Old Man Kards* and how wonderful life can be when he takes a shine to you. The cards keep coming in like homing pigeons. Nothing seems impossible. Every thing is go! *Mistakes?* You've got to be kidding!

This is his philosophy of how to play when the cards just keep coming!"

"When the situation arises, play it for all it's worth. It's like the song goes, 'When you're hot, you're hot!'

Forget about calling, unless of course, you can do it on the first or second card. Set your hand for gin. Go for it! Play wide open. Become open-holed. Speculate like crazy and send out salesmen right and left. Discards? Don't worry about them. If you can't use it, throw it! Add-ons? Hell yes! Go for the inside straight? Damn right! Gamble and enjoy these moments in Paradise. Revel in being unconscious. Make the most of it, because nothing lasts forever. Soon you'll have to go back to playing sensible gin.

So, never mind the guards with the pitchforks. Load your wagon with hay and drive it across the border. When you're hot, you're hot!"

PART THREE:

PRELUDE TO THE SHOWDOWN!

Chapter 34
MONEY

If I could again quote Eddie Colquitt, and I have many times in the past, I would say something like this, "You may not think money is the most important thing in the world, but it's way the hell out in front of what's ever in second place."

Money, I thought. The quest for this all important commodity can make people do strange things, and really can have a profound effect on each and every one of us, even, *The man upstairs*.

A few years ago a young golf professional on the P.G.A tour was playing in his first Las Vegas Open golf tournament. It was overcast and beginning to get a bit chilly, which can happen in the desert in the winter months. A desert course is a bit different in appearance, from a golf course anywhere else. It kind of looks like someone placed a bunch of green ovals on a brown shopping bag you get at the super market. The desert is brown and humans have placed the green grass there, it's real, but also kind of artificial. The water hazards and decorative waterfalls are also artificial to the extent they are man made. They're just like the rest of the town, that's artificial too.

The eighteenth hole on this golf course is a par five, reachable in two strokes if a player hits two near perfect shots. This is also the final hole of the tournament. Looking down the fairway, our hero considers his position. The hole is loaded with trouble. There is water on the left side of the fairway, and in front of the green, bunkers and trees on the right. If he can hit these two near perfect shots, he can be on the green in two and, be putting for an eagle, or maybe take two putts for a birdie. A birdie puts him one shot back, an eagle three will tie him for the lead. A par, a five will keep him two shots back, tied with a few other players, but still a very handsome paycheck, more than he's ever won in his life.

He considers all the trouble on the hole. Decides discretion is the better part of valor, therefore trying for an eagle is out. This isn't "Tin Cup" after all. Hitting par fives in two is great but with all the trouble that would come into play in this case, trying for the eagle would be far fetched, because even if he did crunch two solid wood shots getting the ball close enough to the hole for a one putt was risky. The percentages also didn't favor this; there was just too much trouble involved.

No, he told himself, hit a conservative tee shot, lay up with a long iron, get on in regulation and hope for a birdie, if not, par would be satisfying.

His final decision is, hit a two iron off the tee, lay up with a four iron, and hit a pitching wedge for his third shot, and try to get it close. He reaches for his two iron and is addressing the ball when all of a sudden the clouds part right above him and a beam of light shines down.

"Hit the driver!" he hears a booming voice say.

He looks around, first at his caddy, and then at the gallery, they're all staring at the fairway, or just looking around. No one, it seems, has heard the voice, nor seen the beam of light.

What, am I going crazy? He asks himself, and reaches again for the two iron, and again the clouds part right above him, and he hears the voice *"Hit the driver!"*

"What— !

"Hit the driver!"

He pulls the driver from the bag and ignores his caddy's look of amazement. They had just discussed all this moments ago. He sets up and swings the club. *"CRACK!"* he slams out a massive drive. The ball is hammered! He has never hit a tee shot this far in his life, nor, he thinks, will he ever again.

Walking to the ball he looks up at the sky, complete overcast, silence, and no sign of any openings. "I must be day dreaming!" he decides. Arriving at his ball, he again ponders his position. He is still a long way away, even if he crunches his second shot as well as he hit the first, chances of getting on in two close enough for the eagle is just too risky. He reaches for the four iron.

The clouds part, the beam of light shines down, and there is the booming voice again.

"Hit the driver!"

Too weak kneed to protest, he pulls the driver from the bag. His caddy is aghast. He swings the club. *CRACK!* The ball takes off, flies through the air, two hundred forty yards, it clears the water, lands on the green and rolls into the hole. Double eagle, a two, he wins the tournament, and three hundred thousand dollars.

Getting to the green to retrieve his ball is a madhouse. Everybody wants to pat him on the back, or shake his hand. When he finally arrives, 'everybody', it seems, is replaced by the whole world.

He is reminded of an old song, "*Nobody knows you when you're down and out.*" The second verse of the song says: "*Soon as you get back on your feet again, everybody, anybody is your long lost friend*" And they're all there, '*everybody*' and '*anybody*'. The crowd, the TV people, you name it, they're there.

He gives autographs and interviews. He smiles, and why not, how often does this happen in life? The officials direct him first to the scorekeeper's tent to sign his scorecard.

The United States Golf Association and the Professional Golf Association have a hard fast rule they are in love with, and insist makes sense. Someone else keeps every player's score. This *someone else* would be another player in the same group, however the player himself is responsible for the authenticity of the scorecard, even though he has never laid his hands on it. If it is found incorrect in any way, the player is bound by any mistake or discrepancy that appears. His only recourse is, prior to signing the card, is to check it for discrepancies. If one is found he must have the player responsible for keeping his score correct the card. Then, and only then, should he sign the card.

This actually happened in the Masters Golf Tournament one year. Roberto Di-Vensenzo signed an incorrect scorecard. He had a three on one hole, the player keeping the score, by mistake wrote down a different number. Roberto never checked the numbers on the card, just the total score. The four stood. He had signed an incorrect score card, and finished second, although everyone in the whole world of golf, including the people watching on television knew what the score was. Terrific rule, eh

By the same token, in another tournament, golf professional, Craig Stadler, was about to play a ball, partially under some bushes. The ground was wet, and somewhat muddy, so he placed a towel on the ground so he could kneel on it while playing the shot. For some reason (probably dreamed up by the same person who invented the scorecard rule) this is an infringement. Some super-contentious person watching television noticed this and somehow got through to the TV network covering the golf tournament. Mr. Stadler was disqualified because of a phone call. Can you imagine the World Series or the Super Bowl being run this way? How about major league baseball umpires? If every mistake *they* made calling balls and strikes were subject to a phone call, the game might take a thousand years!

So, off to the scorekeeper's tent they went. I don't know if anyone actually brings an accountant with, but, if it were me, I would.

The press tent is next. Here the people of the media interview the top scoring players every day. On the last day of the tournament it includes the third and second place finishers, and of course, the winner, along with any notables, stars of the tour, no matter where they placed. This procedure, it is said, makes the reporters appear as if they were right there in the line of fire, watching every shot themselves. (Some rumors have them sitting in a tent close to the bar playing gin rummy, but, who the hell would do a *silly* thing like that?)

The interviewee sits on a stool, like some kind of a dunce, with a microphone in front of him, and he fields questions from the television, newspaper and magazine people. Reading about this quagmire, as it were, doesn't quite do it justice. One would have to be there to keep from laughing out loud. Imagine hearing this.

Reporter: "Hi Bobby, how did your round go?":

Golfer: "Hey-Ya—"

Reporter: "I mean, explain a few holes for us."

Golfer: "Okay— One, tee shot, bomb, wedge, six feet, blew it, had it right in the gut, broke off, asshole greens keeper should learn how to set holes. The goddam thing looked like a volcano.

"Two, three par, cut a four iron dead on, caught the corner of the bunker, pin cut too close, asshole greenskee—!"

Then there is the presentation of the winners check, the acceptance, and finally the golfer has some time to himself. He changes shoes in the locker room, pays his caddy and heads to the hotel. He is walking through the casino on his way to his room, (all paths in Las Vegas go through the casino), and he is smiling. This is more money than he's ever had in his life.

"Blink" the beam materializes above him, and he hears the voice.

"*Go to the roulette table!*"

"You've got to be kidding!"

" *Go to the roulette table!*" Our hero proceeds to the roulette table and stands there.

"*Put it all on sixteen red!*"

"C'mon—!"

"*Sixteen Red!*"

He nods at the dealer; the wheel spins, and up it comes, Sixteen Red. *Wow!* This is more money than he could have ever imagined. Terrific! He has money, what's more, he is rich. Holy shit is he rich! He can't wait to get to a phone and call his wife and break the news to her!

"Blink," the light comes on again, and he hears the voice

"*Let it ride!*"

"Give me a break!"

"*Let it ride!*"

"I would rather—!"

"*Let it ride!*"

Looking at the dealer, he nods again. The wheel is spun. It spins, it spins, it spins and the little ball rattles into a hole on the wheel.

"Fourteen black!" cries the dealer.

Holy shit! thinks the golfer, we lost, I lost, all the money is gone! What the hell is this? He looks up toward the beam of light. It has gone out. He listens for the voice. He faintly hears it, it is fading away. The voice says— "*Shit!*"

What did I say before? What *did* I say before? Rich man, poor man, beggar man thief. Only one of these should have any desire for you, the other three are what you could become, if you forget the importance of remembering where you are, and how much money you are playing for.

I guess one could describe my particular style of play as, aggressive, outgoing, gregarious and flamboyant. (Some people call it loaded with bullshit).

I got into a ten-cent game once, and believe me, it's a whole different world. Instead of losing ten dollars in a hand, you could lose a hundred. Flamboyancy is ambushed by conservatism. It is paramount you know and understand the full meaning of how much the game could cost. It does have a marked effect on how you play the hands.

Let me ask you again, "What makes the world go 'round?" I think you know the answer.

Chapter 35
POINT VALUES

Remember when Eddie was talking about "Know where you're at and know the conditions." We'll, you're about to see a good example. In the Chicago area, a point value is put on every game, in a two-man team game, it is two hundred points, and a three-man team game would be worth three hundred points. There is a bonus involved for winning the hand, this is called a box and is worth twenty five points. In most cases this "box" is worth twenty five cents, although at some clubs it is different, maybe fifty points, or a hundred. There is also an additional bonus for winning the game. This is usually equal to the point value of the game. Does it sound confusing? It really isn't. On paper, it would look like this:

CHICAGO AREA COUNTRY CLUB GIN RUMMY GAME
Game value 200 points

Team A. Winning Team	Team B. Losing Team
225 points	125 points
Ten boxes @ twenty-five points	Five boxes @ twenty-five points.

TOTALS:
225 points (winning score)
+125 in boxes (ten boxes @ twenty five points = 350 points.
+200 point bonus for winning the game
550 total points
-125 (team B's total points which must be deducted)
425 (total amount of points won by team A)
425 points @ two cents a point = $8.50. This would be the amount of money won by Team A.

In some locales, the point total is rounded off with a "50" being the dividing line. Hence, any amount below 450 points would be a "four" game, anything 450 and above would be a "five" game. A five game @ two cents a point would be $10.00.

In a "Hollywood" (a three street game), if Team A wins all three games (streets), and they are all five games the total amount of money won would be $30.00, and this would take about an hour. There are situations where a team wins the first street and loses the other two. These winnings and losses are of course pro-rated.

In a. country club in the Chicago area, one will see games running from one cent a point, to one cent, one cent and two cents a point (1-1, & 2 cents a point) to ten cents a point where a player could win or lose from, say twenty five to five hundred dollars in the course of an afternoon. These games are considered low to medium-sized games. There are games at twenty-five cents a point, (quarters), but these are uncommon. The more expensive games can get up to fifty dollars a point (nickels) and five dollars a box.

In Florida, I have seen games that have strictly a dollar value on them, say, ten dollars for the first street, fifteen for the second and twenty dollars for the third street., no boxes involved. In New York City and Los Angeles gin rummy games are played for a hundred dollars a game, the point value for the game would be one hundred points, a gin would be worth twenty-five dollars, and likewise, an under-cut, this would be worth twenty-five dollars. A game such as this would be over in about ten or fifteen minutes with a hundred to a hundred fifty dollars changing hands.

There are, of course "Blitzes" (glossary). This is a situation where one team is shut out, has no points. This is worth double.

There are also games called "Double in spades." Why not hearts, diamonds or clubs? who knows! Suppose you're sitting down to play in a game and someone quietly says "Double in spades?" (They like to sneak this in). *Beware.* Be on guard, know exactly what you are getting into.

If you're fond of gin rummy, and travel a bit, and like to play for a little money, don't, *do not*, automatically raise your hand if someone is looking for a fourth player in a gin rummy game. Find out what the ground rules are, whom you are playing with and for how much. You could get hurt!

In all the games mentioned above, you would find people like Eddie Colquitt. It's like I said, "In for a nickel, in for a dollar! Eddie has turned down invitations to play in tournaments, professional tournaments in Las Vegas, New York and Miami, many times. These tournaments last four days and have purses up to fifty thousand dollars.

Why? Eddie can make almost as much playing in big money games at country clubs all over the country, and the competition is less keen. To sum it up, know what you're getting into, keep your wits about yourself, and remember *"Every hand makes somebody happy."*

Chapter 36
SILENCE IS GOLDEN

"My son, I forgive you. Not only for the sins you have committed in the past, but also for the sins you will, no doubt, commit in the future!"

You may hear this, or a version of it in the confessional booth, and the Priest will probably be quite sincere, You may also hear something like it from your partner (s) when the game is over and you, you, have lost the Lions share of the points, maybe five to ten times the points your partners have lost, but, don't count on it's sincerity. You will probably hear compassionate things like;

"Hey, forget about it, it could happen to anyone."

"Ah, hell, you win some and you lose some."

"Charlie, you fought like a tiger."

"Hey, Charlie, someone's got to lose, it's the nature of the game."

But, What are they really thinking?

"Holy shit, the whole town's under water!"

"I've never been beaten so badly in my life!"

"I've never seen so many Rembrandts in one hand.

"What the hell was he planning on doing? Opening an art gallery?

"He had more bombs in his hand than were dropped on Berlin!"

"Those two cowboys he got stuck with when he had to get under the count looked like, Larry, Curly and Moe, when Moe went to the terlet!"

It does get worse. The things above are usually said out loud, but only out of earshot of the culprit. The thoughts are sometimes worse;

"Holy shit, I hope my wife doesn't look at the checkbook."

"Why the hell did I ever take up this game?"

"Holy shit, I hope my wife doesn't look at the checkbook!"

"Did that asshole ever see a deck of cards before?"

"Holy shit, I hope my wife doesn't look at the checkbook!"

"It'll be a cold day in hell before I play this game again!"

"Holy shit, I hope my wife doesn't look at the checkbook!"

"He should be playing with the blind men at the old people's home!"

"Holy shit, I hope my wife doesn't look at the check book!"

Bearing all this in mind, you will be asked the inevitable question, "How come you didn't get rid of some bombs?" There is no good answer, not one! You played the game for better or for worse, for richer or for poorer. all there is left to do is to turn your hands palms up, shrug your shoulders and walk out of the room. Your next move is to leave the premises of the club, get in your car and say obscene things to the fellow who is looking back at you from the rear view mirror.

Eddie's Thoughts. Let's look at getting rid of the bombs. In most cases a lot of high cards being held indicates a player fell in love with the hand. Falling in love with the hand brings about getting caught with a handful of high cards, and it can happen to anyone.

You are dealt a mitt full of high card possibilities, and there you are with all those Rembrandts. If you can, you think, just draw a couple of key cards, you can make an early gin.

Better you should attempt the seduction of a Venus Fly Trap, than to play for those few key cards, but there you are, and you are in love, and *love* is a many splendored thing, until the other guy says "Gin!" Then the hearts and flowers go right out the window and you are left with thoughts like, "Holy shit, I hope my wife doesn't look at the checkbook!" There is nothing left to do but count.

Let's look at that handful of bombs. You have two kings, three queens, one jack, and Milwaukee Avenue. It does look tempting. Maybe you can draw another king, and maybe you'll draw a 10 to go with the jack, after you've drawn the fourth queen. Maybe "Good Old Charlie" will help you out, he gets rid of high cards quickly, but sometimes, "Good Old Charlie" doesn't show up. Hell, Columbus took a chance! Go for it! When you're hot you're hot!

Tell me about it! When you're hot everything works, but right now we're talking about normalcy. You have thirty sure deadwood points in your hand, plus maybe another twenty or twenty-five depending on how bad Milwaukee Avenue is.

Picture this, and I'll bet it's happened to you at least once in every gin rummy sitting you play in; You are sitting there with all those "Rembrandts." You do not wish to part with any of them. Remember, you are in love.

In your Milwaukee Avenue collection you have a deuce or maybe a three. It's your turn to play. Do you draw one of the badly needed "Rembrandts?" Keep smiling! You draw an ace. Do you hang onto it and reduce your deadwood total? Are you kidding? You are involved with many splendored things.

You find yourself discarding the ace.

"Good Old Charlie" draws from the pile, places the card in his hand, looks at you and prepares to discard. And, here it comes; well, not this time, "Good Old Charlie" discards an ace.

You draw again, a deuce. "Son of a bitch, son of a bitch where the hell are the picture cards?"

You discard the deuce. "Good Old Charlie" draws again, and is ready to discard. Certainly now you'll get a high card. Are you kidding? "Good Old Charlie" got the message long ago; he throws you another mini.

What happens a few picks later? Horrors! "Good Old Charlie" drops the bomb on you, he calls, and there you are, stuck with your "Art gallery."

Why doesn't this work? How come you can't get those badly needed picture cards. Well, you can if *Old Man Kards* is smiling at you, but suppose he's not. Things could be worse. Go back to where you drew the hated ace. You decide to reduce your deadwood; you decide to come off your kings. Taking one from your hand, the safest one, whichever one that is, and you throw it. "Good Old Charlie" promptly picks it up.

Now, where's he going with that card? He's probably using it for three kings, so you decide to hold on to the other one. Your next pick is another ace.

Your strategy now is to get rid of high cards. You are unwilling to part with the other king in your hand; you have three queens, so queens, for the moment are out, so you discard the jack. Charlie picks this one up too. He discards an ace, you grab it and you are now plotting revenge, you discard a middle piece of deadwood. Charlie draws and discards. Nothing. You draw another jack. Fine. You decide to hold onto it and *tap dance* around Charlie's Rembrandts. You discard a deuce. Charlie picks it up and calls.

You are sure you have him under cut. You have a king to play off, a jack to play off, your dead wood total is low. "Good Old Charlie," you always knew he would come through! But, wait, what is this? Where are Charlie's kings? Where are the jacks? Charlie didn't go that way. He made jack queen king. He made 9 10 jack. He had another spread and your deuce gave him the call. And there you are stuck with all your bombs.

"Good Old Charlie!" *The bastard!*

So, gamble if you will, but in the long run the odds favor reducing useless deadwood. If it appears to be a losing hand, try to lose as little as possible, and fall in love at home!

Chapter 37
PARTNERSHIP GIN

There are two men of Jewish extraction, who we'll call Morris (Morey) and Abe. The two of them owned a brokerage firm. They were partners and business associates. One day they went to North Avenue beach in Chicago. While they were splashing around in the surf Abe was caught in the undertow and was pulled into deeper water. He jumped up and down and tried to fight the current, but the more he struggled, the more he floundered, and the farther out he was drawn.

"Morey!" he called, "Come help me, I'm not a strong swimmer, and I'm about to go under!" Morey swam over, but he was of little help. He was not a lifeguard by any stretch of the imagination. The current was just too strong.

"Abe!" Morey yelled, "The current is too strong for me too, I have to go for help!"

"Well hurry, I can't last much longer!"

"I will!" cried Morey, "Can you float alone?

"Morey!" Abe screamed, "This is no time to talk business!"

Although there are many players who swear the purity of the game is one man playing another, going head to head, as they do in the professional tournaments in Las Vegas or Miami, most country club gin rummy games are partnership games.

There are three basic forms of partnership games. 1). Two, two man teams. 2). Two, three man teams. 3). Line Gin. We'll take them in order.

In the two two-man teams version, the partners sit facing one another. One player will play the man on his left. His partner will do likewise. When the hand is over, each partner will play the man on his right. This continues throughout the game.

The Round Robin rule is usually in effect. This is to say Player A has Player B for a partner, then he has Player C for a partner then to complete the round, he has Player D. Each player has the opportunity of having each man for a partner once. A Round Robin is three games. In the course of an evening, or afternoon two or three rounds can be played.

There are many who do not favor the Round Robin format, because there is usually one winner and three losers, or vice versa, three winners and one loser. In the case of the latter, the one loser is referred to as the person who threw the party.

Four cards being dealt, one to each player, determine the partners in the two-man, two-team version.

In some cases the cards are cut. The two high cards are partners, as are the two low. High deals to low for the first hand, or in some cases, black would deal to red. In the case of the Round Robin rule not being in effect, each man would have the same partner throughout the sitting.

In the three men on a team version, the partners sit next to each other. They play the man sitting across the table. After each hand each player on the team that lost the first hand moving to his right one chair changes the partners. The player who was in the right chair moves over to the chair on the left. In some locales this shifting of partners occurs every other hand This reduces the movement of the partners by half.

The partners are determined prior to the game by six cards being turned face up in the middle of the table, three black and three red. The three players drawing the same color first are partners, black deals to red. In some instances the three high cards are partners.

At some clubs there is a rule for which team sits at which side of the table. "High" or "Black" having the choice usually decides this.

Eddie's thoughts: Modern day historians as to their insight and foresight marvel at the people who drew up our constitution. Sometimes I wonder about the people who invented and developed gin rummy. Did they have the insight and foresight to envision all of the rules, including the selection of partners, seating arrangements and the like? If they did all this, how long did it take? And how long did they retain their sanity?

Line gin; Line gin is a great way to introduce a lot of fun into an evening which would otherwise be tame, or dull.

Eight or more players can participate. Expert or non-expert players can play it, and it is not unusual to see both in the same game. In this game one can also see players of, or close to the novice category.

It can be serious, and in most cases it is, however when the amount of players on a team exceeds four it can and does become quite casual and entertaining.

The game is usually played on what are regarded as social nights at most clubs, normally Friday evenings, and Saturday or Sunday afternoons or evenings. It is a very popular after dinner pastime and can get very social with boy, girl, boy, girl, boy girl on a team, or even boy, boy, girl on a team. There is really no set way to do this, no one set of rules.

Most of the time when you see Line gin it is an after dinner fiasco which can be a lot of fun. It goes without saying this is not serious gin rummy. When you have five to ten people on a team how could it be? Certain items must be decided.

1). What type of game is played?

2). How about the call card? How is that little item determined?

Well, the game is usually *Oklahoma gin* with the twenty-first card dealt being turned over. One version is the common call. This would be the lowest card turned over, usually gin. Sometimes a call deck is used. A separate deck is shuffled and placed in a jar, or tumbler. The back of this deck is facing the players. Prior to the beginning of each hand, one card is removed from the back of the deck and turned facing the players. This is the call card for every player playing in the game.

There are games that feature, and this is really quite bizarre, a separate call card for each set of players.— John, is playing Mary, their twenty first card, the one turned up is a five. Their call is a five. Bill and Judy are next in line and are playing one another, their up card is a nine. Their call card is a nine, and so on down the line.

Serious gin? How the hell could it be? And why should it be. It is strictly for fun. Most of the time there is no money involved. There are wagers called *drink stakes*. This would be where the losing team buys the winning team a drink, or halfway through the game the team behind buys the cocktails, more or less similar to the *beer frame* in bowling.

There is a lot of good-natured horseplay involved, and most of the time the games are played for *bragging rights*.

Picture this; you have expert and novice playing one another, one player, very well versed in the game, and his opponent, not versed at all. The non versed player will say things like, "How come you picked up that seven when you didn't want the other one?"

Or a novice getting bored asking "How long does this game last anyway?" Playful answer, "First one to twenty thousand wins."

There are many sayings in the jargon of gin rummy that can be misunderstood. One that comes to mind is a situation where a player is forced into discarding a card that will disclose an undesired amount of information about the hand. This is called *exposing the hand!* Or, in the Jargon of gin rummy, *exposing one's self!*

Bill (expert) is playing Jane (novice). He is about to make a discard that will pretty much disclose how he is using a certain card he just picked up. He forgets he is playing a novice, and a lady at that, and he says,

"Jane, I'm about to expose myself!"

"I beg your pardon!" exclaimed Jane.

Can you just imagine the scorekeeping in a game of ten on a team, where each set of players has a different call card? Suppose someone miscalls? How would you know? What difference would it make? Who would even care? And how about the scorekeeper?

At the end of the game he would become either a mathematical genius or a babbling idiot!

Chapter 38
AIRLINE GIN

There is another version of line gin. It is called airline gin, although you seldom see it any more. It goes like this: Consider a group of young men on a wintertime golf vacation. They will be flying to Arizona to play golf. They have reservations at Tucson National Resort and Country Club, and they are quite excited about it.

All of these young gentlemen, they are sixteen of them, will be getting to the airport, *O'Hare International*, by means of the great Chicago-land expressway system.

This system features eight or nine expressways, that lead into downtown Chicago from all directions, north, northwest, west, southwest, south, and also from northern Indiana.

It is said, in Europe all roads lead to Rome, well, in northern Illinois, all roads lead to downtown Chicago. Traffic during rush Hour is catastrophic. It's unbelievable. The same trip that takes you a half hour in the afternoon can take an hour and a half during morning rush hour.

Keeping all this in mind, picture getting to O'Hare International Airport by means of this same expressway system, only in reverse. All eight or nine expressways have to feed into one of them, the Northwest, or Kennedy Expressway. This is the one expressway that goes directly into O'Hare. It has been referred to, and does look, quite like a parking lot during rush hour.

The flight to Tucson leaves at Nine a.m. The same time most other flights to anywhere are scheduled to leave, or so it would seem. Perhaps this would explain the madhouse getting into O'Hare at that time of the morning.

This flight to the warm weather of Arizona necessitates a wake call up of about Five a.m. Plenty of time for a quick cup of coffee, and then the trek to the airport, chauffeured by an understanding (?) wife who doesn't mind a bit if her beloved goes off to Arizona to play golf with his buddies, while she stays home with the kids in one of the Chicago suburbs and shovels snow for a week.

The sixteen of them arrive at the airport at about the same time, stop at the ticket counter, check in their luggage and proceed to the welcome party the Department of Transportation has planned for them, thanks to our Muslim friends. After an hour of removing shoes, belts, hats, having carry on baggage checked, pockets being emptied, standing in line, and being told (sometimes in Swahili,) that the that the carry on bag is supposed to be upright, not lying down, it is seven o'clock. Boarding is at eight thirty; this leaves over an hour to kill. How do you kill an hour and a half in an airport?

I suppose there are many ways, but for sixteen adventurous souls, not too many are palatable. Too early for drinking! Read the paper? See what's going on in the world? *Shit*, we're going on vacation, who cares? They do the most obvious and sensible thing in the world. They start a gin rummy game.

Cards are readily available at the magazine counter, and reasonably priced, (by airport standards) $6.95 a deck, (but who's counting)? They buy eight decks, and start a game. All of this sounds too easy, but wait!.

First it must be decided what type of game, or games they are going to play. Four games of two on a side? Nah! Too unrealistic! Four guys are finished, while the other guys are still playing? Nope, too disorganized, besides, suppose, when it's boarding time, one or two games are finished, and the others aren't? When would they be continued? Or would they be? *One game of Line gin, eight on a side?* A great idea. This could be continued on the airplane someway somehow, but where the hell would you play it right now? You'd need four or five tables, sixteen chairs, few airports carry this type of equipment.

Necessity is the mother of invention. They spot two rows of those plastic chairs that airport designer's love so much. If you do any flying at all you know the chairs I am talking about. They have seats and backrests made of contoured (or is it contorted?) plastic. They are all connected side by side, and the row of seats to the rear is connected to the one in front so that if both rows of seats are filled, the people are sitting, back to back.

They all look at one another. They all get the same idea at the same time, (except one or two, this always happens), and decide the situation is perfect. They count the seats, twenty-five, perfect, all they really need is sixteen in each row. Line gin, eight men on a team.

Row "A" plays row "B"— Player 1, from row "A" plays player two from row "A," using the seat between them for a table.— Player three plays player four, using the same type of table.—Rows five and six follow suit, and so on down the line with seven and eight playing each other. Row "B" does the same.

(And the head bone connected to the shoulder bone).

The format will be, they all decide, for each man to play his opponent three times before the partners are changed. This is easily accomplished; the players just stand up and do it. How will they change partners on the airplane? Well, as one east coast senator said when running for re-election, "We'll cross that bridge when we come to it!"

This is great, and they all are so proud of themselves. Look at the obstacles they have overcome, and the monumental decisions they have just made. If governments could only think his way, the world wouldn't be in the sorry shape it's in right now. .

Eight–thirty! Boarding call! The hands are picked up because the games are to be continued, and on to the airplane they go.

They are all so pleased with themselves. A camaraderie never imagined before is now present because they loved the way the situation was handled. But how, how in the world are they going to pull this off once on the airplane? Providence intervenes. They get lucky. Their seat assignments are three on one side of the aisle and three on the other side, for two rows, then two on one side and two on the other side for a row.

(And the shoulder bone connected to the backbone).

Picture this: Window seat plays middle seat using middle seat's table. Aisle seat plays aisle seat, using one of the two tables. This involves playing across the aisle, (as we told you, necessity is the mother of invention). This takes place in the first two rows of three players. We now have four players remaining. They sit in the third row, *the row behind the chaos going on in front of them.* Aisle seat plays middle seat, and, after the partner change he plays across the aisle against the other aisle seat.

1-playing 2, then 2 playing 3 while 1 plays 4.

(And the backbone connected to the hipbone).

A-hah! You might say, there's a fly in the ointment. What happens to the middle seat players when the two aisle seat players play against one another? Or, what happens when the inevitable major partner change takes place?

Easy, card players stand up, excuse themselves, beg pardons from other passengers, move this way and that, and cross the aisle when they must. The whole operation resembles a mass exodus.

Picture all of this taking place while cocktails are being served, snacks being enjoyed and safaris to the rest rooms are being made.

It is a lot of fun, but it happened to me so long ago, I don't remember why. I do remember players love it, other passengers tolerate it, and flight attendants hate it!

(Now hear the word of the Lord).

Chapter 39
FROM YOUR LIPS TO GOD'S EARS
OR
SAYING THE RIGHT THING!

There once was a man driving his car down a highway in Tennessee. This would be south of Nashville where the speed limit is fifty-five miles per hour. Our hero in this saga was operating at a speed of eighty-five.

Glancing at the rearview mirror, he noticed a flashing red light. He was being followed by a Tennessee State Police car, and it was closing fast.

Pulling off to the side of the road he stopped, and waited. Moments later the police car pulled up and stopped behind him. The State trooper stepped out of the car. He had to bend his head far forward to accomplish this. He was some kind of big. He looked driver's car over, paused and walked up to the open window of the car.

"You know, son," the trooper said, "You're going a mite too fast for my liking, 'you want to see how fast you were going?"

The driver got out of the car and followed the trooper to the police car. Reaching down inside of the car the trooper pulled out the radar gun he had been using. There is was, lit up with red numbers on a black screen, 86mph. "I'd call that a mite fast, son, wouldn't you?" The culprit had to agree.

"Where 'ya from son?

"Chicago!"

The trooper straightened himself to his full height. He was about fifty with kind of sparse blond hair. He had a red face and a red neck, more than likely products of the Tennessee sunlight. He had a tattoo on his left forearm that read "Bubby."

"What do you do in Chicago?" he asked.

"I'm a bricklayer."

"Is that so? Well you know son, about twenty years ago I used to work construction in Chicago. I was a laborer, I worked with a lot of bricklayers," Bubby said this with a smile.

"Well can't you give a fellow construction worker a break?" Our hero asks.

"Boy, I'd love to because I know you guys from Cook County don't come down here to get traffic tickets, but I like this job, and if I don't write you up, they'll have someone else out here who will. Then I'll probably have to go back to be a construction laborer and I won't like that a bit!"

"C'mon Bubby, give a guy a break."

"You know son," Bubby said after a short period of silence, "I like you, if we didn't happen to meet this way, we'd probably get to be good buddies, go down to the tavern and bend our elbows a bit and all that."

"Well, then give me a warning ticket, you know, a verbal."

"What the hell is that?"

"Well, you tell me I was speeding, it's against the law, and then you warn me never to do it again. I say, 'Okay!' and then both of us go our separate ways. What the hell, that works. You can be a bit generous, *and so can I*— You know what I mean. Everybody could get to know everybody *very* well!"

Bubby laughed. "I'll tell you what son, if you can tell me a story as to why you were going so fast, one I've never heard before, I might consider it, but it's really gonna have to knock my socks off, but that's as far as I can let my generosity extend."

The driver thought for a moment, looked at Bubby, and began, "I used to be married to a woman, in fact I was married to her for five years. In those five years she wouldn't let me watch a ball game on television. She wouldn't let me have a beer with my buddies. She wouldn't cook for me. I had to do all the housework. All this, and it lasted for five years. She just flat out made life miserable for me. A living hell is what it was. Then one day she left me. She ran off with a Tennessee State Trooper of all people. I was so happy. She was gone, I was free! Then, about twenty minutes ago I saw the flashing red light on the top of a State Police car. It was you, but I thought it was him, bringing her back!"

Eddie's thoughts: *There are times in life, and in card games where it is paramount to say the right thing. This can be the difference between winning and losing, getting along, and not getting along. An example of this would be at the beginning of a gin game when it is being decided who is going to be whose partner.*

Consider this: The cards are cut, or dealt and you draw a player that you consider weak. I mean, he knows the fundamentals of the game. He knows the basics and all that, but most of the time he doesn't seem to get it. He doesn't think things through! He's like a six pack of Heinekens two cans short!

Here's the situation, and everybody who plays gin has gone through this once or twice at least. As the cards are being dealt for partners, or the deck is being cut, you look around at the people you will be spending the afternoon or evening with. A quick glance tells you who you would like to have as partners, if you had your "druthers." Partners who would be okay. And players who you wouldn't want at all

"There's Louis; tops. Benny; tops; Lee; good. Donnie; pretty good. Gregg real good; and Charlie!—— Holy shit, I hope to hell I don't draw Charlie!"

It's not that Charlie is bad. He knows what he's doing most of the time, but he has lapses. He will forget what the count is. He will go over the count when he has to reduce his deadwood to save a hand, a game, or, heaven forbid, to avoid a blitz.(glossary)!

You've had him for a partner many times when he had to get under ten to win the game. For example both partners were through playing, the hand was won, and the game is won if Charlie has a deadwood count of under ten. You look at Charlie hand and breath a sigh of relief. Charlie is under ten. All of a sudden when you look back at his hand he has a count of fifteen, then twenty five. He has drawn two picture cards he thought the other guy could use and discarded two minis.

What the hell is he thinking about, you ask yourself as you sit there and wring your hands. You feel like tearing your hair out, one at a time. Son of a bitch, how the hell can anyone be so empty headed. Then you look back a moment or two later. He needs one card for gin, and he draws it. You are elated. Graduation day! The games are over, your team has won. Terrific! You have sweated blood for the last ten minutes. You feel like Christ at Gethsemane. Those ten minutes seemed like ten hours. (Talk about your subjunctive time)! In those ten minutes you have aged ten years. I wonder what kind of time that is called. I'm sure there is a sensible answer, but, it would have to come from a better mind than mine. Is all this worth it? Sometimes you wonder!

How do people like Charlie exist in country club gin? How, in spite of all the mistakes they make, all of the technical errors they commit, in spite of all the ignorance they show when common sense should prevail? Well, best said, they do and they don't. It's like this, if you have *Old Man Kards* on your side you can do anything. Rest assured, he's not going to be there forever, but people like Charlie don't remember that.

In a previous chapter I remembered everything that was good, and outstanding about my Army career. I never once, nor has anyone else I can remember, said anything entirely unpleasant about the service. I suppose if we tried, we could come up with a few beauties, but that's not human nature. Human nature is to remember only the good things.

So here we have Charlie;— Playing the hand wide open!— Go for broke!— Devil may care!— Damn the torpedoes full speed ahead!— Is he successful? Damn right!

Every once in awhile, *Old Man Kards* acts like a stranger, but people never remember this, and this is why Charlie can be, at times, a millstone around your neck, when you get him as a partner, and sometimes a blessing in disguise.

There are two ways to handle this. One is to wallow in self pity.

"Why me, God!" or "If you want me to do penance, let the priest tell me, but don't give me Charlie!"

A lot of players do this, they make the best of it. Their philosophy is; Get the game over with and wait until you draw someone else for a partner.

What I just pointed out, is one way to handle the situation. The other is to turn this so-called disadvantage into an advantage. This is done by *saying and doing the right thing.*

It is done by saying them, and doing them often. Your mission has just taken on weight. Not only do you have to contend with playing your own hand, you are also obligated to play your partner's hand. You can't really do this, it is against all the rules of partnership gin. However, when the hand is over, you can build him up if he had lost, or heap mountains of praise on him if he were successful.

At this point, please allow me to illustrate a very common mistake. You have, out of the corner of your eye, been watching your partner play his hand . You are totally aghast!. You have never in your life seen so many flagrant mistakes. They are outrageous, and, no matter how much *Old Man Kards* is on his side, it's hopeless. He loses, and loses big. You sit there and watch him play the hand. You don't really wish to sit there and be a party to all of this, but what else can you do? You have already been the to the men's room three times. The attendant there is looking at you as if you are a long lost friend. So you sit there. The hand, at long last,comes to an end. You look at how many points Charlie has lost. You think of the national debt. You think of your wife looking at the check book.

It's time to decide what you are going to do about it. The easiest thing to do is, is to do nothing. The easiest thing would be to bite the bullet and try to make the best of the situation.

It would be very easy to criticize Charlie when the hand is over, and the temptation is great. But criticism hardly ever is received graciously. *"What the hell do you mean I did this wrong!"*

Resist that urge. Criticism is designed to correct things. In the course of a game you don't have time for this. The thing to do is to turn on the charm.

"Hey, Charlie, I sure admired you for the way you played that last hand!" You have a

tough time getting this out, bullshit is always difficult.— "*You realized you had a loser on your hands and you tap danced beautifully before the bastard came and got you!*"

Little phrases such as "*Way to go!*" and "*I like your style!*" can go a long way. Doing this, you make him feel like he's a part of the team instead of just a guy the team got stuck with.

It should be said right now; more games are won by how well a team gets along together than by talent alone. *Old age and cheating will beat youth and talent every time!* may be true, but the team that gets along well, and is truly a team, tends to win more games.

There's a word called *schmoozing* that should fit in right about now. *Do it.* Flatter your weaker partner. This is known as the strong player carrying the weaker one. Not just because he is likely to win more hands, but by keeping his partner(s) in the game.

I once was a witness to a game where a very strong player was teamed with two weaker ones. He had just gotten his brains beat out by virtue of a no-brainer. The other guy had called on the second card and caught the strong player with a bundle. This strong player probably had every right in the world to complain about his lack of good luck He probably would have been entitled to complain bitterly. This is not what happened. The man simply laid his cards down and spoke; not to the scorekeeper, but to his partners.

"I have just lost eighty points," he said. He then looked at the scorecard, did a little mental arithmetic and gave his partner(s) the count.

"Here's where we are, and what the eighty points will do for them"— In this way he is bringing his partner(s) together and keeping them in the game.— In one way he is building teamwork and giving his teammates encouragement instead of allowing them to become demoralized.— Little comments regarding how great our team is, and; *how the other team doesn't belong at the same table with us,* can help accomplish this.—.Believe me, teamwork is contagious, and is paramount.

Key cards: gin rummy is a game of key cards. Example; in your hand you have a triangle, a 3-4 of diamonds, and a 4 of hearts. There are three cards that can complete this combination. This is known as a three way hit. The three cards are 2 of diamonds, 5 of diamonds, and any 4. These cards are called key cards. Another example would be 7 and 9 of hearts being held in a hand, the 8 of the same suit would be the key card.

Whether you position yourself to catch these key cards by skill, knowledge of the laws of probability, or just plain dumb luck makes no difference. The end result is the same. If you are the strong player, and your weaker partner is pulling these key cards out of the sky, or whatever, this is like *manna from Heaven,* not just because the hand is being helped, but by the encouragement factor that comes into play.

If you can come up with the right phrase, the right combination of words, you can make this so-called weak player feel like he is ten feet tall. And then watch out. All of a sudden he begins making bigger and better plays.

Look at the football team that has just fumbled and lost the ball. Their defense forces a turnover and gets the ball back. The effect on the entire team is monumental. They have just come up with a big play. The same is true in gin rummy. If you can convince your teammates they are invincible the whole world looks different. Making better plays seems to make *Old Man Cards* sit up and take notice. He will begin to smile. Then more of those key cards will seem to be coming in.

And where did it all start, that's right, with a little bit of encouragement. Would I rather be lucky than good? Damn right!

Chapter 40
TECHNIQUE

Many years ago I was studying the piano. I was working with and taking lessons from a man named Elmer Barron. He was the epitome of the Bavarian music teacher, (mitt der cracking down on der knuckles mitt der baton), that type of teacher. We used to call him "The Baron," behind his back of course.

There was going to be a huge recital. Selected students would be given a chance to perform in Orchestral Hall in downtown Chicago. In the past this was a gala affair. It was looked forward to by all of his students, myself included. I placed my name on the sign up sheet, and began practicing in earnest.

One day he called me into his office.

"Tushilav," he said to me, that was what he called me, sort of a nickname, "Tushilav, you do not have the hands and fingers necessary to become a great concert pianist. Not only that, you don't have the brains for it, you are not enough schmart!"(I always had the feeling Professor Barron's greatest fault was, he didn't lay things on the line, he wasn't outspoken enough).

"For those reasons," he continued, "and because you hit all those god-damn clunkers, I have my doubts." He looked at me again and smiled, "But, Tushilav, you have a great heart, and you have enough bullshit in you to put on a halfway decent performance. You wish to be in the recital? I *think* maybe yah!"

So, I played in the recital. You've heard of Schubert's "Unfinished Symphony"? well mine was almost over before I began. I worked very hard, and somehow got through it. I finished. I rose to take my bow. The audience was applauding (they were very kind).

I took a quick bow, and as I was straightening up I felt a hand on my shoulder. It was The Baron. He was standing there smiling, patting me on my shoulder, and I like to remember him having, maybe a tiny tear in his eye. He stood there and smiled, and all the time he was saying " *Tushilav*, Tushilav!"

It wasn't until many years later that I found out *Tushilav* in Bavarian means Asshole!

Eddie's thoughts:

From day one, in the playing of the game, the novice is taught to pick up the cards, and put them in their proper order. That is arranging them in spreads or possible spreads, with the high cards on the left and low cards on the right. He is also admonished to change the positions of these spreads or combinations periodically, sometimes every hand, maybe sometimes reversing the positions, placing high cards on the right or, the middle. This is to be done so the other guy will not be able to detect a pattern of what value card a player has drawn by where he places it in his hand. All the experts say we should do this.

Great emphasis is also placed on putting a card one has drawn on the extreme right hand portion of the hand, and then put it in its proper place while the other guy is playing his turn. This move further prevents an opponent from gaining information regarding your hand.

Give me a break! I thought. First of all this is country club gin, not a big time tournament in Vegas or Miami. Second, try all this sometime, you will find yourself concentrating so

hard on hiding the position of your cards that soon you will be ignoring the rest of the game.

You could probably do all this with a lot of practice, but, why! I had to disagree. The time spent in learning this could be better spent in other facets of the game.

The first of these is determining where your hand actually is.

Example: You have ten cards in your hand, three high, three middle, and four low. These may, or may not be spreads. Your mission is to decide, by the third card played, which group has the greater possibilities, and then concentrate your attention there. If the middle or low cards are more advantageous, drop off the high cards. Conversely, if high and low have better possibilities, use the middle cards for discarding however watch out for sevens, they can be catalytic.

Perhaps I'm over-simplifying this. The best way for you to find out for yourself is to play a few practice hands alone. You'll soon see what I'm talking about. This is called developing card sense, and having a deck of cards in your hands fifteen or twenty minutes a day will do it.

Let's talk about the count. The words, "The count" can mean a lot of things. It can mean how many points you or your partner have won, and how it will affect the score. Example: Charlie must be made by Louis, Charlie's partner to arrive at a deadwood total in his hand of nine or under. This is known as "Getting under the count."

In the latter stages of the game it can also mean how many points one team or the other needs to "Go out," or end the game. "What do they need to go out?" is the expression most used, another is simply "What's the count?" Example: Suppose the opponents need those same thirty-five points to go out. Your mission is to reduce the deadwood total in your hand to nine or under to keep the game alive. In jest, the expression, "Throw them on the floor, if you have to, but get under!" is sometimes used.

Every time a player concludes a hand, his partner should pause, and then see what happened score wise. This is called "Getting the count." and it must be done, as it has a direct bearing on how you are to play the remainder of your hand. Sometimes it may mean sacrificing your hand, allowing the other guy to win it, even if he gins. If you are under the count the hand you and your partner is won. In this case the "Box" or even the game is the main objective. Said another way, "Don't win the battle and lose the war."

This may be difficult to understand, but, if you look at closely, it's common sense. You are playing partnership gin. You and your partner(s) are a team, and the team is playing the hand. Looking at it this way, it's easy to see why getting under the count is important.

It is said, one of our former presidents was a gin rummy aficionado. He had a sign over the Oval office door stating two rules. " 1.Wipe your feet! —2.Get under the count.

Expect the unexpected.

Sharing with you a baseball story can best emphasize this axiom. There once was a major league batting champion, we'll call him Harry. Harry was a left-handed hitter, and one of the best. Most of his success was due to the fact he had an uncanny ability to pre-determine, to guess as it were, what pitch the opposing pitcher was going to throw, and why he was going to throw it. In a very important game he came up to bat with the bases loaded and his team two runs down. It was the last of the ninth. There were two outs.

Harry had it figured this way. He needed a breaking ball on the outside corner of the plate just above the knees. If he got his pitch he could slice this thing down the left field line, just above the third baseman's head. It would hit just inside the foul line and roll down into the far corner of the outfield. The left fielder would never get to the ball in time to do anything productive with it. Three runs would come in, his team would win, and the ball game would be over.

He also had the pitcher figured out. The man's "Money pitch," the pitch that got people out was a breaking ball over the outside corner that sunk out of the strike zone as it approached the plate. He figured he would see this pitch three times during his at bat. If the pitcher was unfortunate to hang one of these curve balls, that is, to come off the pitch a little where it didn't break as much, Harry would then swing at it full and knock it out of the park He had it figured right down to the wire.

The first pitch was the breaking ball on the outside corner that dove out of the strike zone. The umpire called it a strike. This was understandable, Harry thought, major league umpires are really not noted for their knowledge of the strike zone, in fact, most of them border on the ridiculous when it comes to calling balls and strikes. The instant replay now in use proves that. Harry wondered what they were taught in umpire school.

The second pitch came in, it was a waste pitch, teasing, but not able to be hit. In came the third pitch. There it was again the breaking ball diving for the dirt as it got near the plate. The umpire called this one a strike also. Harry was enough of a hitter to have gotten the bat on it, but the result would have been a ground ball to the third basemen. This was what the pitcher was after. He let it go. The next two pitches were waste balls, close to the strike zone, but difficult to hit. The count was now three and two, a full count. Knowing the pitcher and umpire, Harry was certain the next pitch would be the down and outer. As the pitcher took his stretch, and checked the runners, Harry moved forward in the batter's box, and inched closer to the plate. If the down and out breaking ball came in, Harry, because of his new position, would be able to hit it the way he wanted.

The pitcher came out of the stretch and delivered the ball. Harry tensed, ready for the breaking ball, down and outside. The pitch was a heater, a fastball on the inside corner. The pitcher didn't have much of a fastball, but in this case it he didn't have to. Harry picked it up halfway to the plate, but he was unable to pull the trigger. He stood there with his bat on his shoulder and watched the pitch cut the inside corner letter high while the umpire rang him up. Hell, a blind man could have called this one. There is was, strike three, and the game was over. The pitcher had outguessed Harry and had done the unexpected.

This type of thing happens a lot in gin rummy. Consider this. It is a close three men on a side game, with both teams in the two hundred ninety range. Either team could go out. Your team has just won fifteen points, enough to go out and end the game. All you have to do is hold it. You have the misfortune to have been dealt Milwaukee Avenue. As the hand progresses, you are able to get rid of a lot of deadwood, make a few great key card picks, and by sheer luck and a lot of tap dancing, you are ready for gin. The fly in the ointment is you need a queen to go with your two-queen combination.

You are fairly certain this card, the queen will be forthcoming. kings have been played, Jacks have been played, and one queen has been played. The deck is down to twelve cards, enough for each player to have five picks. With only five picks left, you either have to draw this card or get it from Charlie, fat chance! Charlie, at times is sharp, and can be a little tough. He is sharp enough to realize, if he calls, and gets undercut, the game will be over and he will have lost the game for his team. Charlie is not going to call.

You draw a card, it is not a queen, and you discard a safe card. Charlie draws and discards. The situation repeats. You draw and discard, Charlie draws and discards. No queen. You sweat blood. You draw an ace. What to do? If Charlie is looking for a low card so he can call, this may be it. No, you tell yourself, if Charlie were going to call, he would have done it by now. You are so totally convinced you discard the ace. Charlie picks it up and calls. Not only is he not undercut, he wins twenty points by virtue of your two queens, plus the one card piece of deadwood you are holding. In this case a safe nine. He wins enough to put his team out.

By whatever means he was able to do this, be it skill, luck or brains he did it. He did the unexpected. Of course he had a bit of help from *Old Man Kards*, because when you looked at the deck to see where the accursed queen of spades was, there she was, *that black whore*, right on the bottom, but be that as it may, Charlie did the unexpected, and won the game for his team. Had you considered the unexpected, the outcome of the game might have been different.

PART FOUR:

WORLD WAR THREE

Chapter 41
THE BLITZ

Our glossary defines the blitz (also known as a Schneider) as a situation where one team shuts out the other. This is to say, the winning team has ended the game, has gone out with the other team having no points at all. There is a penalty for this, or a bonus, depending on which team you are on. The team that loses, loses double. In other words, the three-cent game you were playing just became a six-cent game.

This is where the count really becomes important. In the early stages of the game, getting on board becomes paramount, super important. It's called "Playing for half price."

Let's take a good look at this. The game is in its early stages. Your team is not on board. Your partner has just won forty points. Your mission is to reduce the deadwood total in your hand to fourteen or under in case the other guy gins. At this point winning the hand, for the moment, becomes secondary. If you are under fourteen points your team is automatically on board, even if the man you are playing gins his hand.

You do anything you can to accomplish this. You shun high cards; you pick up every mini card that comes along. Its called *diving for the sewer*! Winning the hand becomes secondary. The team must get on board.

This situation prevails for all three streets of the game.

Chapter 42
THE PSYCHOLOGY OF THE BLITZ

One of Eddie's favorite subjects while discussing gin rummy is called the psychology of the blitz. This subject would take in all three of the points covered in the preceding chapters, The hand, the Count and the blitz.

Most of you have been blitzed if you have played any gin rummy at all, and I would venture to say you would all agree on one thing. It hurts. How much it hurts depends on the individual. Eddie would say, "Getting hurt by being blitzed depends on the circumstances .Your outlook on the game. Your ego. If you are ahead or behind for the course of the evening comes into play. Also whether or not your wife looks at the checkbook in the morning. Suffice to say it hurts."

The very fact that it hurts brings the psychology into the game. Pain affects different people in different manners. You can think of the blitz as a penalty, or you can be aggressive and consider it a weapon. Considering the blitz a penalty suggests fear.

There is fear of not getting on, fear of being chastised by your partners, fear of losing double. Fear!

The person, or player who is aggressive takes advantage of that fear and uses it to further his own cause. In a precious chapter we spoke of self-doubt and indecision leading to mistakes, well, fear breeds both of these commodities, and they all lead to mistakes. Blitzes just don't happen. They are caused! Eddie told me a long time ago, if players kept their heads and didn't become afraid of their own shadows during a gin game, half of the blitzes that take place would never happen. In this chapter we will be talking about mistakes, fear and pressure.

There are people who regard the blitz as something relatively unimportant.

"Hell, why even think about it, it doesn't happen that often."

Well, I've got news for people who think that way. *Yes it does*, and because it does it's necessary for it to be looked upon as something very important. Even if the people in doubt were correct, if it really didn't happen very often, it would still have to be considered. It would still have to be placed in a very high position when playing one's hand. This is because of pressure, pressure that builds when hand after hand is lost without being on board.

Suppose you are playing in a six-man game, three players on each side. Two of the players on the other team have recently been blitzed, maybe in the last day or so. Not only have they been blitzed, but blitzed big time. Your team has just won six or seven hands in a row. The hands haven't been won big, but big enough to remind these two players of the fiasco two or three days ago.

"Goddammit, is this shit going to happen again? What the hell is going on? What did I get myself into for Pete's sake!" You hear it all the time.— Self doubt rears it's ugly head and mistakes begin to creep in, pressure builds. You and your team now have a mission, to keep the pressure on. Being blitzed hurts, we've already been into that, and the other team, especially the two players who have suffered recently, have to be kept thinking about it. A little chatter never hurts.

"Hey, you guys had better get on!" From one opponent.

"Didn't you just get blitzed recently?" From another. This is said with a soulful look.

"Doesn't your wife look at the checkbook in the morning?"

"C'mon, we don't want to blitz anybody."

You don't want to blitz anybody? Of course you do, but that's not the point. The point is you and your partners want to keep the words "Get on!" and "Blitz!" first and foremost in their minds. This is called keeping the pressure on and this is called using the blitz as a weapon.

While you are doing this, all efforts must be redoubled in preventing the other team from getting on board. Everything you can think of becomes fair. You are now; not playing for survival, as you were when you were trying to get on, this is no longer the case. You are "Going for the throat!" The jugular!" The kill!"

For this reason your style of play must change. There must be a change in attitude. You are no longer trying to win points for the advancement of the team. You are now trying to keep the other team from getting on board. In other words, you are trying to win enough points, as a team, to keep the enemy locked in their trenches, unable to mount a charge.

Example: your partner(s) have just called and gotten you somewhat of a cushion, but under twenty five points. Your thoughts should be "Have they won enough points for me to be thinking of calling, thus preserving their points, and the box, or should I be thinking of going for gin in defense of an undercut." Much depends on this type of thinking. Many players would get to the call and automatically call. The situation should carefully be thought out.

There are many times when this would be successful, however the action should not be considered automatic. Take a few seconds to review what the call card is and how deep into the deck the hand is. For instance, if there is a high value call card, say a nine or ten, and more than three quarter of the deck has been played, it may be wise to wait a bit before calling before calling with a high number. Who you are playing, at this time, should be considered

I've got an eight for a call, but I'm playing Charlie, and everyone knows what a sidewinder he is! He loves to hide in the weeds and undercut people. In most cases, the call would, and should be automatic, however, when a blitz is involved, the strategy may be different.

The reverse is also true. Your partner(s) have just lost an appreciable amount. Your move is to go for gin, even if all indications point in the other direction. You may be down forty points, and the thought "Winning back forty points is improbable, I'll just call and save something." Aggressive thinking has just been thrown right out the window.

Calling just to save something may be the way to go in ordinary circumstances, but right now you are trying to keep the other team off, and every attitude, every play should lead to that end. To do otherwise is to chance letting the other team on for nothing. That is, without a fight. There will be plenty of time later on in the game to "call and save something." Your mission right now is to preserve the blitz.

An example of negative thinking is Charlie and Don had just lost a total of forty points. The hand was reaching its later stages. Their partner, Joe, draws a card, making his hand low enough for him to call, to knock. "I'll just call and save a little, no sense letting them get a bigger hit." So he calls, and gets undercut. The opponent was doing a bit of tap dancing with a few high cards. When these cards played off, Joe was cut and the other team was on board, the blitz in the first street was gone.

Had Joe been thinking aggressively and was making every effort to preserve the blitz, he would have forgot about saving something and played for gin. Even if his attempt was unsuccessful at least he tried. His partners say *Ah shit* to no one in particular, and life goes on. If he does make gin and catches his man with a minimum of sixteen points the blitz is still intact, and the pressure continues to mount.

This, then, is the true psychology of using the blitz as a weapon. Pressure. Pressure is the key word. Keep it on and let it mount, especially if you know one or two players on the other team have been blitzed in the last few days. With the proper amount of pressure, you won't have to work too hard to beat them, they'll do it all by themselves.

Once again, don't win the battle and lose the war.

Chapter 43
THE WINNING ATTITUDE

"Winning isn't everything, it's the only thing." This is the world-famous quote from Vince Lombardi, when he was the coach of the Green Bay Packers.

"The thought of losing never entered my mind." Eddie Colquitt, gin rummy expert.

Vince Lombardi and Eddie Colquitt, two masters at their respective games using different words to say the same thing. Let's take it a bit further. Think of the word "Execution!" both men were true believers in that word. Let's take Vince Lombardi first.

If you've ever read a book about Vince Lombardi, and there are several, you would come away with the feeling; if you do everything correctly, you will be successful most of the time. Vince believed this. Doing everything correctly is called execution, and the thing that makes it work is dedication. Every player on that team was dedicated to one another. Thorndike-Barnhart puts it this way: "Execution: to carry out, to do, to perform, a way of carrying out or doing; skill."

"Dedication: A mark of respect."

The greatest example of execution that I can think of, is the now famous, "Packer Sweep."— This was a very simple, very basic play; it was a sweep of either end, an end run. If the play were going to the right, the front line of the Packer offense would be unbalanced to that side. This is to say; there would be more men on one side of the football than the other, the right side.

The play as it was called in the huddle was, simply "Sweep Right!" The quarter back, Bart Starr, in this case, would take the snap from center, and pitch it to the full back, Jimmy Taylor, who was moving to his right at the time. He would follow the entire right side of the Packer team, and some of the players from the left side, who would move right also, around the right end, and the necessary yardage was usually picked up.

This particular play was usually called in a third down situation, and every player on the other team knew it was coming; there was no deception at all. It was a straight power play, going around right end, and the Packers made no pretense about it.

The play was no different in design than the sweep used by every other team in the National Football League. What made it succeed for The Packers was execution. Every man knew exactly what he had to do. Each man knew who he was supposed to block, that man's strengths, and his weaknesses. It was almost as if every man on the defensive team had been "kibitzed." and he probably was. Vince was that kind of a coach.

The fact that every team the Packers faced, knew on third down this play was coming, and was powerless to stop it, is a tribute to Vince Lombardi's philosophy,

"If every man does his job the way he is supposed to, the play is unstoppable!" Once again, the word, and the attitude is "Execution."

Let's look at Eddie Colquitt, and his feelings about "winning attitudes."

Many years ago, Eddie was talking about execution, making the correct play. "If you are a player who truly loves card games, and the desire to be a winner is great, you will have to, like it or not, become a student of the game. You will want to know all there is to know about every facet of every game, honesty, strategy, kibitzing, advertising, bluffing and the like. You will need to and want to develop a sense of discipline. This discipline will force you, whether you realize it or not, to make the correct play, to execute."

Sometimes the correct play is not the winning play. This is God's truth. The reason is, nobody is perfect. Situations arise that the player involved has no control over." The words no control are very important.

In Vince Lombardi's case everything is done to perfection. The pulling guard, Jerry Kramer in this case, has knocked his man flat, the blocking back, Paul Horning has taken out his man. Every man on the team has done his job. But wait, someone's shoestring breaks, and he loses his balance, and he doesn't take out his man. Or, maybe someone slips on the soggy turf and partially misses his block, and the play is unsuccessful. This happens because nothing is one hundred per cent.

In gin rummy, the same thing is true. You can sit there sometimes and know every card in the other guy's hand and still get beat. Nothing is one hundred per cent. The best a player can do is making as many correct plays as he can. As I said, sometimes the correct play is not the winning play or the play that works; nonetheless, it must be made. This is execution.

It's there. Partnership gin rummy is a team game. Like him or not, you must be dedicated to your partner(s) for the brief time you are together, otherwise the advantage of teamwork is lost. No one man can do it all by himself.

One day Eddie happened to get into a game where one of his partners wanted to play only for the lowest stakes he could get.

The reason being "I don't want to win a lot of money from my friends." and "You can lose enough money playing for a penny a point."

Eddie's reply was, "First of all, if you don't want to win a lot of money, what the hell did you sit down for? And second, as far as me losing, the thought never enters my mind!"

In a later conversation, Eddie told me," A guy like that, you don't even want on your team, he'll be a millstone around your neck because he has a losing attitude. Any man who wants to play for bragging rights only, should go out and get a game with the ladies." Eddie's entire point can be summed up in one sentence. The thought of losing never does not enter Eddie's mind, nor should it enter yours.

Winning, whether it's serious, thrifty, casual or amusing is fun. Don't ever let anyone tell you different, not that you can't have a good time and go home with less money than you came with, you can, but I never met anyone who actually enjoyed it.

From the moment you sit down at that table, every move you make, every thought that comes to mind, every word you utter, be it serious or not should be geared to one thing, winning.

The only attitude to be considered is the winning attitude. Take steps to develop it. It can take on many forms, and every form it takes comes down to just one thing, an absolute refusal to lose. Eddie has said this many times.

He has also said, "Done correctly, your winning attitude can become contagious."

Let me share a story with you. I call it the story of the Owl's nest!

Joe, Ronnie and Bob were on in all three streets and needed only a few points to go out in all three. This is called "Being in the Owl's nest." Bill, Charlie and Lou were on in all three streets, but just barely. This is when Charlie began building the *Winning attitude*.

"I've seen it happen a thousand times!" he said, slyly nudging one of his partners with his elbow, and winking at the other, "The top of the mountain is so steep, it takes a superhuman effort to get there. The last few feet are killers."

Lou would hop in, "Yeah, in football, they call it 'the red zone. First and goal from the five, and you feel as if you're never going to get there." They would win a few more hands, and inject more seeds of doubt. This is fun to watch, if you know what's going on. You see three guys, who have been getting their butts whipped, and they decide enough is enough. They are going to do something about it. Do you remember what Eddie said about the winning attitude being contagious? Well, that's what's happening. Just by looking at the three of them, you'd think *they* were wining. They are laughing it up, joking and having a merry old time. The three guys who are winning look like death warmed over. Bill jumped in again.

"The sheriff didn't even know they were missing until he saw the buzzards circling!" and they would win a couple more hands.

This could possibly be called "Coffee Housing." Coffee Housing is meaningless chatter designed to upset, or break another player's concentration. In many areas it is more than frowned upon, it is regarded as gross, but, in this case, it is not. It is three guys pulling together toward a common goal. All three of them realize this, they realize they have a job to do, and they are doing everything in their power, mentally, physically and verbally to get it done. This is called dedication, and it's also called developing a winning attitude.

This goes on in all sports, or games.

Bill Charlie and Lou kept it up.

"Nothing worse than someone creeping up and breathing down your neck."

"Boy it's a shame to come so close and fall flat on your face!" and they would win a few more hands. I'll leave it to your imagination to see if Bill Charlie and Lou were successful in coming from behind to overtake the other guys and become winners, but I'll say this, I've seen stranger things happen in gin games.

Let's get back to the winning attitude. Every move, every thought, every word should be geared toward winning. This can all be summed up by saying; It's developing a philosophy that's predicated on a refusal to lose, and it's doing everything in your power to prevent it. It's saying the right thing, and making the correct play. This is called execution. It's pulling together with your partners toward a common goal. This is called dedication. Put all three of them together, refusal to lose, execution and dedication and you have *the winning attitude.*

And, believe me, there's nothing like it!

Chapter 44
THE GIN RUMMY COACH

Eddie and me were talking about some of the more entertaining aspects of card games, Gin in particular. Sometimes, we decided, the game does get a bit serious. After a few drinks I left the club, went home, and before dinner I sat in my office and thought about the not so serious things about card games in general.

In my lifetime I have taken any number of golf lessons. If I had to innumerate them, I'm afraid I couldn't. If I were to keep track of all the lessons I have taken from actual teaching professionals, the number would go into the hundreds. If I were to go a bit further and include the many tips I have received from playing partners, friends, or relatives (my son, handicap eight), at dinner parties or cook outs, the number would reach into the thousands.

Do, or possibly I should say did, any of these lessons or tips do any good? Well, maybe. When I was in my forties I had an eleven handicap, which I couldn't play to.

I am now seventy and I have a twenty-three handicap, which I can't play to. Draw your own conclusions. During this span of time, I have discovered one inescapable fact. One fact that is wrapped with incontrovertible proof: No low handicapper can ever help a high handicapper in trouble. This can only be done by another high handicapper, one who has read all the golf magazines, or instruction books written by Arnold Palmer et al. Where else could you learn how many knuckles to expose while activating the strong grip? How about the position of the hands at the top of the back swing? The hips? What role do the hips play?

No, my friends, you will never learn this from your average low handicapper, or teaching professional. "*The hips?*" they say, "*The hands?* Forget all that crap! The shoulders are the key. *The wrists?* Shit, turn the goddamn shoulders!"

One sleepless night after suffering a horrendous loss on the golf course, followed by an equally devastating defeat at the gin table, I lie awake asking myself this question; Who does a golf professional visit when he is in trouble?

Would this be similar to asking whom the doctor sees when he isn't felling well? ——Or, whom does the priest seek out for confession?

In the olden days, prior to instruction books, or videotapes, touring professionals sought help from their cohorts. After all they were all professionals. They would not, in any way shape or form seek help from the teacher at the local driving range (handicap ten), than they would take up in rummy for a living. No, if Arnold Palmer were having trouble with his putting, he'd get next to Gary Player on the putting green.

"Hey Gary" he would say. " I know this knock kneed stance I use is unique, I mean no one else in his right mind would use it. I think, maybe, if I kept my stance the same and pointed my big toe of the left foot more toward the hole, maybe, just maybe, more putts would probably go in!"

Gary would probably look at Arnold and tell him; "No my man, no way at all. It's the shoulders! Turn the god-dam shoulders."

In this day and age, asking for help from a fellow competitor is not done. Most successful tour players employ a golf coach. There are several kinds. One is a man who has been a successful instructor of long standing, who knows everything there is to know about the golf swing. He is a virtuoso. Men such as he are few and far between. Another form of golf coach is a former tour player no longer playing the tour for one reason or another, back problems, shoulder problems, loss of hand to eye coordination, etc. He has long since discovered it is far easier to charge a leading money winner a thousand dollars or so, for an hour, than it is to submit his own body to the physical rigors of the golf swing. This would be your most of your golf coaches. Make no mistake about it, while appearing to be the easiest thing in the world, the golf swing can, and will cause pain if done improperly for any length of time. I am living proof.

Golf, however, does teach you something vitally needed in gin rummy. Besides teaching you a lot of words you wouldn't know had you never set foot on a golf course, it teaches you patience. There is no better lesson in patience than the one learned by waiting for a half hour to hit up to a green occupied by four other players pursuing their own worthless putting.

While confident sleep would come (it didn't), I wondered if there was anything as a gin rummy coach? Really, think about it, suppose you were a stellar player down on your luck, out of touch with *Old Man Kards*, and getting your brains beat out day in and day out, you could go into coaching.

Actually the closest thing I've ever heard of as far as someone being a gin rummy coach was Eddie Colquitt.

As the story goes, he was in the process of building an addition on his house and needed a land survey. This is one of the requirements for any type of construction. There was a member at Itasca Country Club who was a land surveyor; we'll call him Charlie. Eddie looked him up and asked how much surveys cost. Charlie inquired as to what it was for. Eddie told him and Charlie said "About two hundred fifty dollars ($250.00.)

"That sounds like an awful lot of money for a piece of paper." Eddie said.

"Well," said Charlie, we have to make a trip to your house, measure up a few things, go over to the Village Hall, look up the existing survey, it all takes time, and time is money. "I'll tell you what," Charlie went on, "You're one of the best gin rummy players around. If your can take me on as a pupil, teach me a lot about the game, really make me a winner, I'll do the survey for free." Eddie agreed, and they made arrangements for Eddie to watch Charlie play. About a week later Eddie stood in back of Charlie and watched for a while. After about a half hour Charlie turned around and asked, "Well, what do you think?" Eddie looked at him, smiled, and said

"I'd rather pay the two fifty!"

In gin rummy, there would be coaching in the more physical aspects of the game just as there are on a football team. I envision coaches in shuffling, cutting, and dealing. Where else could you go to find out how many knuckles to expose on your left hand while dealing the cards? There would be a specialty coach giving instruction on how to hold the cards in your left hand while drawing from the pile with your right. This is, of course if your right-handed, although I have seen lefthanders do it this way if the popcorn bowl is on the left side.

I lay awake at night and envision other types of specialty coaches, coaches in kibitzing, fishing, technique or coffee housing. These would, of course, be true specialists, vastly knowledgeable in all aspects of their particular fields, and masters of all they survey.

I close my eyes struggling for sleep. No such luck. I begin to fantasize. I see a huge man. He is wearing a green uniform with black stripes, a red armband, and a black swastika. He is tall with blonde hair and blue eyes. A perfect blonde mustache accentuates his suntan. He has broad shoulders and a wisplike waist. He is the epitome of what Adolph Hitler envisioned when he dreamed up the master race. I'm sure you've seen him in the television commercials. He is standing on a pedestal, looking down at a strikingly beautiful blond lady, also complete with blue eyes and suntan. She was the other half of the "Master Race." No doubt.

"Helmut!" she says in a sexy voice, "*I luff* you!"

Helmut looks down his nose at her and says, "Of *course* you do *fraulien*, and you couldn't help yourself!"

I am seated at a card table in the card room at his club. (You don't think for a moment *he* was going to come to *my* club)? It has taken me an hour and a half, driving through a snowstorm, to get there.

"*Achtung!*" *says Helmut.* "*You vill pick up ze cards und you vill practice ze shuffle*"
I wanted sleep. I got Helmut.

I have seen many commercials on television, usually at four o'clock in the morning, when any sane person would be asleep. These would be commercials professing to cure anything and everything wrong with your, in this case, golf game.

"Friends, for six small payments of $29.99 we'll send you Doctor Divot's video tape guaranteed to get rid of each and every flaw in your golf swing, you now, or ever will have. We will put you right back on track to playing winning and enjoyable golf, or, double your money back. *Plus!* And I did say *Plus?* If you phone 1-800 -7448, in the next five seconds, we'll throw in, free of charge, at no cost to you, a genuine golf umbrella, autographed by Doctor Divot himself." (It's amazing how much the announcer resembled Leon Sitkowitz).

I get out of bed. Sleep is impossible. I go into the family room, sit down and click on the TV. I turn the volume down and begin channel surfing. I start at one hundred and work backwards for fear I might miss something. I run the entire gamut all the way down to channel two *Why isn't there a channel one?* to see, if, by some miracle there is a video tape offered about gin rummy.

"Friends, has it been *too* long since you've won at gin rummy? Has it been an eternity? Do your friends laugh at you behind your back? Does the back of your checkbook, you know, the checkbook your wife doesn't know about, look like the government's estimate of the national debt? Are your friends telling you their threesome is full? Are you sick of being kicked around the gin rummy table by Mister Meany?"

Mister Meany is depicted as a man wearing a black suit, white shirt, black string tie, and has Ten-dollar bills sticking out of his pockets. He is semi bald, wears black horn rimmed glasses, and has a pointy nose and perpetual frown. (He is probably an attorney).

"Well friends, your problems are *over,* yes I did say *over!* No more will you have to worry about Mister Meany. No more will you have to worry about your buddies sneaking out of the club to avoid playing cards with you. You will be able to laugh at people who are avoiding you. You can become the *darling* of the gin table again, you can become Mister Meany yourself, and *last,* but not *least,* your wife need *never* discover the truth about your mystery vault, the secret check book. Get smart! Get some peace of mind, and a good night's sleep!" (Hah!)

"Friends, for ten measly payments of fifty dollars each, or *six* hundred dollars cash or credit card, plus twenty two fifty for shipping and handling, we'll send you Doctor Stephen Schneider's video tape *Win at gin rummy, or die trying.* Place your fifty dollar deposit in a plain brown eight by ten, self addressed, stamped envelope and mail it to Post office box 28557448, New York, New York, or phone us at 1-800-7448 in the next five seconds and give us your credit card number and social security number. Confidentiality is guaranteed by Doctor Schneider.

"You will learn to shuffle properly, deal properly, get no-brainers properly, even eat popcorn properly, or we will cheerfully, gladly, willingly, even eagerly refund triple your money back beginning in the year 2099."

This is the type of commercial I was looking for, but try as I might, I managed to come up empty. I would sit in front of that accursed television set and see countless commercials about *"Get rid of arthritis forever."* or *"The only mattress guaranteed to let you wake up refreshed".* Thirty small payments of $339.95 —— double your money back— Not sold in stores.

There were commercials going on into the night, into the wee small hours of the morning about weight reduction, or exercise equipment. "Doctor, my husband thinks my ass is too

Big!" —$39.95—not sold in stores— double your— But no gin rummy commercials.

The next night I managed to fall asleep. I was dreaming, dreaming of all things, how to shuffle cards. All of a sudden a little round man who was green in color visited me. He had one eye way up on his forehead, three arms, all in front, and six legs, five on the bottom of his body, and one on top of his head, *don't ask!* He claimed to have recently escaped from a lunatic asylum on Mars, making his way through the galaxy by stowing away on space stations, landing in Arizona and hitch hiking to Chicago. *Don't Ask!* He looked at me sitting in front of the television set, idly moving cards around in my hands. He questioned what I was doing. "I'm practicing shuffling the cards."

"Shuffling?"

"Yeah, shuffling, I'm using both hands to mix the cards up, this is called shuffling."

"What an odd name, why do you call it that?"

"Well, I never really thought about it, it's just what they call it."

"Who?"

"They! —— Well it doesn't really matter, it's just what they call it." He gave me a rather odd look, which, I guess was difficult, when you consider he only had one eye. He went on with his questioning.

"Why are you shuffling the cards, or, mixing them up? I like that better."

I explained I was going to mix them thoroughly, then proffer the deck to my opponent, who would then cut the cards.

"Cut the cards?" I explained that my opponent was going to place the top half portion of the deck to the right, then take the bottom half and place it on top of the first.

"Whatever for?"

"Well," I explained, "All this shuffling is to ensure the cards are thoroughly mixed. Cutting is supposed to guarantee this, so no one feels cheated after the cards are dealt." He looked a bit unconvinced, and then asked the inevitable question.

"Dealt?"

I went through the entire procedure with him, explaining how the cards are shuffled, and cut prior to dealing them. I then explained dealing. "I give my opponent ten cards, and I give myself ten cards."

"All at once?"

"No-no-no-no, I give him one, then I give myself one, then I give him another, then me another, until each of us ten cards, we then pick up these cards, ten cards each, and hold them in one hand, and play begins."

"Play begins?"

"Yeah, my opponent picks a card from the top of the deck and places it in his hand. Then he takes another card from the ones he is holding and places it next to the pile of cards on the table."

"Uh-huh, what happens next?

Well, then it's my turn, and I do the same thing, I pick up a card, put it with the cards I am holding, and put another card on top of the card he just laid down."

"How long does this go on?"

"It goes on," I replied. "Until we get to the end of the pile, or one of us ends the game." I could see my explanation was coming off as quite feeble, but I'd never looked at the game that way. I could see how he was about to ask how one of us would end the game, but I think he changed his mind. I was happy, because I had no desire to get into ginning, calling or undercutting, at the time.

"Let me get this straight," said, the Martian, "First you mix the cards, no, you *shuffle* them."— I nodded.— "Then, you give him some, no, excuse me, I forgot, he has to separate them, no, *cut them*!" I nodded again. "Then you give him some, and you give yourself some" Another nod. "Then you sit there for hours picking up cards and replacing them with other cards?'

"That's about it!" I said.

"He gave me that rather odd look again. "You know," he said, "I'm gonna catch the next space shuttle leaving out of Cape Canaveral. You're nuttier than I am!"

Chapter 45
THE STING!

"How many drinks is your local tavern supposed to get from a quart of hooch?" Leon asked Anton. They were playing in a golf outing. The course was crowded and there was a wait on every hole.

"Well," said Anton, "There's thirty-two shots in that bottle."

"True," said Leon. " But if it's a decent place they over pour a little to make a better drink. The customer appreciates it and he will keep patronizing the bar."

"They don't measure the shots anymore?"

"No, because the drinks are not as good!"

"It doesn't sound like good business to me," Anton replied

"It's very good business. Look at it this way. If the place decides to over-pour a bit they get maybe twenty drinks out of that bottle. The bottle of whiskey, say Canadian Club, wholesale's out at about ten bucks a bottle. The better places charge about five bucks a drink no matter what you cut the whiskey with, ginger ale, seven up, vermouth, water or just plain on the rocks. That's twenty drinks out of a bottle that costs ten bucks. Twenty drinks ads up to a hundred dollars. That's one hell of a mark up. I'd say it was damn good business."

"Aren't the drinks overly strong?" asked Anton.

"No," said Leon. "Not at all; it's an honest drink. When you serve a man an honest drink it tastes good and he appreciates it. Now there are places where the owner will tell the bartender to use more ice and less liquor, but that's cheating and this type of place doesn't last long. Word spreads."

It was time to play. Leon walked to the tee, addressed the ball, swung the club and hit he usual fade into the middle of the fairway. He looked at Anton, smiled and said" Not far but straight!" Anton also hit his tee shots from left to right but there was a difference. Anton did not hit a fade; he hit an out and out slice. The ball flew off the club head and headed due left. About a hundred yards out it changed direction and started back toward the fairway finishing some ten yards in front of Leon's ball. Smiling he said to Leon,

"They don't ask you how, my man, they ask you how many!" They put their drivers back into their bags, got into the cart and went down the fairway.

Leon was driving, Anton riding shotgun. He looked at Leon. " Hey Bro"' he said, "All this talk about liquor, What's that all about?" He knew there had to be a great reason for Leon to spend the amount of time he did with the subject. Leon never did anything profound without great forethought and a justifying motive.

"It's like this!" Leon told him. "I made arrangements with Eddie Colquitt, when I bought this car from him, for the two of us to play gin with him and Kenny Allen, I told you this didn't I?"

"Yeah!"

"Well, it's very important where this gin game takes place. It has to be at a place where they have a good bar and this bar has to serve honest drinks."

Anton looked over at Leon and he could almost hear the gears turning inside of Leon's head. "Why's that?" he asked. Leon smiled."

"Anton," he said, " One of the smartest human beings in this world. One of the cleverest people God ever created is Kenny Allen with two honest drinks in him. Believe me he becomes sharp as a tack. The man moves up to a higher plane and does and says things he could in no way shape or form do without those two CC Manhattans or Skyy vodkas in him. He becomes unbelievable.

Now, take that same Kenny Allen and add one more cocktail and he's back to square one. That's why he can go into a place, have three drinks and walk out without any apparent ill effects. But watch out for the next one. Add one more cocktail and he's a different person entirely. After four drinks he doesn't look any different, or act different, but the entire thinking process is altered. Mentally he becomes someone else, and that someone else is a very sloppy gin rummy player.

This is something we have to exploit. About the only place that serves a super honest drink and also has a card room is Itasca Country Club. There are other places, of course, but Itasca is so convenient to the four of us. I say, all we should have to do is find a way to play this game at Itasca, get four CC's into Kenny and the two of us can go back home *with a pocket full of dough!*"

"Leon, my brother, you've always got an angle!" Leon smiled.

The years had passed, I became a bricklayer, then a contractor, then and a homebuilder. I had my own construction company. I was making money, and I was married now. I took up golf and joined a country club. It seems at country clubs, golf and gin rummy go hand in hand. Most of the guys, when finished with their round of golf, would break out a couple decks of cards and start a gin rummy game.

The games would be played for various amounts of money ranging from a penny a point sometimes a quarter a point. Winning or losing ten bucks in the course of a day was commonplace. Also was winning or losing several thousand dollars. The games were quite cliquish. The high rollers more or less kept to themselves, as did the penny ante players. I would bounce around from nickel games to ten cents a point.

I considered myself a top-notch player. Eddie had taught me well. I did enjoy playing for a lot of money. I had a lot of time invested in learning all facets of the game and I wanted to, in no uncertain terms get paid for it. At first I had a little trouble finding the more expensive games, but word gets around and soon I had my hands full with players who wanted to see if they could trim the 'old master.'

I would still see Eddie from time to time. He not only belonged to our club, but to two others in the area. With his talent at golf he played in a lot of good sized money games, and played a lot of business golf, plus, with his flair for gin rummy he had to make himself available as much as possible. One must make a living, mustn't one?

Eddie's sons were in the used car business with him. They were his partners, and they were responsible for running the business. Eddie would bounce around from one country club to another picking up a *few pennies here* at golf, and a *few pennies there* at gin. "Just keeping the wolf from the door." he would say.

One evening, when the two of us were having dinner with our wives, Eddie gave me a peculiar look. I recognized it; it was the same look he wore when he was trying to sell something.

"Leon and Anton Sitkowitz" He said.

"Yeah, what about them?"

"Well just after we saw them in Vegas, I ran into them at a golf outing"

"What are they up to now, outside of trying to scam everybody in the country?"

"Well. I guess they're doing pretty good," he said, "They're both in the construction business with their father. Being in the business yourself, I'm surprised you haven't run into them yourself. I nodded. They did ask about you."

"It was nice of them," I said.

Eddie went on, "I took the liberty of setting up a gin game with me, you, and the two of them for next Saturday if you're available."

"They play gin rummy now?" I asked.

"Yeah!" replied Eddie, " and pretty well from what I hear. As I told you, I set up a little game for Saturday."

"How little of a game?" I asked.

"You mean how much?" he said laughing.

I looked at him. "Yeah, that's the general idea."

"Well," he began, "We were talking in the neighborhood of ten cents a point, nothing exciting."

"That's some neighborhood," I replied, "Who the hell lives there, Bill Gates?"

"Hey, for Pete's sake, a dime a point won't kill you. It's not the end of the world!"

Fifteen cents a point! I told myself, a man could easily lose a grand or two if he were unlucky and didn't keep his wits about him. Ten cents a point, the *bastard!* Not the end of the world! He says, *that son of a bitch!*

"Hell," said Eddie, ordering another round of drinks for the four of us. " They're just a couple of dumb bricklayers, what the hell are you so worried about? This is September. You're up what? Maybe Fifty grand for the year. You've been beating the crap out of everybody, including me. Let's have a little fun!"

Yeah, let's have a little fun, I thought.

Looking back, I remembered one day Leon, Anton and a few of us other guys went fishing at the Horseshoe. The "Horseshoe" was a horseshoe shaped pier that extended out into Lake Michigan about six or seven hundred feet. The pier was lined with fishermen of all shapes and sizes. There were many of them, some sport fishermen, some who were fishing for their supper, some unemployed and some derelicts. They would make their way to the pier in the nice weather months. They would sit down, and cast their lines into the water and dream of the salmon, bullheads, or mostly lake perch they would catch.

Most of these nomads would buy their bait from the bait concession and coffee stand located at the beginning of the pier. This stand was really a series of card tables put together, and manned by two Greeks, who later on in life, would probably own fancy restaurants on State Street. Most of the fishermen would buy their bait from these two gentlemen, although some of them would use earthworms dug up from backyards, or parks along the way to the pier. Most of the bait sold at the concession stand was minnows (shiners), seined out of the lake by the two concession stand owners.

Fishing on the whole was terrible that particular morning. No action at all. One, two, three hours went by, nothing, not even a bite. An atmosphere of gloom was settling in.

Suddenly Leon's pole bent a little. He had a nibble. Watching the bobber floating in the water, he saw it flutter, then disappear. Leon set the hook and began reeling in the fish. From the action the pole was getting and the fight the fish was putting up, it had to be a fish of some size. Leon was about to cry out "Jumbo!" the yell fishermen use at The Horseshoe, to announce they have a *lunker* on the line. Crying "Jumbo!" would certainly seem to be the thing to do.

Something made Leon hesitate. Leon had an idea, he didn't yell, instead he coaxed the fish in close where Anton was waiting with the net. Anton lifted the fish slightly out of the water. Leon had been right. It was a lake perch about twenty inches long. It would weigh in at about two pounds.

"Keep him in the net, and hold him here," he told Anton. Leon looked around. No one had noticed his catch. Getting to his feet, he looked at Anton "I'll be right back," he called as he made his way back to the coffee and bait stand.

"How's business?" he asked one of the Greeks.

"Lousy!"

"What are you stuck with?" Leon asked.

"Twenty dozen big shiners."

Leon asked the man if he would like to *sell out* on the bait. Of course he would!

"Give me and my brother free coffee and free bait for the rest of the week," Leon told the man, "and I'll see if I can help you out!"

The deal was made. Leon, upon arriving back to his spot on the pier, sat down and took the pole from Anton. He played the fish out of the net and let it swim around a bit.

"*JUMBO!*" he yelled, and let the pole bend a bit. "*JUMBO!*" he yelled again and began reeling in the fish.

A small group gathered around and watched Leon pull the fish in, It was a beauty, all brown and gold and shimmering in the water

"What are you using for bait?' Leon was asked.

"Big shiners!" he replied.

The group disappeared and headed for the bait stand.

Lowering the fish back into the water, Leon allowed him to swim a bit.

"*JUMBO!*"

"What are you using for bait?"

"Big shiners!"

Another group headed for the bait stand.

Leon caught that same fish ten times. The bait man sold out his stock of big shiners. Leon and Anton got free bait and coffee for the week, and they all lived happily ever after.

And I'm supposed to play gin rummy for fifteen a point against minds like these? I've got to have rocks in my head.

"Why fifteen cents?" I asked after thinking it over.

"Well," said Eddie, "I just thought we'd keep it interesting, of course, if you're worried about anything, short on guts, we could always make it two cents, or a penny even.

Worried about anything? I told myself, *"Me?* Short on guts? *Me?* Who the hell did he think he was talking to? After all, am I not the guy he taught to be proficient at the game? Am I not the big money winner around this club?"

Years ago, a friend of mine was in the process of buying a new sport coat. An hour went by as the salesman put garment after garment on my friend's shoulders. Nothing! After my friend had rejected ten or fifteen items, the salesman went into the back room. He came out with a rather gaudy, loud piece of apparel and put it on my friend. He ran his hand across the shoulders as if to smooth the material out.

"Of course," the sales man said, "A man would need the shoulders necessary to wear a coat such as this!" (The bait had been cast.) *"I'll take it"* was my friend's reply. (The hook had been set).

I continued talking to myself. *Am I not the big money winner this year? Am I not the man who every one desires to have as a partner?* An end to this petty gouging, it will give me a bad reputation. One does not trifle with a determined man!"

"Knock your socks off guys, ten cents a point is will be!"

Needless to say, I got my ears pinned back. I threw the party.

Chapter 46
THE CRITIQUE

Jack a diamonds
Jack a diamonds
You're a villain of old.
You rob my coat pocket,
Of the silver and gold!

It's whiskey, you villain,
You've been my downfall.
You rob my coat pocket,
But I love you for all!

It was later on that afternoon. I was with Eddie at the bar having a drink. Leon and Anton had long since departed counting their money. To the victors go the spoils, and clearly they were the victors.

Eddie had won a little, but I was the big loser. Hell I was the only loser. We had played a series of round robins, where everyone gets to be each other's partner once. This went on all afternoon, and well into the evening. I had just finished losing every game with every partner. And yes, there were blitzes involved. I had just thrown a twelve thousand dollar party. I kind of felt sorry for Eddie. Every time he would get a little ahead he would wind up with me as his partner, and lose it all back, plus.

I looked at my drink. "It's too late to throw a drunk," I said, "I've already had enough hooch with the gin game and all that.

"Hell yes," Eddie told me, "You had enough to float a battleship, and I want to talk about it. I thought you had more sense."

"What are you talking about?"

"Well, picture this, Leon calls the waitress over and offers to buy drinks for the table. Five minutes later she comes back with three iced teas and one vodka on the rocks, guess who the vodka was for?"

"Well, sometimes it loosens me up!" Eddie looked at me, there was a short silence, and he went on,

"Yeah sometimes, but not today. Didn't you notice what happened when you took that first sip of vodka? *Old Man Kards* began to frown. Then Leon bought another, and then Anton bought one. Hell, it's the oldest trick in the book, buy a man three stiff ones in the course of an hour, and you'll probably own him."

"That wasn't the case!" I ventured.

"Maybe yes, and maybe no," he said, "But how do you account for all those bait cards they threw that you went after like a lake perch after a big shiner. Hell you did things I never ever saw you do. You were so out of it you even passed up quick calls when you had them!"

"Well I was desperate." Eddie looked at me and ran his fingers through his hair.

"Yeah," he said," And the more of that yocky-dock Leon was feeding you, the more desperate you became."

"Hey, I can handle it."

"Not when you're playing for high stakes against qualified opponents. No man can. The concentration just gets up and walks away."

I thought back and started to re-hash some of the things that had happened that afternoon. It was like putting pieces of a puzzle back together. I remembered all the tricks they had played on me, and all the bait cards they threw that I was a sucker for.

"Yeah, I guess they baited me pretty good."

Eddie nodded, "Sure they did, then when they figured they could get away with it, they started to reverse bait you."

"How so?"

"Look at all the times Leon undercut you." Eddie said with a frown. I was beginning to feel like a grammar school kid getting reprimanded by the principal.

"Take a good look." he went on, "Both of them pulled stuff where, if you had not had a drink, you never would have allowed it."

"What do you mean?" I asked.

"Leon would get down to two, or three. He'd break his rhythm intentionally. He'd act like he was in trouble. He would hesitate, scratch his head or even pull his ear lobe. You would fall for this, and when you got down to seven or eight, you would call, and *bingo*! Undercut city. Then he would celebrate by ordering another round of drinks. Good old Leon, He didn't miss a trick. He didn't have to out think you, he just out drank you."

"Maybe *Old man cards* had something to do with it!" I said a little loudly. I was starting to get pissed off, getting chewed out is not my idea of fun. "Maybe they were just lucky, I'm not that bad of a player."

"Sure they were lucky," Eddie replied, ignoring my dirty look. "And you're right, you are not that bad of a player, but remember the old story about *Old Man Kards*. You never want to give him a chance to get his dander up. Doing stupid things like drinking while you are in a big game, will do it every time.

"The thing to do, if you are ever in that situation again, is to stop at one, or not even have the first one. Have something soft, do your real drinking later. This is the way it's done. Hell, you should know that. I taught you, I brought you along. You're about as good as the cards are, and it doesn't get much better than that."

"I know," I told him, "Maybe it was the hooch. The situation was kind of unique, I think under different circumstances I could have handled them a little better."

" Sure you could." Eddie called the waitress over and ordered a Heinekens for himself, he told me I could have an Iced Tea; it would be good for my character. I smiled and let Eddie go on. He was just getting warmed up, and perhaps, maybe after an Iced tea or two I might be ready again for a real drink

Eddie went on. " The thing to do is keep your cool. Figure out his style and then go after him. Make it work against him. Anticipate his moves and act accordingly. You didn't do that today you let him play you. You've been on kind of a hot streak lately, and maybe you thought it would continue. Maybe you got the idea you were invincible. But remember, all good things have to end sometime.'

The waitress arrived with our drinks; she popped the cap on the beer and set it down in front of Eddie.

Eddie smiled. This was his way of thanking her for not pouring it. A true beer drinker likes to do this for himself.

I looked longingly at the Heinekens, then at my iced tea. The Latin words *Remissionem Pecatorem*, (Latin: In forgiveness for your sins), came to mind.

"Look at the way you played." Eddie said. He seemed to be enjoying this. Sometimes I picture him lecturing students in a college class.

"You began by setting up triangles, high ones at that, even speculating to get them. I can't remember the last time I saw you pick up the first card off the deal. Then he bought you a drink, and you still wouldn't change your pattern. Hell, he saw right through you. Every time he played you he knew exactly where you were going. He spun you like a top."

I usually tend to drift when people are criticizing me. I mean I really let my mind wander.

I mumbled something about the game not being my idea. This really seemed to set him off. He then went on for about a half hour non-stop, touching on different approaches to the game, and how not to get trapped into situations where you could get hurt. He finished by giving me a sorry look; one like a parent would give a child when the child had been caught with his hand in the cookie jar. He called the waitress over and asked her to bring me a Heinekens. I guess he felt sorry for me.

"Take that Iced tea away, he's had enough penance." When she brought the beer over he said, "Go ahead, the battle's over, you can soothe a few wounds if you like."

"What the hell," I said, "I guess now is the time for it."

"Damn right!" replied Eddie. "During the game is definitely not the time. Look at it this way," he pointed his finger at me. "When I was bringing you along I never mentioned the alcohol aspects of the game. That's why it was so easy for you to fall into Leon's trap."

I looked at him; I was getting the critique of my life, also the most costly and most embarrassing.

"Now before we speak of the techniques and styles of Leon and Anton," He said, "let me touch briefly on drinking and playing cards.— Alcohol, booze, a touch, whatever you wish to call it, can seriously impair your thinking when playing in a serious game. You don't have to be drunk for this to happen, just like you weren't drunk this afternoon. Far from it. But, you can put yourself into a mental block by just having one or two. And yeah, it does loosen you up. It can make you feel happy, giddy and yes loose. But the brain cannot begin to make the adjustments it has to make when you are involved in a competitive situation . Remember this trilogy. You have to out think them, out drink them, and then maybe you will be able to out play them.

"Let's dwell on the drinking a bit. When the other guy offers to buy a drink, it's all right to accept. You don't want to be considered anti social, or any thing like that, but, watch what he orders. If he orders something soft, you do the same. If he orders a real drink you can do the same, but hold it at one. Even that first one should be allowed to sit for a while until some of the ice melts. Take a sip, and let is sit. Most bars use what is called 'cocktail ice.' The cubes are smaller and they melt quickly. They do this because you can handle more drinks. Therefore you will buy more.

"Later on in the game, if you have a commanding lead, you can even offer to buy a round of drinks, just so you can *loosen the other guy up.* If you do this, remember the cocktail ice principal. Play your hand and ignore the drink. After several minutes some of the ice will have melted, and the drink will be somewhat watered down.

"Another tip. Between hands, go to the men's room a lot. Splash cold water on your face. Do this often it will keep you fresh. Do you see where I'm going with all this? Keep yourself fresh and you will have given yourself the edge."

Eddie stood up and stretched.

"Gee, I didn't mean to go on like this," he said. "But, what the hell, I didn't do all that well myself today. I didn't lose, thanks to you, but most of what I took off them, I gave right back when it was my turn to be your partner, so allow me to continue with three cardinal rules, then we'll get some cheeseburgers."

"I suppose I'm buying?" I said.

He babbled something about his fee and signaled for the waitress.

"First of all," Eddie began, "There are people who will refuse to play for anything of consequence. Bragging right are all they are interested in. At three cents a point you'd own most of them, they become that predictable, but, for pennies, they speculate a lot, and do crazy things and *Old Man Kards* kind of watches over them. Why bother with the likes of them? You've got better things to do.

"There are also a lot of good players, genuine good players who normally don't play for anything of consequence, who you will see in a three cents game once and awhile. They kind of sneak in there when they're feeling hot. They're like people in Las Vegas who stand near the blackjack tables and watch the cards that have been turned up. If they notice a lot of small cards have been played they figure a lot of ten value cards are coming up. Then they hop right in. These are the kind of people I am talking about. They refuse to keep score, but they watch the score sheet like a hawk, and they treat every penny like it's the last one that's ever going to be minted.

"You want to avoid people like this because it's a matter of economics. If you beat them in a small game you are not winning anything. And the few times you see them in a money game they can hurt you if they're getting cards. Most of these people are super cautious and super slow. You don't have time for all of that! There are better games to be found. Look for opponents who are courageous and knowledgeable. You'll have more success."

Eddie picked up his glass and looked at me. I guess he was waiting for a response. I gave him one.

"Yeah," I told him, "I know all that, but I did have a tough time figuring out the Sitkowitz brothers."

Eddie smiled. "That's because you had a few drinks and lost your patience. A lot of people think temperance is a virtue, believe me, patience has it beat eight ways to breakfast."

We finished our drinks and headed into the restaurant section of the club. A waitress came to take our orders. She asked if we'd like something from the bar.

"Hell yes!" Eddie said to her, then to me; "Hey my man, buy me a drink, I have to charge you something for the lessons I just gave you."

I laughed and said to Eddie, "Have a ball, sport," then to the waitress, "Give Mr. Colquitt two, make it three of anything he wants." Eddie gave the waitress that sly grin he had and turned his attention back to me.

"Look at gin rummy this way. There are three basic types of successful players.

There are a lot more types of styles, but the successful players fall into three main

categories. There are players who play for the call. They very seldom go for gin. Then there

are players who are going for gin every hand, and seldom call, and there is the player

who is a combination of the first two. He would be the most dangerous.

"Then there are the speculators. A little speculation is a good thing. Nothing ventured, nothing gained! But the player who makes a habit of *devil may care* speculating is flirting with disaster. Not that there aren't successful speculators, there are!

"Another type of speculator is the player who tries to intimidate his opponent. They like to sit back with a four card spread, a three card spread, two queens and a piece of deadwood well into the game looking for you to throw them a queen, or snatch it from the pile. These are players who will win sometimes, lose sometimes, types of players. But they lose more than they win. They will play you for anything up to ten cents a point because they can afford it. They figure the high stakes will intimidate most people.

They win big sometimes, but in the long run, the ax will fall, it has to, the laws of probability work that way. In the end they lose much more than they win. Now, let's talk about Leon and Anton."

Chapter 47
THE BROTHERS "SITKOWITZ"

A man walked into a bar and sat down. He ordered three beers. "One right next to the other!" he said to the bartender.

He then sat there and drank one, then started on the second, finished that, and began drinking the third. The bartender looked at all this and asked the man why he didn't just order one beer, drink it, then the second and finally the third. In this way each beer would be cold and fresh when the man was ready to drink them.

"Well, it's like this," the man began. "It's sort of a ritual my two brothers and me have. Every afternoon at Three o'clock, where ever we are, we stop whatever we are doing, go to the nearest tavern, order three beers just the way I just did, then we toast each other with the first beer, then the other two and we Thank the Good Lord for all he has given us." The bartender smiled knowingly and walked away.

One afternoon about three weeks later the same man walked into the bar and ordered two beers and an empty glass. The bartender suspecting a death in the family offered some sympathy.

"I'm truly sorry for your loss, he began—"

"No, it's nothing like that!" said the beer drinker, lifting up one of the full glasses and taking a sip. "You see last week my wife changed our religion, and we became Quakers and if you know anything about that religion you know they allow absolutely no drinking in the family. I am allowed no alcohol, which explains the empty glass."

"What about the other two full glasses?" asked the bartender?

"Well, my two brothers didn't become Quakers," was the reply.

Eddie was on a roll. When this happens he becomes much like a snow ball rolling down a steep hill.

"Let's look at the Sitlowitz brothers and take them part piece by piece. Listen carefully and you'll learn something.

"Leon is a breakdown type of player. He is always reducing his hand. He gets rid of high cards quickly, sometimes recklessly. He's not hard to figure, just hard to beat."

"Hard to beat?" asked.

"Yes, hard to beat!

" Do you remember when we were kids?— The Cubs had a second baseman named Eddie Stanky." I nodded. "Stanky couldn't run," said Eddie. "He couldn't throw. He couldn't hit. All he could do was beat you and he always found a way!

"He would bunt and drop his bat on the catcher's ankles. This caused the catcher to trip over the bat while he was trying to field the ball.

"Another thing he was famous for, and he did invent this trick. If there was a runner on first base and a ground ball was hit to the shortstop, Eddie who was a second baseman would take the relay throw, step on second, and while throwing the ball to first to complete the double play, he would aim the ball right between the runners eyes. This would sometimes cause the runner to slide prematurely. Stuff like that! He was a team player with an intense desire to win. Leon is a lot like him. He's not hard to figure, just hard to beat.

"The most important thing Leon does is to decide where his hand is, and where he wants to take it. And he's smart, make no mistake about that. Take a trip over to where he plays cards. Have a drink and walk around. Your main objective is to scout him. Watch his style of play closely, and you'll soon learn it. Probably because you've seen it a hundred times before.

"Here's how it goes. He can be dealt some good possibilities in the low end of the hand. Then, maybe a middle spread, and a high triangle. Most people will play with these "Rembrandts," for a while, and then start to get rid of them. There are also people who would disdain throwing one of these high cards, until they have seen one on the discard pile, because they fear they are going to complete someone's high combination. Not Leon, he will begin dumping these bombs right away.

"Another ploy of Leon's, and it's a good one, is to give an add on after seeing the other guy pick up a card that will give him a sure spread. Example: You are playing Leon. He has Milwaukee Avenue in his hand. He also has a pair of kings. He is looking for a safe discard. He decides to come off the kings. They look safe. He discards the king of spades. You pick it up and make kings. Leon doesn't know this, but he is counting on it. At his next turn to discard he adds on to your kings. That is to say, he gives you the fourth king. He has his reasons. First of all you may need the card for your fourth king. If this is the case, he is certain you will pick it up. If you do you are involuntarily helping him. First of all, by virtue of your picking up this card he is forcing you to maybe come off a possible combination. He is willing to take that chance. Plus, what the hell was he going to do with that fourth king in the first place? Hold it for the undercut? *Old Man Kards* would laugh, then turn his back.

"No, Leon would give the add on, and gamble on the next few discards from the other guy."

"Isn't that falling right into the other guy's hands," I asked, "Giving him a four card spread?"

"Maybe yes," Eddie said, "Maybe no" Leon's philosophy is; the remaining king in his hand is a meaningless piece of deadwood taking up space. Leon wants to make room for the future. He drops off the king. Charlie mentally says thank you so much. In the meantime, Leon has made room in his hand for a possible card that can help him. Charlie, on the other hand, now has less room for a possible combination. This is how Leon plays, and the odds, or laws of probability favor it!"

The cheeseburgers came. I ordered a Heinekens and Eddie did the same. The restaurant was starting to fill up, but Eddie paid the oncoming people no heed. He was like a snowball, and there would be no stopping him. He went on talking about breaking the hand down.

"Once Leon has given the fourth king to the other guy, it's breakdown time. Reduce the deadwood value of the hand at every opportunity. At that point, Leon is busy discarding middle and high pairs, or high cards. It's like; someone yelled, "Run for the hills," or "Abandon ship!" *First man to the lifeboats*, that's Leon.

"This method works more often than not, and it does give you a lot of safe discards, so if the other guy is to make a hand he has to do it all by himself. Reducing the deadwood total is another benefit of this move, and it does get him near the call quickly. The downside to all this is it is not hard figure out. When a man is running for the hills, all you have to do is look for the foot prints.

"Once Leon's hand gets near the calling stage he has three choices, call, play for the undercut, or play for gin. It's actually fun to watch him do this, because if he decides on the second or third option, playing for the cut, or going for gin, this is where the theatrics begin. The chatter starts, Leon's mouth is constantly open. That brass band full of bullshit that is usually Leon, now becomes a full-scale orchestra. And the one-liners start coming out one right after another. You'd think he was Rodney Dangerfield."

I called for another Heinekens. Eddie still had most of his left. One of the principal laws of physics is; one cannot drink beer at the same time while one is talking. That's not really in the textbook, but it sounds great! Eddie went on.

"Take a look at that number he pulled on you when you were my partner the second time."

I thought back, and remembered. Eddie had just ginned and won thirty-five points. I had to get less than ten points in my hand to ensure the box, or win the hand. Winning the hand was somewhat remote because I had been dealt Milwaukee Avenue, getting under the count had to be my move, we weren't on board as yet.

Leon had just drawn from the deck and was about to discard. He had his hand halfway to the pile when he stopped, hesitated, and pulled the card back. He looked at a kibitzer standing in back of me.

"Lou," he said, "Look in Kenny's hand and smile if he is under ten."

Now this is a loaded question because almost everyone when put in this position will smile. It is human nature working. I turned around and looked at Lou. He had a broad smile on his face.

Well, I lost it. I really did! I became so flustered at the audacity of the remark that I flat out lost it, my composure, my concentration, everything! Call it anger, frustration, aggravation from being kicked around all afternoon, or just plain stupidity. I lost my head. I came apart at the seams. Eddie's count was no longer the priority in my mind; I had to beat that sonuva bitch or die trying. I went for gin. I didn't make it, Leon did and I was not under the count. My one chance to get us on that street flew right out the window just as if I had held it in my hands and dropped kicked it through the uprights. Field goal!

Did they blitz us? Of course they did. *Old Man Kards* looked at my action, became enraged, and that was that. How does the saying go, "Look in the mirror and you'll see an idiot?" That was me.

"Yeah, I remember," I said almost tearfully.

"You *should*," countered Eddie. He had eaten most of his cheeseburger while I was in the think tank, and was now ready for another beer. I had another one too; getting chewed out is thirsty work.

"He played you like a piano, and look at some of the comments he threw around, 'Anton, we own 'em, we *own* 'em!' or, 'Get the wagon out honey, we goin' for a ride tonight!'"

"Yeah, it wasn't pretty." I told him.

"Well, learn from it," he said.

This lesson was taking longer than I realized, but I was starting to enjoy it. Maybe it was the Heinekens. I hoped the bar didn't run out.

Eddie pointed a finger at me, it was the third or forth time he had done that. I probably deserved it. I was starting to hope he'd run out of steam soon, but it sure didn't look that way.

"Now," he said, "I'm going to point out a play that I thought was a sheer stroke of genius. It happened during one of the few hands you won when he was your partner. If you remember, I was standing behind him watching."

"Is that the time he ginned and put us out across the board?" I asked.

"It sure as hell is. Let me tell you how it happened. You had just made gin if you remember."

"I do," I said.

"Well, "Eddie said with a smile, "He went over the count"

I thought for a moment. Going over the count, when your partner has just ginned, violates just about every rule in the game. In particular, it violates the *bird in the hand* rule. That is, the hand is won; don't risk ruining things by not staying under. Most partners take a dim view of this, and *Old Man Kards* begins to growl.

There are many experts who, from time to time, will advocate going over the count. This is a risk, but if successful, will put a player into a position where he will reap great rewards. If the ploy is successful, your partner beams and calls you things like "Genius!" and *Old Man Kards* begins to smile. Here is what happened.

I had just ginned and won five over, thirty points. If Leon can get under five, we win the first game.

Anton discards a deuce. Leon looks at it. Three things cross his mind. First, he has a six way hit going, any one of six cards can gin him if he draws it, or if Anton throws it. If he plays for the six way hit, he has to stay over the count. We need only fifteen more points to win the second street, and twenty-five more to go out all the way. *Graduation day!* The situation is risky because if Leon is over the count and Anton gins we do not go out in the first street. Not only that, it gives the other guys another shot at winning the first street. Nothing would be stopping them from coming up with a few no-brainers of their own and going out themselves.

Second if he doesn't take the risk, he puts himself and me in the position where Anton and Eddie can get super lucky and win games two and three.

Third. If he is unsuccessful, stays over the count, and the other guys mount a successful charge and wipe us out, he has to listen to me bitch at him the rest of the day.

The temptation is almost insurmountable. He is in love with the hand. He decides to go for it. He passes the deuce and draws from the pile; it is the ten of clubs. He discards it, and is still over the count. He has in his hand 2-3-4-of hearts, 6-7-8-of clubs. 7-8-9-of spades. The six cards that can gin him are ace or 5 of hearts. The 5 or 9 of clubs, and the 6 and 10 of spades.

Anton, who he is playing, draws from the pile. The card is the ten of spades.

He looks at the ten of clubs Leon has just thrown, decides his ten of spades is reasonably safe, and throws it.

Leon says "Thank you so much!" picks up the ten of spades and says "Gin!" We win all three games and I get a few of my dollars back. I don't necessarily advocate going over the count, it can lead to big trouble, but sometimes—!

I looked at Eddie. He was wearing that sly grin he sometimes had on his face when he thought he was being cute.

"That's right, "I said in retrospect, "He did, he went over the count, and made it work. He's quite a player."

"Yes he is," replied Eddie, "And the next question you should be asking me is how do you beat him?" agreed, and I did indeed ask Eddie how to beat him.

"Okay I said, "Tell me how."

Eddie looked at me a long time, and finally said, "I don't really have to tell you that. When you get home tonight, just think of all the people just like him you have been beating for years. Today was just pay back time with a few things thrown in. There is a certain amount of unpleasantness in life we all have to put up with. We don't have to like it, but we still have to put up with it. You can beat Leon eight ways to breakfast because you have been doing just that for a long time. Put your memory to work, and you'll come up the answers.

"One more thing," he went on, "I know you didn't have much choice in the matter today, but I thought you were up to it. Try to avoid playing with people you don't know too well for a lot of money until you have had a chance to scout them. If you don't, most of the time in the game will be spent on experimentation, trying to get a handle on how the other guy plays. When money is involved, you don't have time for this."

"Learn a lesson from today."

Chapter 48
DO YOUR HOMEWORK!

A salesman walked into a hotel bar, looked at the bartender an asked,

"Do you want to see something interesting, something you've never seen before, and if I prove my point will you let me have two drinks on the house? I guarantee you'll lose, and you will immensely enjoy losing."

"Go ahead, make my day!" said the bartender.

Reaching into his suitcase he had brought with him, the salesman took out a tiny piano about eight inches high and placed it on the bar. He then took out a little man about a foot high and sat him on a bench at the piano. The little man began playing the piano.

"That's amazing!" said the bartender, placing two drinks on the bar. "Where the hell did you find him?"

"Go ahead, wise guy," said the little man, "Tell the bartender how you told the witch doctor you wanted a twelve-inch pianist."

Eddie smiled and handed me the check. "My bill!" he said. I paid the tab, *again!* And we went our separate ways. I lingered in the parking lot and reflected a bit on what had taken place today.

"Learn something" Eddie had said. "Learn something."

I looked up at the sky. It was star clustered and bright. The kind you can get in the Midwest in late October. I could smell smoke in the air from burning leaves, and the breeze seemed semi-balmy. It was the type of weather you sometimes get just before the temperature plummets, the wind picks up, and *Old King Winter* gives you an idea of what's in store. Sometimes I wonder if he's related to *Old Man Kards*.

I got into the car. I drive a Cadillac Deville. To me it's the *only* car! I know I would get some argument from Eddie. He has owned a red Ford convertible with a white top ever since I've known him. I decided to drive around for a while. It was a good night to be on the road with the windows open. Traffic was light so I decided to tool the car around the open roads of the northwest suburbs. I accelerated from one quiet country back road to another. It was dark, but not so dark one couldn't see the shapes of trees, long horizontal fencing and the silhouette of a farmhouse here and there. I drove, felt the wind on my face, and I went over in my mind the things Eddie had been talking about.

"Out drink him." Eddie had said. Boy, I thought I was an expert on drinking.

"Do you drink?" I was once asked.

"Well it depends." is my stock answer. "If it's wet, I drink it." I thought I knew everything there was to know about the subject. Well you never know, I always thought watering down drinks was something bartenders or "B Girls" did!

Out think him Hell yes, you've got to do that. Day in and day out a man has to think, and continue to do it. If you're going to just sit there and wait for the no-brainers to come, you may as well hang out a sign that reads "Pigeon for hire!" Think, and keep your eyes open. *This ain't no game for a blind man!*

There once was a young lady who had just arrived in town. She had taken a new job. A job that was very important to her. It was one that was full of opportunity, and would pay very well. She was about to check into a hotel for a few nights until she got settled when she heard from a girlfriend of hers. The friend offered her apartment for a week, as she would be out of town for that time.

Happily accepting the offer she let herself into the apartment. It had been a long hot day and a nice shower would be just the thing to relax her. Stripping down to a pair of briefs she turned on the water and was about to shed the briefs and step into the tub.

The doorbell rang! "What to do?" she asked herself. She stood there semi naked. The doorbell rang again.

"Who's there?" she heard herself exclaim!"

"Blind man!" was the reply.

"What the hell,"she told herself, "he's blind, can't see anything" She flung the door open.

"Nice boobs!" said the man, " Now where do you want the blinds?"

Leon is an easy man to figure, but a hard man to beat, Eddie had told me. How was that possible? I let it sink in for a moment of two. Easy to figure, I let it roll off my tongue, and thought about it some more. Easy to figure, why? Why? *Bingo!* I had it! It was just like the light bulb that appears in the comic strips when an idea takes shape. He is easy to figure, *because he does the same thing all of the time.* Two or three cards into the hand he is reducing the deadwood in his hand, diving for the sewer, running for the hills.

A long time ago Eddie had told me "If a man is predictable in a card game—sooner or later he'll belong to you."

The trees along the road whizzed by, whoosh, whoosh, whoosh.

"Hard to beat! Hard to beat! Why? Why?" Simple, he gets down fast, and he's smart. But so am I!

I thought back to that "Blood bath" the first time I played Eddie at the club. Before I had played him I told myself ; He can be had! Well, so can Leon.

The evening was cool and pleasant. The driving was enjoyable. Eddie had told me to go home and think about all the people just like Leon, who I have beaten over the years, and this is where the answers would be found. I didn't really have to think about them; hell I could do better than that.

I kept a book on most of them. That's right. I had a profile, a dossier as it were; on each and every gin player at the club how much they could play for comfortably, and where was the choke quotient. By this I mean, if they were comfortable at two cents a point, where would they tend to become uncomfortable? Maybe three cents a point, maybe a nickel?

Would this pressure affect their play to the extent it would cause mistakes to creep in? Would they have a tendency to dive for the sewer right from the start if the stakes were a bit higher? Would they have the guts to play awhile?

Leon is usually diving right away, unless he is in love with the hand. It's as if he was playing poker.

"Getting out of the hand, and waiting for a better one," he calls it.

The more expert money players use the term, "Gag reflex." to measure a player's ability to withstand pressure, to absorb financial discomfort. (How much will he play for)?

I don't go quite that far, but I do like to know many things about the other guy that are important to me. Things such as; what kind of business is he in? Does he have problems on the job, or at home? Does he get uncomfortable when he is asked how his investments are doing? Does he give the impression you can cause his mind to wander if you hit him with a little chatter? All these things are important to me, and they are right down there on the chart.

In the military this is known as *Mind Fudging* Actually the phrase a little stronger than that, but this is a clean book! In the first Gulf war in Iraq our military wanted to drop leaflets over the enemy positions. Leaflets showing pictures of young ladies in very scanty costumes, or no costumes at all, such as what you see in the more gamy girlie magazines. While this was done in World War II, it never was in Iraq because a lot of *Bleeding hearts* in this country, mostly in the media, didn't think it was playing fair. Imagine that! Our guys are getting killed, and it's unfair to *Mind Fudge.*

Well, in gin rummy, it is entirely fair to *Mind Fudge*.

Like most any other contest or sport, it is part of the game. In your contact sports such as football, or hockey, or even in baseball where a ninety-five mile per hour fast ball coming at you, there is the intimidation factor. In football or hockey, the message is "You're going to be hit, and hit hard!" In baseball it's "Hey, that ball can hurt if it hits you!" Well in a card game the message is similar. The fact that you came prepared to lose a *hundred* and you're already down *two hundred* can be very intimidating.

If you should decide to dabble in *Mind Fudging*, you should remember it's an art. It has to be done with discretion, but not too often, else you tip your hand.

The charts, or sheets I have been referring to disclose everything I have learned from kibitzing. That is, scouting an opponent.

Eddie was right, I had played people exactly like Leon, and I just didn't realize it. If I were to compose a sheet on Leon based on what I now know, it would have some very basic facts about him. Facts about his business, work habits, family, bank account, and a general description section pertaining to his card game.

The general description section would look something like this:

Leon Sasecasewicz: Gin rummy pattern:

Leon's entire game can be described as a get down and call pattern. He goes for gin only when he has what he considers a great gin hand, a couple of spreads dealt and maybe a six way hit combination. Lacking this he will play for the call, and if he senses his opponent is in trouble, he will play for the under cut. To beat him one needs a lot card sense and card memory. His opponent must be able to *tap dance* a lot, and build his hand around what he thinks Leon is holding.

If a player can do this with any amount of regularity he will be in a position to undercut Leon. The more he is undercut, the more profound an effect it will have on him.

If an opponent can bring this about, Leon is no longer difficult to beat; in fact, he becomes quite easy because he has lost his main weapon.

You have to beat him at his own game to hurt him. Once you get into his head, it's not too long before you can get in his face. Little tricks such as intentionally mis-dealing when you detect impatience, or dropping the cards on the floor can go a long way to distract him, and can raise havoc with his concentration.

There are description sheets about many players. Anton was a horse of another color.

I headed down the tree-lined driveway leading to my garage making a mental note to look for charts in my collection that would categorize Anton. This I would have to do tomorrow because I was now becoming tired. Today had been a very busy day.

Chapter 49
THE WAR ROOM

The night passed swiftly. I slept like a log despite the blood bath I had been through the day before. I was thinking about Anton, and what type of player he was. I had played him, and despite my ineptness and anger the few hours I played against him, I had a fair idea of what kind of gin rummy pattern I was planning to write about him.

I had breakfast with my wife in the kitchen. I finished, read the paper, took out the garbage and went into my office. I work out of my house, in this way I am never far from anything related to my business, even gin rummy. I answered the few messages that were on the machine, and then I got to work.

Anton: I began pulling sheets out of the file. I thought back to yesterday, and I realized I had had the opportunity to stand behind him a few times. I had in fact, kibitzed him without realizing it. Think, I told myself, remember! Slowly it began to take shape.

The way I read Anton was, he is a middle player. He likes to go for spreads and combinations in the middle of the deck. He likes to tie up all the middle value cards so the other guy can't use them.

I looked through the file and pulled out five charts on middle players. Oh yes, I do have them cross-filed. Looking at all five I discovered they all played the same way. The only difference I could see was the varying amounts of money they would be comfortable playing for.

Middle players like to establish three card runs in the middle of the deck, hence the name middle player. The ideal hand for a middle player is; 6, 7, 8 in three of the four suits, plus a piece of deadwood. On paper it would look like this:

6- Diamonds- 7-diamond -8-diamonds.
6- clubs-7 clubs-8 clubs.
6-hearts-7 hearts-8 hearts.

Note: This is a nine way hit. Any one of nine cards will gin this hand. 5 and 9 of each suit, and the 6, 7 and 8 of spades. Naturally this is an ideal hand for anyone if dealt, which it is not very often. The middle player will strive to put this combination or a form of it together as the hand progresses.

When he was alive Bob Elson, was recognized as "The dean of American Sportscasters" he also was recognized as one of the finest and most astute gin rummy players in the country. Many of the younger players reading this book may not recognize some of the names you will read in a moment, you're a bit too young. The era I'm speaking of lasted some fifty years, from 1925 -1975. During that time Bob Elson reined supreme on the gin rummy tables wherever he went.

During the daytime hours and some nights he would broadcast sporting events. All one had to do was select the correct station and you would hear his voice describing the actions of The Chicago Cubs, The Chicago White Sox, and during the winter months the Chicago Black Hawks hockey team.

His off duty hours were spent playing gin rummy. He was such a fantastic card player he could have easily forsaken broadcasting and made his living playing cards. He enjoyed broadcasting so much he didn't do this, but he did find a lot of time to play gin.

Most of his opponents were baseball, football, hockey players, and professional golfers. He played cards with Babe Ruth, Leo Durocher, Sam Snead, and he was quoted as once saying;— "If he didn't have every cent Dizzy Dean owned, he soon would."

Bob Elson was a middle player, and a great one. He had one steadfast rule. *Never throw a seven*! Re-read this rule, then go back and look at the diagram on the last page. It's easy to see how the lack of a couple of sevens would wreak havoc on this hand. This rule, not to throw a seven, would be the first line of defense against a middle player!

Players such as Anton tend to be a shade unconventional. While this can be rewarded handsomely, it also borders on being reckless. In my profile sheets of players I have scouted, I grade each player on how unconventional, or reckless they can become. For example, I have seen players with gin in their hands and not declare it because, in their opinion the other guy's deadwood total was too low. They would wait patiently until Charlie (him again) would break up his hand in order to throw a safe card, then the boom would be lowered.

Let's look at this a little closer. The call is two. Charlie's deadwood total is four. Lou, who is Charlie's opponent, draws a card giving him gin. The hand is nearing the end of the deck, and judging by what has been played, and what is in his own hand Lou believes Charlie is going nowhere with the hand. He doesn't think Charlie will be able to call the hand, and his possibilities for gin are remote.

Lou can lay down the hand and announce gin right now, but what will he win. He is under the assumption Charlie has four or five points in his hand. If he declares gin now, he will win gin plus four, or five, twenty-nine points say.

He decides to gamble and wait a bit, if Charlie's situation changes, he can gin then and win a lot more. He is certain Charlie is holding three Kings. The hand is in its late stages.

Sooner or later Charlie will need a safe discard. He waits, and sure enough on the forty-ninth card played, Charlie breaks his three Kings to avoid throwing a hot card.

Lou turns the discarded King over and says "What Do they make in Peoria?" Unconventional? Sure, reckless? Certainly! The whole point in this little saga is to alert you to expect some recklessness and unconventionality when you are playing an unconventional type of player. And most middle players are just that.

Defense: When playing a middle player, every effort must be made to tie up the middle yourself. If you are holding a middle card, or draw one, hang onto it. Don't discard them until you see like cards appear on the discard pile. Do a little *tap dancing* and try to form your own middle hand. If you can do that, take some sevens and eights out of play all that is left for the other guy are a few scraps on either end.

It was now becoming time for me to review everything in my files about other players who were comparable to Leon and Anton. After I finished this I began pulling sheets on known speculators.

An idea was beginning to take shape in my brain. It had started out as a small gem of a flame, but was now approaching the intensity of a four-alarm fire.

Speculating.—Conflicting statements: "He who speculates wears tattered clothes!" "Nothing ventured, nothing gained!"

A card picked up from the deck, or discard pile that doesn't immediately help the hand, but is taken for it's possible true value, is a card taken for speculation, and is called a "Spec" card. There are gin players who believe in its value and swear by it. There are just as many players who do not. There are players who do it occasionally, and players who do it not at all.

Speculating in gin rummy has been compared to drawing to an inside straight in poker, or betting on one roll of the dice in a crap game in Vegas. The saying in poker is "A player who draws to an inside straight deserves everything he gets" This saying is, of course, a double-edged sword. So too in gin rummy. If you can make good on a spec, you deserve all the good fortune that befalls you. Conversely, if the spec is unsuccessful, and you get caught with the now useless card, you deserve the kick in the pants you get.

Players who play the middle of the deck favor spec cards. It takes a lot of work and a low value call card to build a good middle hand. They all need something to work with. They pick up cards from the discard pile with little regard as to hiding what they are doing. They believe the end justifies the means, and sometimes it does.

There are also players who speculate from the stock only. They feel any card taken from the discard pile discloses too much information about the hand. Triangles: There are speculators who take a spec card only if it forms a triangle. An example of this is a person holding, say, a 5 and 6 of hearts will speculate with a 6 of diamonds forming what is known as a triangle. This is a four way hit, 6 of spades, 6 of clubs, 4 of hearts and the 7 of hearts.

Speculating on triangles is done by some players, mostly very early in the hand. Many times it is done on the very first card turned up. The reasoning is if the spec doesn't work, the speculator has time to break it up, get rid of it, and go on to better things. The danger in this is the opponent may be defending and may use the discard in his own hand.

Some speculators will pick up a high card very early in the hand. The card actually has no value in the player's hand, it is done to induce the other guy to hold high. *Tap dancing* here is a must. Eddie has said many times There is no man alive who can hold onto a useless piece of deadwood without getting hurt in the long run. They have a habit of jumping up and biting you in the butt."

The basic thoughts advocating speculating are; the chances of making a spread and improving the hand are increased, especially if you are dealt Milwaukee Avenue.

Another reason, and this you have to pay attention to, is one man's spec card may cause the other guy to *tap dance* and hold useless cards in defense. I've seen Eddie; when he is playing Oklahoma gin, take the *up* card (the twenty first card dealt), if he considered it hot, just to keep it away from the other guy.

A good example of this is; if he is playing a known middle player, and the up card is a seven, he will take this card if it is his turn.

Those who do not favor speculating have these opinions. First, the speculator gives away information about his hand. Second, and most important, the speculator is penalized because he loses a chance to draw from the pile by choosing the discard pile. A good defense for this is verbal, and a lot of people use it.

"You mean to tell me you're going to pass up a shot at the pile to pick up a piece of crap like that?" Sometimes it works.

Chapter 50
SETTING THE TRAP

There once was a couple who were on a Caribbean cruise. They had left Miami and were cruising southwest. The ship had the misfortune to sail into the Bermuda Triangle. Lines drawn through Bermuda, Puerto Rico, and a point west of Miami border this oceanic phenomenon, which is believed by more than a few people to be a death trap.

There have been any number of aircraft and ships that have mysteriously disappeared after allegedly sailing into this area. Legend has it that any small fishing boat, or airplane venturing into these waters run the risk of never being seen again.

This couple, a Florida business man and his wife were standing on one of the forward decks when a mysterious gust of wind came up, plucked the lady from the deck, carried her some miles away, and dropped her into the ocean. The lifeboats went out, but to no avail, the lady was hopelessly lost. *Gone!*

Six weeks passed and the businessman received a telegram from the Coast Guard.

"We have located your wife at the rocky bottom of a bay just south of Bermuda. Needless to say she is dead, however, in her mouth we found a half open oyster shell, and in it was a pearl that appraised out for fifty thousand dollars. Please advise!"

A few days later the Coast Guard received a telegram that read *"Mail me a check, and re-set the trap!"*

If my sitting in my office pulling up information sheets of people who's card playing techniques resemble those of the Sitkowitz brothers, gives the impression I am setting a trap for them. I have to plead guilty. Let's look at the sheets of spec card proponents I settled upon and we'll try to pick their brains a bit. We'll go right into their heads.

Lee: Lee has a fantastic memory for discards, great card sense, will almost never throw a hot card, and, if the first card up has any value to him, he will pick it up. The reasoning for this move is it creates a greater possibility of future help in the hand, plus it may force an opponent to tap dance around it. The reasoning against such a move is two fold.

First, Lee must make a safe discard to avoid getting into trouble.

The second reason is, and this is major, he is passing up a chance at the pile where a card of real value may be hiding.

Lee will hold this spec card to almost the very end if he is unsuccessful. If the opponent *tap dances* around it, the hand is usually played to a draw. This happens frequently with players such as Lee. Many times Lee will make the spec good, and if he has any valuable cards at all he will win a lot of hands. He will depend on his defensive ability, and his ability to keep you off balance to be a winner.— So, how does one combat this?

Well, first of all you will have to take a look at super serious, strictly defensive players. Most of them have attitude problems.

I call it the "Nobody's going to put anything over on me!" syndrome. Very seldom will you see players like this part with a hot card. They will break up pairs first. They always operate on the theory that dictates undercutting the opponent if he should call; in the meantime they are trying to turn every one of these possible hot cards into spreads. It's not hard to understand when someone gins on them they have a lot of deadwood in their hand.

Lee goes mentally "bananas" when someone picks up two or three discards. It forces him to move from an offensive, defending strategy, into a game where he has to defend against cards he didn't figure on defending against. In a way the other guy is beating Lee at his own game. When Lee is making his specs good, he is a tiger; otherwise he is a pussycat.

Most of the time he is hard to beat because he ties up your hand, but when he is beat, it is usually for a lot. Eddie likes to quick call him, or wait for the no-brainers and go for the throat.

Pete: Where Lee is a defensive player to the 'nth degree, Pete is wide open. He is always speculating. When one spec card doesn't work, he will get rid of it and go for another. He is easy to recognize because he plays a lot from the discard pile. Handled correctly he becomes very easy. Players such as Leon own him. A player who reduces his hand quickly will win a lot of hands from Pete. Playing for the call is a must. There's no need to go for gin, one can win just as much by calling.

One more thing should be said about players like Pete. They are all in love with the high cards, the bombs. When kibitzing Pete you will usually see him try to develop a hand that has a four-card spread, a three-card spread and a high triangle such as jack-jack- queen. The player who calls the hand will win a lot from Pete. If you try to get down into the *gutter* and play his game, he'll own you.

Frank: Frank is strictly a money player. He enjoys playing for a lot of money in the hope of intimidating his opponents, or possibly the team he is playing against. He is always trying to find your "Gag reflex" button. He believes in streaks, and when he is on a roll he can really pile up the points. But he will give back just as many because of faulty play or reckless discards. He is easy to spot because when *Old Man Kards* is sitting on his shoulder. He plays quickly, and is full of chatter. But when the old guy disappears he *clams up* and his pace is much slower.

It was nearing six Pm. I was by myself sitting in the family room, my wife having gone shopping with some of her friends. I had some eighteen-technique sheets to review. It was a good night to sit in front of a fireplace to study, and make plans. By ten o'clock I had finished. I had completed part one of my plan.

The next morning I was up early. I had breakfast, watched the news for a while, read the paper, and was in my office by nine. It was time to put part two of my plan into action. Part of it included a crash course in Polish. I reached for the phone.

Chapter 51
MOUNTING THE ATTACK

It was late April, some six months later. The sun was shining and the temperature was pushing seventy-five degrees, very balmy for that time of the year.

I was with Eddie; we were sitting in his car, which was parked in the lot at the club. The car was a red Ford convertible with a white top that was down. Some things never change. Eddie was dropping me off, he had a few errands to take care of, and then he would return.

I too had a mission.

Eddie was looking at the flowerbeds ringing each tree in the driveway. They were beginning to bloom. He ran his fingers through his hair, and turned to face me.

"So," he said," You're going to play those two guys, Leon and Anton, first one, than the other, for twenty cents a point. You could lose three or four grand! Who the hells idea was this?"

"Mine really," I replied, "Although they went for it in a big way. They think I'm easy."

"Well," he said looking seriously at me, "You'd better be on your toes, 'less you lose the farm!"

I explained to Eddie about the technique sheets, the dossiers I had on players just like them. I told him I would know what each of them were going to do and when they were going to do it.

"Uh-huh," said Eddie, "You got one of those on me?"

I laughed. "Yeah, about four inches thick."

He looked at me. "Let's be serious, I think you're about to get your head handed to you!"

"How so?"

"One of them will be sitting behind you talking Polish to the other. They'll have you coming and going."

"Do you know where I've been the last six months?"

"Well," said Eddie, "I do know you haven't been around here too much. Where have you been?"

"I've been seeing a language teacher in *Buck town*." Buck town is one of the last few Polish strongholds in the city. It is on Milwaukee Avenue and completely surrounded by minority neighborhoods.

"Don't tell me, let me guess, you've been in Buck town learning Polish."

I nodded. "That's right, I worked hard and got pretty good."

"I'm impressed," Eddie said. "It will stop them from using the language trick on you, but it won't stop them from using hand signals behind your back, I've seen them do that!"

"You'll be back in a half hour or so, won't you?"

"Uh-huh!"

"Well then, watch my back, Mr. Colquitt, watch my back!"

Eddie looked at me and flashed that sly grin he used so often.── "Knock them dead, my man, knock them dead" he said as I stepped away.

He put out his hand. We shook. I glanced at the car's interior. It had red carpeting, white seats, red door interiors and a red dashboard. Eddie was wearing a red shirt with white flowers, white slacks and of course the sunglasses. The hair was still blonde and wavy. I couldn't help but smile as I thought again; *some things really never change!*

"Colquitt," I said, "What the hell kind of a name is that?"

"A little French," he told me, " With a lot of Irish thrown in, that's why I've got such poetry in my veins."

I looked at Eddie sitting in that car and I let my mind wander back some fifty years or so, to Fort Campbell, Gate three, US. Highway 41.

I gave him a quick grin and said; "Are you sure it's not bullshit?"

He smiled, put the car in gear and drove away.

Epilogue

So, there you have it, my little saga. In it I've told you a story, introduced you to some people, and tried to show you how you could play the game a little better, enjoy it a little more, and make a few pennies doing it. The three go hand in hand, don't they?

The key word in that sentence is enjoying. Whether you're playing the game for a little or a lot, the element of enjoyment is the key factor. Even people who play gin rummy for a living would consider doing something else if they didn't enjoy it so much.

I like to think that throughout history, famous men, no matter what their walk in life, sat down and enjoyed a game of gin rummy together. Sometimes, in my whimsy, I can almost visualize George Washington and General Cornwallis playing a few Hollywood's back in 1781, but I don't think *that* ever happened!

Enjoy!

J.S.

GLOSSARY

Most of you who read this book will be familiar with the following terms. They do, however, vary throughout the country, and locally from club to club.

Add on: A defensive move where a player knowingly adds on to a known spread in an opponent's hand, to avoid introducing a fresh card.

Blitz: A situation where one team shuts out another. The winning team's points are usually doubled. A.K.A. Schneider.

Bait: Card of one numerical value discarded to entice an opponent to discard the same valued card in another suit. A.K.A. Salesman.

Bombs: High valued cards.

Call: A time when a player can terminate the hand by lying down his spreads and unrelated cards (deadwood). The deadwood must be equal to, or lower than the call value. A.K.A. knocks.

Call card: A card specifying the number at which a call can be made.

Call deck: A separate deck of cards used for determining the call, or knock.

Chatter: A line of conversation used by one player to annoy or distract another. A.K.A. Coffee housing.

Count: A total of points won or lost, and how it affects the score.

Deadwood: Unrelated cards in a player's hand.

Fish: Another word for baiting an opponent.

Hand: The actual cards you hold in your hands, or part of a game Example: This hand is over!

"Hiding in the weeds" A person who holds deadwood under the number of the call for the purposes of undercutting an opponent is said to be "Hiding in the Weeds."

Hollywood scoring: A scoring system where three games are scored simultaneously. These games are also known as streets.

Kibitzer: One who looks on as an outsider. One who watches a card game over a player's shoulder, where he can observe the player's cards?

Make the cards! Shuffle thoroughly.

Misdeal: An incorrect amount of cards dealt.

Miscall: A situation where a player calls, or knocks with an amount of points over the designated call amount (call card).

Mini's: Low value cards.

No-Brainer: "A hand that is dealt, or develops quickly by sheer luck, requiring no skill at all to play.

Open hole. A player who plays loosely is said to be open holed

On the over: A situation where a new game begins while an existing game is still in progress.

On board: The first point or points a player or team wins in a street.

Oklahoma Gin: A form of gin rummy where ten cards are dealt to each player, with the next card turned over. This card then becomes the call card. In a partnership game the lower of the cards turned over becomes the call card.

Playing cards off (A.K.A. layoff). A situation where a player takes cards from his hand and plays them on related cards in his opponent's hand after the opponent has called. Playing cards off is not allowed where the opponent has ginned.

"Play him down!" Cause a standoff. Play the hand until there are no more cards left in the deck (stock).

Rembrandts: Picture cards.

Run: Three or more cards of the same value, or three or more cards in sequence in the same suit.

Spread: See Run.

Spec. Card: A card taken from the deck or discard pile for speculation.

Street: See Hollywood scoring.

Tap dancing: The playing of a hand according to what the opponent has picked up from the discard pile.

Triangle: A combination of three cards, where any one of four cards drawn will result in a spread. (Example: 7D 7H 8H. Seven, the 7S or 7C or 6H or 9H.). Any one of these four cards if drawn will result in a spread

Undercut: A situation where a player has a lesser point value in his hand, than the opponent has when the opponent calls.

CPSIA information can be obtained at www.ICGtesting.com
Printed in the USA
LVOW10s0536051115

461161LV00001B/23/P